Sons of Sparta

Books by Jeffrey Siger

Chief Inspector Andreas Kaldis Mysteries
Murder in Mykonos
Assassins of Athens
Target: Tinos
Prey on Patmos
Mykonos After Midnight
Sons of Sparta

Sons of Sparta

A Chief Inspector Andreas Kaldis Mystery

Jeffrey Siger

Poisoned Pen
PRESS

Published by Poisoned Pen Press, an imprint of Sourcebooks
P.O. Box 4410, Naperville, Illinois 60567-4410
(630) 961-3900
sourcebooks.com

Library of Congress Cataloging-in-Publication data is on file with the publisher.

Printed and bound in The United States of America.
POD 10 9 8 7 6 5 4 3 2

In memory of Leighton Gage, a true friend, dedicated mentor, and gifted writer.

Acknowledgments

Randolph Amengual; Roz and Mihalis Apostolou; Nikolaos Chorvalakos; Christos Exarchacos; Andreas, Aleca, Nikos, Mihalis and Anna Fiorentinos; Giorgios Giorgariou; Nicholas Gryblas; Panagiotis Iordanopoulos; Nikos Ipiotis; Flora and Yanni Katsaounis; Chris Kay; Olga Kefalogianni; Panos Kelaidis; Dimitris Kordalis; George Kyrtsos; Ioanna Lalaounis; Linda Marshall; Terrence McLaughlin, Karen Siger-McLaughlin, and Rachel Ida McLaughlin; Lambros Panagiotakopoulos; Dimitris Petropoulakis; Poppy Psinakis Patterson; Barbara G. Peters and Robert Rosenwald; Ioannis Pikakos; John Sfakianakis; Alan and Pat Siger; Jonathan, Jennifer, Azriel, and Gavriella Siger; Ed Stackler; Christos Stampoulis; Nolan and Chris Stripling; Spiros, Vassiliki and Eleni Theodorakakis; Pavlos Tiftikidis; Elias Tsaoussakis; Vassilis Tsiligiris; Sotiris Varotsis; Christos Vlachos; Nicholaos Zigouris; Barbara Zilly; Elias Zuckerman;

And, of course, Aikaterini Lalaouni.

"[I]n this century, scarcely a word has been written on the remote and barren but astonishing region of the Mani...but the name of the Mani at once suggests four ideas to any Greek: the custom of the blood feud, dirges, Petrobey Mavromichalis, the leader of the Maniots in the Greek War of Independence and the fact that the Mani...wrested its freedom from the Turks and maintained a precarious independence."
—Patrick Leigh Fermor (1915-2011)
MANI: Travels in the Southern Peloponnese
(1958)

Mani Peninsula Map

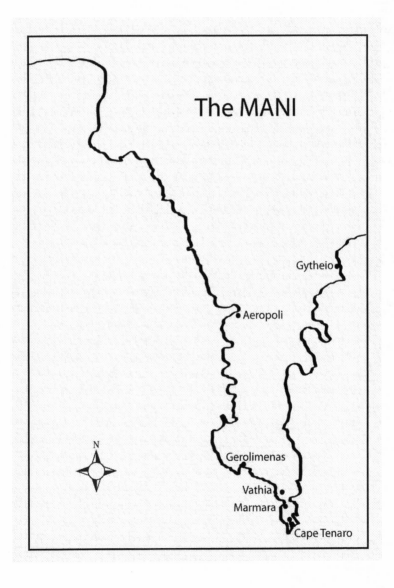

General Map

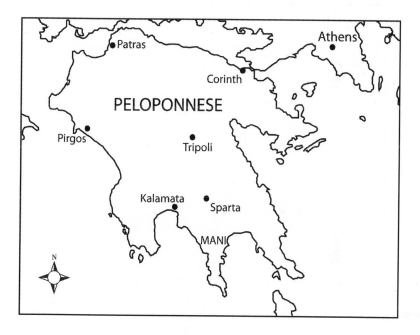

Chapter One

As he drove alone down the highway the tune kept running through his head. An old Greek ballad. He couldn't shake it. Not since early morning, when his father's brother called to say, "Come home at once," offering no more of an explanation than "It's a family matter."

Everyone in his family knew the words that went with the tune, lyrics that spoke of family honor and all that was expected of those duty-bound to protect it. The song told the story of his father's father and what his family had demanded of him a hundred years before:

In the early 1900s a young medical student studying in Athens received a message from his father to return home at once. The trip from Athens to the Mani, in the southernmost part of Greece's Peloponnese, took several days. When the student arrived home he learned that his younger sister had humiliated their father by becoming pregnant by a young man in their village. Her lover had proposed to marry his sister, but their father refused. Instead, in front of his sister and her lover he told his son to shoot and kill them both.

The lovers ran from the house, but the brother caught up with his sister in the courtyard and murdered her there. His sister's lover he caught and killed at the port as he tried to escape by boat.

At the trial of the brother for killing his sister and her lover, the Judge was about to render his decision when the Judge's mother stood and shouted at her son, "Just remember before you pass judgment that you murdered your own sister for the very same reason."

The brother was acquitted and returned to medical school.

The driver shot a quick glance down at the Corinth canal as he passed west from the Greek mainland onto the Peloponnese peninsula.

I wonder what Uncle has in mind, thought Greece's Special Crimes Division detective Yianni Kouros. Judges weren't as forgiving these days as they had been in his grandfather's day.

The Peloponnese stood as the southernmost part of mainland Greece, about the same size as the American state of Massachusetts. It had served as the setting for much of the blood-soaked drama that played out across ancient Greece, as well as the ancestral home to Spartan power that had rattled the ancient world even more than its legend resonated in popular imagination today. Many said the ancient Spartans simply vanished from the Earth without a trace, same as their city. Others believed they had gone farther south and found sanctuary deep in the mountain-spined, middle peninsula of the trident-shaped tip of the Peloponnese, to the region known as the Mani.

Kouros smiled as he recalled his father blasting anyone who dared question the Mani's claim to Spartan origins. Maniots took great pride in their region's colorful, notorious history as home to their pirate, highwayman, and warrior ancestors; in men and women fighting ferociously alongside other Maniots to defeat every foreign force foolish enough to attempt to occupy their part of Greece; and in being the first to declare war on the Turks in Greece's 1821 War of Independence.

But the smile faded as he thought of his uncle, the last male of his generation. The others had all died young, Kouros' father the only one from natural causes.

West of Corinth, Kouros turned south at Tripoli onto a two-lane road toward Sparta. In these late October days, with most tourists gone, he'd made good time, but still had halfway to go, and beyond Sparta the road would slow him down even more. This wasn't the Sparta of ancient times, whose inhabitants lived a warrior life disinterested in erecting the magnificent edifices so important to their northern Peloponnese neighbors and the far-off Athenians. No, this was modern Sparta, a town of government offices, businesses, and residences where prosperity depended upon groves of oranges and olives, not on war.

North of Sparta the road coursed through a five-mile stretch of lush, high, mountain passes overlooking broad green valleys and a horizon of jagged mountain giants. He always wondered as he traveled through this wilderness why nearly one-half of Greece's eleven million people chose to live crammed together around Athens with so much of Greece this green and uninhabited.

And I'm one of them.

South of Sparta, Kouros passed into the Mani. The land turned harsher, wilder, tougher, less forgiving, though still green and filled with citrus, olives, and corn. But once he turned west and began climbing the rugged north-south Taygetos mountain range, greens swiftly turned to browns and grays. On the other side of those mountains lay the region of the Mani his family called home—arid rocky land penned in by the

Ionian Sea to the west and worn-down limestone mountains to the east, a place where olive trees battled with boulders for the region's arable land.

The source of this part of the Mani's only significant modern economy loomed like sentinels along the ridges and hillsides: ancient four- and five-story, square, stone battle towers, historical treasures erected by Mani families as far back as the thirteenth century, which today drew tourists in flocks.

But to Kouros the towers were stark reminders of another side to the Maniots' fierce character, for although they offered strong defensive positions against bandits, pirates, and foreign invaders, their principal purpose served the families' ruthless battles with their neighbors. Here the concept of family vendetta was so deeply engrained that Mani society had rules on how, when, and against whom vengeance could and could not be taken. Doctors and priests, for instance, were considered too valuable to the community to serve as targets of an offended family.

At the southern end of a long, wide plateau running between the road and the mountains, Kouros turned left and followed a rock and dirt lane up toward a sharp-edged, two-story stone farmhouse. Decade-old cars and a couple of beat-up pickups sat parked every which way next to a five-story, beige and gray tower made of the same stone as the farmhouse a hundred feet away.

He parked next to one of the pickups and sat for a moment, staring at the farmhouse. Everything about it, from the color of its walls, its roughhewn wooden front door, and its traditional Peloponnesian terra-cotta-tiled roof, brought one word to mind: nondescript.

Precisely how his uncle wanted his home to appear to the outside world.

On the other side of the farmhouse door lay what few could imagine existed in historically impoverished, southwest Mani. This was *Mesa* or Deep Mani, where people struggled with virtually waterless, salt-wind-driven land, enduring lives far more difficult than did Maniots living in the fertile, olive- and honey-rich areas of *Exo* or Outer Mani to the north, or to the east, beyond the Taygetos mountain range, in *Kato* or Lower Mani.

Amid land so poor and scarce that not even the deeply held Greek tradition of dowry was practiced, Uncle's home featured artwork and furnishings as fine as any to be found in a ship owner's Athenian mansion. Its ground floor, which once functioned as stables, mangers, and a barrier from the damp ground, now served as the main living area.

Kouros' grandfather had lived in this house after finishing medical school. He'd returned to his village to practice medicine, serving what he called his penance for taking his sister's and her lover's lives. He spent his life committed to helping any woman in trouble, defending her however necessary, knowing he'd be spared vendetta assassination by reason of his position as a doctor. In this same house, he'd lived to die in his sleep after fathering four sons and two daughters.

Regrettably, his children did not share their father's immunity from revenge, and the savagery that had plagued the Deep Mani for so much of its history claimed three of his children—retribution for acts by their father considered insults to the honor of another family.

Kouros' father and one aunt survived because they were sent away to live in Athens. His uncle had been spared, according to him, because the village's council of elders—charged with ruling on feuds among warring clan families—placed Uncle outside the bounds of vendetta, fearing that his father would abandon the village and leave it without a doctor should Uncle, his last surviving child there, be killed.

Kouros' father, however, had a different explanation for his brother's longevity. He attributed Uncle's survival to his uncanny skill at modernizing traditional Mani techniques for augmenting their barely subsistence standard of living: piracy and banditry.

Throughout its history the Mani welcomed pirates on its seas and bandits to its hills. With the introduction in the 1960s of paved roads across mountains that once isolated much of the Mani from the rest of Greece, Uncle had seen his opportunity to spread proven Mani methods to the rest of Greece.

Soon, Uncle had not only feuding families but also rival clans working together as their Maniot ancestors had once united solely to battle foreign invaders. But now their rallying cry was a call to rack up profits in a united criminal enterprise. Up until a decade before, when Kouros' uncle "retired," as he called it, Uncle had been the most significant criminal leader in the region. A position in obvious counterpoint to his nephew's current role as right hand to Andreas Kaldis, feared chief of the Greek police's national anticrime and political corruption division.

Kouros' and his uncle's different approaches to life had never been an issue between the two men. Kouros' father had passed away and his uncle retired before Kouros became a cop, and on the occasions they'd been together since, Kouros had sensed an unstated bit of pride in Uncle that his older brother's son had made it to the "other" side.

Then again, nothing before had ever put their differences in conflict. As Kouros knocked on the front door, he hoped that wasn't about to change.

Chapter Two

A dark-haired, barely teenage girl in jeans and a pink hoodie opened the door. "It's Yianni," she said to seven men in jeans and work shirts sitting at a white linen-covered table in a room just beyond the entryway.

"She means Athens Yianni," said one of the men.

"Of course she does," said a white-haired man at the far end of the table, his face lit up in a broad smile, eyes sparkling. "The rest of you *malaka* Yiannis are already here." Uncle had just affectionately lumped nearly half of Kouros' cousins into the category of wankers.

Uncle stood up and spread his arms wide, like a bear waiting to embrace a bull.

"You look terrific, Uncle. I see you let your hair grow longer."

The two men hugged and exchanged kisses on both cheeks. "Stop bullshitting a bullshitter. I'm a fat old man and you know it. Everyone knows it."

Kouros' reply was lost in barrage of comments and catcalls from the men at the table as they shuffled back chairs and stood to embrace and exchange kisses with their cousin.

Uncle stood by his chair, watching and smiling.

"Where shall I sit?" asked Kouros.

"Next to your uncle," said a man about Kouros' age, but a head taller and far broader. "We have to put up with him all the time. You haven't had the pleasure since our cousin's wedding."

"And that was three years ago. It's way past your turn to suffer through his stories," said a younger and shorter man.

The group laughed as Uncle shook his head and looked at Kouros. "They're very lucky your aunt is no longer with us to hear them speak like that about her husband."

"*Theos singhorese tin,*" nodded the big man. "If mother were still alive, no one would dare speak like that. She'd whip us all."

More laughter, and more wishes that "God forgive her soul."

Uncle raised a bottle of beer. "A toast. To all of us. Together again. *Yia sas.*"

Kouros picked up a beer and clinked the bottle against his uncle's, "*Yia sas.*" He went around the table doing the same with each cousin, every one a bull. Some small, some large. Kouros fell into the middle of the herd.

Though it was still early afternoon, Kouros figured from the number of soiled plates, empty beer bottles, and overflowing ashtrays on the table that they'd been carrying on like this for hours. But no one seemed drunk, as if everyone realized there was a serious purpose for this get-together.

A woman in her thirties walked in from the kitchen, carrying plates filled with food, followed by the girl in the pink sweatshirt carrying more food.

"Here, Yianni, you must be starved. Eat," said the woman.

"Cousin Calliope! I can't believe it's you."

"Why, do I look so bad?"

Kouros nodded toward the girl. "No, you look like your niece's sister, not her aunt."

The teenage girl rolled her eyes.

Calliope smiled. "Father," she said to Uncle, "if this is how men from Athens talk, I understand why you and Mother never let me leave home." She bent over and gave Kouros a big kiss on each cheek, then a smack to the back of his head.

Kouros smiled, "Glad to see you picked up where your mother left off."

Calliope waved a hand at the men at the table. "Someone has to keep this family in line."

The men laughed. But not too hard, for they knew there was truth in her words. Historically, Mani fathers were rarely home, leaving Mani mothers to decide family matters, such as selecting which of her sons would face death to avenge a slight to the honor of the family.

"Come," she said to her niece. "Back to the kitchen. Time to leave the men alone to tell more lies to each another."

Uncle leaned over to Kouros. "I've been blessed with two daughters and three sons. Luckily, only Calliope lives with me. For she's the *less* strong-willed of the sisters. I think your aunt trained them to haunt me." He smiled. "Eat. We'll talk later."

Kouros ate as Uncle's oldest son, the biggest of the cousins, talked about a tourism explosion in their part of the Mani. "The land's yielding more euros per acre from visitors than any crop ever did."

"Later, Mangas," said Uncle. "Let your cousin finish his meal in peace."

He'd used his eldest son's nickname, not his given name, Yianni. Greek tradition had the first-born son named after his paternal grandfather and the second son after his maternal grandfather. That's why four of the seven cousins sitting around Uncle's table were Yiannis: Mangas, Kouros, Uncle's slain brother's son, and his surviving sister's second son. The non-Yianni cousins were Uncle's two younger sons, Theo and Giorgos, and the surviving sister's older son, Pericles. To the extent the interests of the female members of the family were affected by this meeting, it would be up to their brothers and sons to protect them.

"Don't worry about me, Uncle. I can chew and listen at the same time," said Kouros.

"No. You'll finish, then we'll talk." Uncle's voice was hard.

Kouros finished as quickly as he could without offending his uncle.

"Would you like more?"

"No, thank you."

Uncle nodded, paused for a few seconds, and smacked his hands firmly on the table.

Seven bulls jerked to attention.

"It is time."

"Our ancestors have lived on this land for hundreds of years. We *are* Mani. No one can ever change that. No government, no foreigner, no neighbor. And while some of our neighbors may choose to sell their birthrights, we shall *never* sell."

Some cousins nodded.

"But I also appreciate the times in which we live, and the struggles many of you face. And will continue to face. We are a family and no one of us should benefit at the expense of another."

Where is he headed with this? thought Kouros. He caught a puzzled look on the face of his slain uncle's son. *I guess I'm not the only one wondering.*

"I've decided to accept a proposal for our property."

"*What?*" said Uncle's youngest son, Giorgos. "You can't. You just said you'd never sell."

"Giorgos is right," said his brother, Theo. "This is our home. We can't leave it except through death."

Uncle raised his hands to calm his sons. "Spoken as true sons of Mani, for which I'm proud. But hear me out."

Giorgos' face was blood red, but he said not a word. In the Mani you dared not disrespect your elders.

"I've not sold the property. I've agreed to lease all of our land on the plateau for ninety-nine years except for this house, the tower, and the surrounding ten acres, which will remain ours. The rest will return to our family in your children's children's lifetimes."

Giorgos exploded. "What are you talking about? This is our land. No one else can ever live on it."

"What's the rent?" asked Theo.

Uncle smiled. "A sensible question. One I

would expect from my son the accountant." He paused. "Until the property is developed, the rent will be equal to twice what we could earn if used as farm land. Once it's developed, we'll receive a net rent equal to three percent of the project's gross annual proceeds."

"But who would make such a deal?" said Theo.

"One desperate for the land who realized that was the only deal I would make."

Giorgos still fumed, but less so. "Who are you leasing it to?"

"Someone who wants to build a luxury resort hotel, complete with a golf course."

"They must be crazy," said Giorgos. "A golf course here? In this waterless oven?"

"And an airstrip." Uncle shrugged. "I don't know about such things. I just know the terms will bring us far more money than we could ever hope to see from the land, and the land will still be ours."

Kouros cleared his throat. "May I speak, Uncle?"

"Of course."

"I'm very happy for you and hope it's as good a deal for you and your family as you say, but I don't think you asked me or Yianni—" he pointed at his slain uncle's son—"here for our advice. You and our aunt inherited the property from Grandfather when he died. It is yours for the two of you to do with as you wish."

Uncle waved his finger. "You're wrong. It is not just a good deal for *me* and *my* sister and *our* children. It's a good deal for *all* of our family."

Now puzzled looks came from all around the table.

"When I die, Calliope will continue to live in this house. But all of the cousins, including your sisters, will share equally in the rents. I do not need the money, and I will take care of my sister. She has agreed. And when you pass on, your children will inherit your shares."

"I don't understand," said the surviving aunt's son, Pericles. "Why are you doing this?"

"Because your mother and I think it's fair. Two of our brothers and a sister died on this land defending our honor, and if my mother had not forced my sister and Athens Yianni's father to flee, they too, would likely have died here. We all suffered, we all endured. We shall now all share in the family's good fortune."

Uncle looked at each face sitting around the table and fixed his eyes on Kouros.

"I don't know what to say, Uncle," said Kouros. "Thank you."

"Yes, thank you," said the slain brother's son.

Uncle nodded. "You're welcome."

Kouros glanced around the table for any sign of disappointment on the faces of those who now shared their inheritance, but they'd all had time to regain whatever composure they might have lost.

"I think this calls for some serious drinking," said Pericles.

"Yes," said Uncle. "Calliope, bring in the whiskey. Please."

Kouros had come prepared for a clash with his family over what he feared would be an effort to compromise his position as a cop, not to learn that he'd now have an income for life. How much didn't matter. He just felt relieved that his worries were unfounded.

Kouros was on his third celebratory shot of whiskey with his cousins when Uncle touched his arm.

"Yiannis, may I speak with you for a moment?"

"Sure, Uncle. What is it?"

"It's private. Come with me out to the tower."

So much for unfounded, thought Kouros.

The sun wouldn't set for another few hours, but Uncle still carried a flashlight. The five-story, effectively windowless tower had been built for war, not comfortable dwelling, and its narrow vertical slits were designed for taking aim at an enemy, not for admitting light.

As they walked to the tower, Kouros looked

west across a rock-strewn patchwork of fields sloping down toward the Ionian Sea and a cove with a tiny beach from which pirate ships once sailed. He wondered what Uncle had on his mind. Family intrigues played as much a part in life here as struggles to survive on land as fertile as chalk. Gray chalk. Even the sea yielded little food here. Nature's bounty had forgotten this place, blessing it in consolation with magnificent sunsets and quiet solitude.

Perhaps Uncle was right to lease the property. Tourism just might be God's plan for this long-suffering land.

"You never knew my father's father," said Uncle, scratching his ear. "He was good at his trade and provided well for his family."

"As I recall, he was a pirate," said Kouros.

"Yes, but not an ordinary one. He preferred guile to battle. Did you ever hear about his 'priest routine'?"

Kouros gave a quick upward nod of his head, the Greek gesture for "no." "And I'm not sure I want to know."

Uncle grinned. "I think you're old enough to handle this family secret. Your great-grandfather liked to pose as a priest for rich visitors and officers who'd come ashore from ships anchored off the coast. He'd gain their confidence, find out what they desired and, on the pretext of taking them somewhere to satisfy their itch, lure them to where his crew waited to kidnap them all. His men treated him as if he were one of their captives, and he'd convince the real captives to appoint him their intermediary in ransom negotiations between the captors and the victims' ship. That was his way of pirating a ship without risking the life of his men."

Uncle stopped at the door to the tower and looked at Kouros. "Some of the victims even gave him a reward for saving them from 'cutthroat Mani brigands.' Yes, your great-grandfather was creative in his business. Successful, too."

"Sounds like someone else I've heard tell of."

Uncle laughed. "I guess you could say I came by my trade honestly. I certainly shared his desire to protect his men as best he could. My way was to insist that they prey only on the outside world, drawing blood if necessary from other Greeks, Albanians, *Tsigani*, Europeans, North Africans, anyone but fellow Maniots." He turned to unlock the door. "And therein also lay the greatest difference between us. I abhorred our Mani blood feud history and did whatever I could to prevent that plague from spreading. That's not to say I haven't done a lot of very bad things, caused many to lose their lives, and taken some myself, but always outsiders, never Maniots."

Uncle paused. "Unless, of course, there wasn't a choice."

Uncle stepped inside and Kouros followed.

Towers always looked so much roomier from the outside, but their necessarily thick walls drastically reduced their inner dimensions. Though considered larger than most, this tower had less than one hundred square feet of first floor space, and each ascending story was smaller than the one below. The open, west-facing doorway filled the room with light. It was empty except for a freestanding ladder in the southeast corner running up through a trapdoor in the floor above. More ladders ran between the other stories, each capable of being pulled up quickly.

"Do I sound like an old man on the edge of making his confession?"

"The thought did cross my mind," said Kouros.

"But you'd think I'd know better than to pick an honest cop as my confessor." He put his hands on Kouros' shoulders. "What I'm about to tell you I've never told another living soul."

"Uncle, I'm not the right person to hear this."

"I'll be the judge of that." He drew in and let out a deep breath. "There is nothing more important to me than my children. Nothing."

Uncle walked to the front door and closed it,

shutting out all but a narrow spray of light cutting across the room through a tiny, barred window on the north wall and a pale glow fanning down through the trapdoor from tiny windows and narrow gun slits above. He stayed in the shadows by the door.

"Until the day I die I will never understand what drove my grandfather to have my father kill his sister. She was his *daughter*."

Kouros looked down at the floor.

"I could never bring myself to cause someone to kill my child. Or my sister or my brother. I am not a fool, I know it happens, it is part of our culture, but for me…no…never. Not after all that I saw in this house.

"My father never got over killing his sister. He never spoke of it, but he lived his life as if he'd died the day he murdered her. And when his own children began falling victim to vendetta, he took no steps to save them. As if he saw their deaths as the price God had placed upon his soul to pay for his sin. It was my mother who sent your father and aunt to Athens, and pleaded with the council of elders on my behalf.

"And all the many things he did for all those women he cared for in the village, he did seeking a forgiveness that never came."

He took a step toward Kouros. "The strangest

thing of all is, I don't think my father's father ever forgave his son for the killing. My father's return to the village as a doctor was not just my father's penance, but became his father's as well. Every day, the father saw the son and remembered what he'd made him do. It was a festering wound impossible to heal. And when his first grandchild fell to vendetta, Grandfather did not leave his grandson's burial site for two days and two nights. He returned home with fever but did not send word to his son for help. He stayed in his bed and died of pneumonia as his wife—my grandmother—sat patiently in the corner of the room watching him pass on."

He took another step closer to Kouros. "They were all sad people. Sad every day of their lives."

Silence.

"That's quite a burden you carry, Uncle. But I'm really not the one to help you with this. Perhaps a priest, a—"

He raised his hand for Kouros to stop. "No, that is not the sort of help I need. I've lived with this all my life, and will live with it for the rest of it. I have something I want to show you." He walked past Kouros into the darkest corner of the room and shone his flashlight into a stone, trough-like structure once used to store powder kegs and shot for musket battles.

"My grandmother never uttered a word to her

husband about his decision to have their daughter killed, but he knew she never forgave him. He'd murdered her pride and joy."

"How do you know?" said Kouros.

"She told me after Grandfather died. Long before that, when I was the baby of the family, she took care of me so that my mother could do other things. Like all grandmothers, she liked talking to babies. She had much she wanted to tell, but dared not tell an adult, so she opened up to me. She got used to talking to me about her secrets, and the older I grew the more she revealed. From her I learned things different from what others told me. Proud talk about the honor of vendetta she tempered by showing me the inevitable emptiness of it all, mourning her beloved Calliope every day of her life.

"My Calliope is named after her, Theo and Giorgos after my slain brothers, and their sister after my slain sister. So that I never forget what our family has lost to vendetta."

Kouros watched as his uncle began removing stones from inside the bottom of the trough.

"I've spent my life trying to spare my family the curse of vendetta. I made my decision to lease our land for that same reason. I don't want my sons and their cousins fighting over what should happen to our land after I am gone. Some, like Giorgos, want to keep it as it is, no matter what. Others, like

Theo, see the benefit of selling. Who knows what my sister's son Pericles may be thinking? He and his brother like the high life in Athens but don't have the money to afford it. Mangas is only interested in living life as it comes."

"Following in his father's footsteps?"

"I hope with the same attitude toward family. One that will never bring the two of you into conflict. But that's not why I brought you in here."

He piled up the stones next to the trough and on top of them placed several boards that had lain beneath the stones. He reached into the trough and lifted out a large box covered in cloth.

"What's that?" said Kouros.

"Calliope's chest."

"The murdered Calliope?"

He nodded. "Grandmother hid it here the night of her murder. She feared Grandfather would destroy it. Later, she worried that showing it to my father would only bring deeper sadness to his life. She showed me where she'd hidden it just before she died and made me promise to pass it on to my daughter when I had one, or someone else I thought would treasure the memory of Calliope and 'could forgive her for the mistake of loving a boy too much.'

"She made me promise to follow her instructions to the letter." He stood and carried the chest to Kouros. "But I never could bring myself to open old wounds. So I left it here, buried in my grandmother's shawl."

"But what does this have to do with me?"

He put the chest down at Kouros' feet. "Because the vendetta isn't over."

"You can't be serious."

Uncle sighed. "I wish I weren't. But vendettas can go on for generations."

"This isn't that sort of vendetta, Uncle. There's been no bad blood between the families for fifty years."

"I thought the same thing until last week. When I received a threat."

"What sort of threat?"

"One written across the back of my morning paper." He pulled a folded newspaper page out of his back pocket and read: "*Your father took his sister's and her lover's lives to preserve our ways. We shall take yours to save our Mani. You have one week to change your plans or die.*"

"That sounds crazy."

"I know."

"May I see it?"

Uncle handed him the page. The message had been carefully pasted onto the newspaper with words cut out of other newspapers.

"Any idea who did this?"

Uncle gestured no.

"What plans are they talking about?"

"My guess is the hotel."

Kouros scratched the back of his head. "In your line of work, Uncle, you must have made a lot of enemies. What makes you think the threat didn't come from one of them?"

"I thought that, too, at first. But I've had death threats before and my enemies know they don't scare me. Besides, if any of them wanted to make a macho point to impress some third party with how tough they could be by taking me on, I can assure you it would be for a flesh-and-blood real reason, not some generations-old vendetta bullshit. They'd know this sort of threat would make me think the sender a fool, one I'd never take seriously. And I didn't. Besides, I was too busy working on completing the hotel deal to worry about it."

"Then why are you taking it seriously now?"

He reached into his shirt pocket and pulled out a mobile phone. "Yesterday, I received this anonymous SMS." He held the phone so Kouros could read the message: YOUR TIME TO CHOOSE IS OVER. NOW IT IS YOUR TIME TO DIE.

"I will die someday. How, when, and where is in God's hands. Or maybe the devil's. But I don't want my death resurrecting a vendetta that will take more of my family. My sons are hotheads. Proud of being Maniots, but they don't know what it means to mourn a lost sibling or child, or to live in fear of what your neighbor might be about to do to you at any moment."

"What can I do for you?"

"I want you to find out who's threatening me."

"Then what?"

Uncle locked eyes with Kouros. "I'll take care of it."

"Uncle, I can't set someone up for execution."

He put a hand on Kouros' shoulder. "That's not what I have in mind. That would only fuel the vendetta. If I know who is behind this, perhaps I can reach out and make peace."

"And if not?"

Uncle shrugged. "All I ask is that you think about it on your drive back to Athens. See if there's some way you can bring yourself to help that won't compromise your principles. If you can, I'd be grateful. In the meantime, I'd appreciate it if you'd take Calliope's chest with you."

"Me?"

"Yes. As I said, I promised my grandmother to give it to someone who would treasure her daughter's memory and not judge her for her mistake. I don't see that in either of my daughters, as much as I love them. So, just in case I never get around to keeping that promise, I'd like you to be the one to do it for me."

Kouros swallowed. "I'm honored."

He picked up the chest and handed it to Kouros. "And if you do decide to help me find who's behind this threat, I promise you no one will die because of it."

Kouros smiled. "Promise?"

"My word of honor."

Chapter Three

"*Maggie!*"

The door to Chief Inspector Andreas Kaldis' office on the fourth floor of Athens' General Police Headquarters swung open and a sturdy, five-foot three-inch redhead stuck her head in the doorway. "You rang, Chief?"

They'd long ago settled on his yelling as far more efficient than the intercom.

"Where's Yianni?"

"On the way back from the Mani." She looked at her watch. "Should be here in about an hour."

"What's he doing on the Peloponnese?"

"How should I know?"

"Because you know everything about everyone in GADA." GADA was the nickname for central police headquarters and Maggie served as its unofficial mother superior. She'd ended up as Andreas' secretary when the retirement of her longtime boss coincided with Andreas' promotion back to GADA from a brief stint as chief of police for the Aegean island of Mykonos.

"He said it was a family matter."

Andreas nodded. "Okay, but tell him I want to see him as soon as he gets in."

"Your wish is my command."

Andreas waved his hand in the air. "Please, Maggie, not this early in the morning. I've a meeting this afternoon with the minister and need practice at being respectful to my boss. You're not setting a good example."

"As if you'll be able to carry off that act for long."

He smiled. "I wonder what's on Spiros' mind."

Maggie stepped inside the office and closed the door.

"According to his secretary, our distinguished minister of public order is scared to death about something having to do with Crete."

"How do you know that?"

"Spiros Renatis is your boss, and so that makes him my boss, and I like to keep up with what's going on in my bosses' lives. It makes mine easier."

Andreas sighed. "Why do I even bother to ask? So what do you know?"

"He's insecure, worried about every little thing. Ever since his wife's name showed up on that list the French gave our finance minister of two thousand Greeks with undisclosed bank accounts in Switzerland, he's been afraid of being booted out of his ministry position."

"Doesn't seem like much to worry about to me," said Andreas. "For two years, all the finance ministry did with that list was hide it. It took a journalist to make it public and the only one prosecuted was the journalist. Twice, and both times unsuccessfully."

Maggie grinned. "Well, at least it got the prosecutors finally doing something."

Andreas threw an open hand curse gesture at the windows of his office. "I'm still waiting for the first crooked bastard on the list to go to jail."

"Aren't we all? Spiros' story is that the account held earnings on his wife's investments outside of Greece on which all taxes were paid. But he's worried some hot-shot prosecutor out to earn a reputation might not buy that and decide to make his wife the first to stand trial, dragging Spiros into the middle of it."

Andreas shrugged. "But what's any of that got to do with whatever has him worked up over Crete?"

Maggie shrugged. "That's all I know. Would you like me to guess?"

Andreas patted his forehead with the fingers of his right hand. "Maggie…"

"Someone's squeezing his privates big-time."

"Who?"

"No idea, but whoever it is has a vise grip on them. So, be careful of your own."

"Thanks for the motherly advice."

"You're welcome." She smiled and left.

Andreas leaned back in his chair. He knew he ought to head down to the gym for a workout. Too much time behind the desk these days. He was coming up on forty and needed to keep a handle on the old waistline. Better yet, keep a handle off of it. He stood up, stretched his arms, and bent his six-foot, two-inch frame in half, fingers aimed at the toes. *Can still touch them.*

He straightened up and stretched again. He stared at the windows, walked over, and pulled back a curtain. There wasn't much to see. The interesting sites—Greece's Supreme Court and the stadium of one of the country's two most popular soccer teams—lay in other directions. Andreas let the curtain fall back in place.

I wonder what flaming bag of shit Spiros plans on dumping in my lap this time.

Andreas looked at his watch. He'd been waiting half an hour. His mobile phone rang. "Kaldis here."

"It's Yianni, Chief. Am I interrupting something?"

"No, Spiros has me waiting out here with his secretary trying to make me think he's actually busy. Even had the poor woman tell me, 'The minister's on a very important international conference call.'" Andreas spoke loud enough for the secretary to hear but she acted as if she weren't listening. "She deserves a raise for all the bullshit he puts her through."

She smiled.

"Sorry I missed you at the office, Chief. I got hung up in traffic. Farmers protesting tax increases blocked the highway with tractors. It was a mess for hours."

"So what else is new? Everything's a mess these days. How are things with your family?"

"Terrific."

"That's what I like to hear. Good news."

The secretary's phone buzzed, she picked it up, listened, and nodded at Andreas.

"Got to go, Yianni, his majesty will see me now."

Andreas crossed in front of the secretary's desk and opened the door to the minister's office. Before stepping inside he looked at the secretary and said loudly. "I meant what I said about you deserving a raise." He turned to Spiros. "Don't you agree?"

"Please," said Spiros, "just close the door and sit down."

Andreas closed the door and sat in one of the chairs by Spiros' desk.

"You must learn to show me more respect," said Spiros.

Andreas smiled.

"Did you hear me?"

"Are you recording this?"

A flash of anger crossed Spiros' face. He drew in a breath, reached for a glass of water on a silver tray sitting atop his desk, and took a sip. "Okay, so we've had some rocky times. Can't we put them behind us?"

"Did you bring me here to have that conversation?"

Spiros gestured no.

"I didn't think so."

"I could fire you."

Andreas shrugged. "Or I could resign. Either way you'd have the media to contend with. They know me, remember. And like me." He didn't have to add, *far more than they do you.*

The anger had returned on Spiros' face.

"Don't forget who I am," said Andreas. "I'm that 'crazy bastard who can't be bought or fired or set up.' I'm the only excuse you have to all those potbellied patrons of yours pressuring you to make nasty things about them on your desk go away." Andreas pressed his forefinger on Spiros' desktop.

"Without me to blame you'd have long ago lost your ministry for not doing favors, or be facing prison time if you had."

Andreas pulled his finger back from the desk. Greece's track record for prosecuting corrupt ministers hovered at just above zero, but times were changing so the risk was there and Andreas knew Spiros wasn't a risk taker. "We both know you need me more than I need this lousy-paying job." That part wasn't a bluff. Andreas had married the socially prominent daughter of one of Greece's oldest and wealthiest families.

Spiros took another sip of water. "Like I said, I don't think we should dwell on the past." He put down the glass.

"Okay, so let's talk about the *now*. Why am I here?"

Spiros bit at his lower lip. "I'm not a crook."

Andreas leaned back in his chair. "And precisely what's that supposed to mean?"

"You're right about the pressures exerted on this office. More so today than ever before. The people are screaming for prosecutors to cut off every politician's head. The corrupt are looking for ways to make as much as they can while they still can, and opportunists are trying to buy up government assets on the cheap." Spiros brought his hands up to his face and rubbed at his eyes. "Now I'm being dragged into the mess."

"Is this about your wife's bank account in Switzerland?"

Spiros gestured no as he kept rubbing at his eyes. "For now that's just an annoyance." He dropped his hands. "I'm talking about serious pressures involving more than a trillion euros."

Andreas cleared his throat.

"It shouldn't come as a surprise to you that all the talk about huge natural gas deposits off the southern coast of Crete has a lot of people wanting in on the action. And not just Greeks."

"I'd be surprised if that weren't the situation," said Andreas.

"We're talking pipelines, drilling rights, construction, shipping, maintenance. Everything you can imagine, all the way down to who gets the right to open a taverna. There's enormous money in play."

"And claims by Libyans to the same gas deposits."

Spiros nodded. "If Gaddafi were still in power, our government could have worked things out with him. But who knows what the Libyans will do now, or more likely, who will tell them what to do? The Americans, Chinese, Europeans, and Russians are all jockeying for influence in the region."

Andreas shrugged. "Big money attracts big players."

"I know. Look what happened after gas and oil were discovered in the Mediterranean off Cyprus. Every country in the area laid claim to the deposits. It has Israel teamed up with the Republic of Cyprus against Turkey's claim through Northern Cyprus. And with Cyprus' banking economy shot to hell, the Russians are licking their chops to get a piece of it."

"But how does the gas find in Crete involve you?"

"There are rumors that certain private foreign interests are attempting to influence Greek government officials improperly in the awarding of drilling and pipeline rights."

Andreas smiled. "I get it. Our countrymen are pissed off at having to compete with non-Greeks in a free-for-all bidding war for the favors of our accommodating government officials."

"This isn't funny."

"I know. Real wars are fought over oil. Just ask the Americans. But you have to admit it's ironic." Andreas smiled again.

"A lot of powerful people are clamoring for me to start an investigation."

"I assume you've been asked to be selective in choosing targets."

Spiros nodded. "All of them want me to go after their competition. The trouble is, in something this big everyone in the hunt has powerful friends asking me to do the same thing to everyone else."

"In other words, you're caught in the middle."

Spiros put his hand to his forehead. "Tied to a spit like an Easter lamb waiting to be slow-roasted the moment any of the losers starts shouting 'government corruption.'"

"Because their corruptors weren't as good as the winner's?"

"The reason won't matter. They'll point to our investigation, find something we missed, and say the other side obviously bought me off. The corrupt in government who actually were part of it all will righteously agree and make me their sacrificial scapegoat."

"Isn't that the way it's always been? Set up the good to protect the bad? If you think everyone's corrupt and an investigation won't make a difference, why bother to open one? Just say no."

"Everyone may not be corrupt, and even if they all are, I still can't say no. If I refuse, the big players demanding I act are powerful enough to drive me out of office and put someone in this chair that they can control."

"Don't tell me you're doing this out of loyalty to country."

"Is that so hard for you to believe?"

Andreas studied him. "What do you want from me?"

"I want you to look into this and come up with something I can use to get everyone off my back."

"Do you have any idea what that 'something' might be?"

"No."

"You do realize, Spiros, that you're sounding a bit crazy?"

"No, 'desperate' is the word. I don't want to end my public life under a cloud. If I can't find a way out of this I'm ruined."

"You could resign before this goes any further."

"If I resigned now, the media would say it's because of that bank account in Switzerland."

Andreas shook his head. "I wish I could help you, but if anywhere near a trillion euros is involved, I have about as much a chance at finding the lost city of Atlantis as that 'something' to get your alphabet list of world powers and who-knows-how-many connected Greeks off your back."

"All I can ask is that you try. You're the only one I know who might be able to pull it off."

Andreas fixed on Spiros' eyes. "Spare me the

Vaseline. Just don't forget two things. One, if I start, there's no going back, no matter who's involved."

Spiros nodded. "Understood."

Andreas leaned forward. "And, two, if I find out you're trying to set me up to take a fall for you…" Andreas let his voice trail off.

Spiros did not look away. "No need to say it. I understand that, too."

Andreas leaned back in the chair. "Fine. I need a copy of your files on this mess."

"There are no files." Spiros picked up a pencil, wrote something on a piece of paper, and handed it to Andreas. "But here's whom you should speak to."

Andreas read the name, looked up, and stared at Spiros. "You weren't kidding about who's involved."

Spiros nodded. "As you said, 'Big money attracts big players.'"

Kouros was in his office when the call came through. "Detective Kouros here."

"It's me." The voice sounded strained. It was Uncle's oldest son, Mangas, successor to his father's criminal enterprises.

"You sound gloomy," said Kouros. "What's the matter, did I leave my toothbrush at your father's house?"

"I've bad news."

Kouros' heart skipped a beat.

"My father's dead."

Kouros held the phone, frozen, and didn't speak.

"Did you hear me?"

Kouros nodded at the phone. "Yes." He drew in a deep breath. "What happened?"

"He was driving back alone from morning coffee with his friends at the taverna in Marmari on the road to Cape Tenaro…"

Kouros listened to his cousin struggle against tears. Cape Tenaro sits at the southernmost point of mainland Greece where the Ionian and Aegean seas meet and Greek mythology placed as the entrance to Hades, home to the god of the dead. Some moderns called it by its Italian name, Cape Matapan; the ancients had called it Tainaron.

"His car went off the road at a cliff and…"

Kouros waited.

"The ambulance driver said he didn't suffer. But they always say that. I can't stop wondering what was going through his mind in those last seconds."

Kouros had an idea of what it might have been, but this was not the time to bring up the death threats. Not with his cousin's temper. "I'm sure he was thinking about your family. When is the funeral?"

"Tomorrow at eleven."

"I'll be there."

"Thanks. He used to say you and I were 'two sides of a gold coin, each facing in different directions, but both made of the same stuff.'"

Now Kouros struggled with tears. "Your father was a very special man."

"He drove that road every day. I don't understand how it could have happened."

"Maybe he had a heart attack?"

"There was nothing wrong with his heart. But there's an autopsy going on right now."

"Anything wrong with the car?"

"I have people checking on that as we speak."

Kouros heard anger growing in his cousin's voice.

"Have the police looked at the car?"

"The cops in this part of the Mani wouldn't know where to start. I called the same guy they use, a friend who has a repair garage. He'll tell me all I need to know."

"All you 'need to know' to do what?" said Kouros.

Silence.

"Mangas, you're angry and looking for someone to blame. I understand, it's only natural. But that doesn't mean you'll make the right decision if you find something wrong with the car."

More silence.

"Now it's my turn to ask, 'Did you hear me?'"

"Yeah, I heard you."

"Just promise me you won't run with your temper until the funeral is over and we've had the chance to talk."

Again silence.

"You know your father would have wanted it that way."

"Okay. You have my word. Nothing until after the funeral."

"And we get to talk?" said Kouros.

"Yeah. Bye."

The line went dead but Kouros kept staring at the handset. He'd often wondered how his cousin picked up the nickname "Mangas." It came out of Greece's Roaring Twenties as a term used to describe young, urban, working class men attracted to the *rebetiko* Greek folk music of their times, Greece's equivalent of America's blues. Hatched in prisons, hashish dens, and ouzo parlors, it attracted long-mustached men partial to an idiosyncratic style of dress—woolen hat, arm through only one sleeve of a jacket, striped trousers, knife snugly tucked into a belt around the waist, pointy shoes—and a distinctive John Wayne style of limp-walking. Old time *mangas* tough guys were long gone and today the word held many potential meanings, ranging from "strong or brave or crafty," through "swaggerer," and on down to "bully, henchman, or hooligan." Some even said it was Greece's equivalent for "dude," as in the iconic Jeff Bridges character in the American film, *The Big Lebowski*.

No matter what prompted his cousin's nick-name, if Uncle had been murdered there'd be no holding Mangas and his brothers back from taking revenge. And if Kouros didn't tell them what he knew, they might end up going after the wrong people. But who were the right people?

Kouros hung up the phone. A new bloody clan war was about to break out in the Mani.

Time to speak to the chief.

Chapter Four

When Andreas returned to his office he found Kouros sitting on his couch. "Why do I doubt you're sitting here anxiously awaiting to talk about soccer?"

"I need time off, Chief. Family business."

Andreas walked behind his desk and sat down. "I thought you said everything was terrific."

"It was. Until I got a call from my cousin. My uncle died this morning in an automobile accident in the Mani."

Andreas shook his head. "I'm sorry to hear that. When's the funeral?"

"Tomorrow. But that's not the reason I need the time."

"Are we talking about the uncle who, shall we say, walked a different path than you?"

Kouros nodded. "He hasn't been involved in that for years."

"Didn't his son take over for him?"

"That's who called me."

Andreas leaned across the desk. "Yianni, we've been together a long time—"

"Since I was a rookie on Mykonos, I know. But it's not what you think."

"How do you know what I'm thinking?"

"You're about to warn me to be careful about someone in that part of my family trying to draw me into their business."

Andreas leaned back. "Okay, consider yourself warned."

"I think my uncle was murdered. And if my cousins start thinking the same way, all hell will break loose down there."

"What makes you think murder?"

Kouros told him about the death threats his uncle had received. "He died on his way home from the same taverna where he received the first threat."

Andreas rubbed his forehead. "Why does crap always come in piles? Wait until you hear what Spiros just dropped on me."

Kouros listened, and when Andreas finished he shook his head. "How does he expect you to help with *that*?"

"Beats me. Maybe I'll have a better idea after I talk with this guy." He waved the piece of paper containing the phone number given him by Spiros.

"Chief, we've been together a long time...." Kouros let the words trail off.

Andreas smiled. "Since Mykonos, and I know what you're thinking. All fat cat bad guys are looking for a friendly cop willing to look the other way, and I'm sure this one's no different."

"At least my cousin came by his ways honestly. He was born to that life. Corrupt political types make a conscious decision not to play by the rules."

"Fine, so we're both warned."

"I do need the time off."

"I know. Take what you need. But keep me in the loop. And you're on duty, not off. The last thing we need down there is a clan war. That part of the Mani is just beginning to get a toehold on tourism and a breakout of vendetta violence could wreck its prospects."

"Funny you should say that. The reason my uncle wanted to see me yesterday was to tell the family he'd reached a deal to lease out the family property as a big-time resort."

"Like I said, for everyone's sake, let's hope that if your uncle was murdered it's not tied into a vendetta or likely to start one. But whatever it is, try to wrap it up quickly because I really do need your help with this Crete thing."

"Mind if I ask you a question, Chief?"

"As if I have a choice."

"Why are you doing this for Spiros? You know better than anyone that he'll turn on you faster than a hooker on a nonpaying trick if he thinks it could take the heat off him."

Andreas nodded. "I made it perfectly clear to him I knew all of that. Though I didn't put it quite as thoughtfully as you just did."

"So, like I said, why are you doing this? He's just sticking you with another mess he can't get anyone else to touch."

Andreas spread open his arms. "That's just the point. If I don't take it on, who will? We might as well hand over the keys to Greece to the bad guys. As I see it, either I do my job and risk Spiros turning on me, or I resign." Andreas rubbed at his eyes with the thumb and forefinger of his right hand. "If I resigned I'd be out of the fight, powerless against the wolves descending on our country in packs. Just the thought of being helpless drives me close to crazy. I'd have to move my family out of Greece to save my sanity. And that's something I never want to do. So, for now, I risk another betrayal by Spiros as my price for staying in the battle." Andreas dropped his hand from his eyes and stared out the window. "But if that little bastard tries to screw me this time…"

"We can always call in my cousin." Kouros smiled.

Andreas chuckled. "Do you want to take anyone with you?"

Kouros gestured no. "It would attract too much attention. Make my cousins think I suspect something might be wrong. I'll just poke around and try to keep a lid on things until I get a better handle on who might be involved. If I need help, I'll yell."

"Don't be a hero."

"I know."

Andreas smiled. "There's only enough room for one in this unit."

Kouros picked up his mother at her apartment at evening twilight. He'd wanted to leave earlier but she said she needed more time to prepare for the funeral. He knew there was nothing he could say to hurry her along, for in virtually no other aspect of Greek life was the role of women as dominant as in the matter of funerals.

Greek funerals differ from those in other parts of Western Europe, and in the Mani even more so. There, funerals evoked memories of ancient rites and pagan practices followed in the Mani six centuries after the rest of Greece had accepted Christianity in the fourth century.

Greek Orthodox funerals took place as soon

as possible after death, usually within a day or so. Generally, the poorer and less educated the family, the greater the intensity of the mourning, drawing anguished female mourners sobbing, crying, shrieking, and wailing into such frenzies that some risked falling in upon the coffin. But in the Mani—perhaps the poorest province of Greece— the women conducted their traditional mourning in a relatively structured manner.

Unlike the uncoordinated dirges and lamentations staged in other parts of Greece, the women of the Mani expressed their mourning in long funeral hymns, guided by a strict poetic meter different from any other Greek rhyme. Mani women improvised their *mirologia* or "words of lament" while sitting with the body at the home of the deceased, each working herself into a sufficiently emotional state of grief to signal that another should take over. The *mirologia* employed an ancient literary form, first welcoming the guests, extolling the deceased, the deceased's children, and the deceased life's work, and—if killed in a feud—ending in curses and vows of vengeance.

Kouros and his mother wouldn't make it to Uncle's home in time for the *mirologia*. Uncle's body would spend the night in church and *mirologia* wouldn't be said there. He wondered what his mother might have said had she chosen to participate. There was no requirement that she do so, and for someone as important as his uncle, plenty of women would be competing to out-mourn one another.

His mother fell asleep just south of the Corinth canal. Good, he thought. It would be a long day. He wondered if his cousin had any news about Uncle's car. He thought to call him but that would wake his mother. Besides, no reason to risk winding up his cousin with a phone call. Mangas had promised to do nothing until they'd had the chance to talk after the funeral. A phone call now might give him the opportunity to change their deal.

If Mangas found something wrong with the car, his headstrong temper could send him after an otherwise innocent mechanic. Yet if Kouros told him it might not be the mechanic's fault, but sabotage, it chanced launching his cousin on a rampage against anyone he might think to blame. Kouros let out a deep breath. And if he mentioned the death threats received by his uncle, it risked stoking unrestrained vendetta violence of the sort his uncle had spent a lifetime trying to avoid.

Kouros needed to get a grip on things quickly. But where to begin? He yawned.

"With staying awake," he mumbled to himself. He reached for the thermos of coffee his mother had packed for their trip…along with enough food to feed all of the Mani for a week.

God bless mothers.

And heaven help those who dared cross the child of a Mani mother.

"*Kalo vradi,* Chief Kaldis," said the doorman at Andreas' apartment building.

"Good evening, Angelo."

"Mrs. Kaldis said to tell you that she and your son are at your mother's house for dinner."

Which was precisely where Andreas should have been an hour and a half ago. "Thank you."

He guessed that by now his mother was having so much fun playing with her grandson that she'd probably forgotten all about Tassaki's AWOL father. Besides, Andreas' late father had been a cop so his mother was used to her men missing dinners. He doubted his wife would be as forgiving. Andreas wasn't complaining. As he saw it, Lila Vardi had sacrificed far more than he when she became Mrs. Kaldis. Andreas' biggest struggle was learning to cope with what it meant to be living in a penthouse apartment on the most prestigious street in Athens, next door to the presidential palace.

The elevator opened into the apartment's foyer

and Andreas walked through the front rooms into the kitchen. He saw a note taped to the refrigerator:

"On the off chance you don't make it to your mother's, dinner's inside. :-) Marietta will warm it up for you. Love, L."

Perhaps I've misjudged her.

He opened the refrigerator door and found his favorite dish: chicken and fresh tomatoes slow cooked in *oyvetsi* pasta. He put the pot on the black-and-gray counter on the kitchen island, found a fork, and started eating out of the pot.

The man Spiros wanted him to call came from a politically connected family that had skyrocketed to great wealth in the 1980s and remained in orbit ever since. It was rumored he could "fix anything" regardless of the political party in power.

"*Mister Kaldis*," said a woman in the doorway behind him.

Andreas acted startled. "Marietta, you should wear a bell so I know when you're sneaking up on me."

"Missus Kaldis would shoot me if I let you eat your dinner cold. And out of the pot! Give it to me."

"You'll have to kill me first. I like my *oyvetsi* cold. And don't worry about Missus Kaldis. If she shoots you, I promise to conduct a thorough investigation."

She reached for the pot but Andreas shielded it from her with his body.

"Just give me the pot, please."

"Let's make a deal. If I let you get me a glass of wine, could we call it a draw?"

The maid shook her head, turned, and walked into the pantry. She returned with an opened bottle of white wine and a wineglass.

"At least I can tell Missus Kaldis I gave you a good wine."

Andreas looked at the label: KIR YIANNIS. He smiled. That wine company was owned by the current mayor of Greece's second-largest city, Thessaloniki, who, unlike his predecessor sentenced to serve a life term for corruption, had a reputation for honesty. A quite different sort from the man he was about to call.

"Can I get you anything else?"

"No, thank you, Marietta."

She left him sitting on a barstool by the counter, sipping his wine and picking at his dinner. Andreas liked the kitchen. Most of the other rooms had spectacular, unobstructed views of the Acropolis or its majestic sister hill, Lykavitos, but this one offered only walls, with just a glimpse of the sky through windows in the room beyond its doorway. It reminded him of his old fourth floor, maybe the elevator was operating, slight view, one-bedroom apartment. This room kept him in touch with his roots, or so he liked to think. Roots were important. He hoped Kouros' own roots wouldn't create a problem for him, but the kid was tough enough to figure out the right thing to do.

Andreas looked at his watch. It was coming up on eleven, the perfect time to call Spiros' man with all the answers. He ran with a crowd that partied until the early morning hours, entertaining many of the same folks they'd be compromising later.

Andreas stood up and carried his wineglass into the library. He closed the door and sat down behind the desk. He mumbled to himself as he picked up the phone. "I guess it's my time to figure out the right thing to do."

He dialed the number on the piece of paper. The phone rang five times.

"Orestes here." There was the sound of loud music and the clatter of plates in the background.

Andreas took a sip of wine. "Sorry to bother you, sir, my name is Andreas Kaldis and—"

"Your minister said you'd be calling. Does it always take you so long to do what you're told?"

Andreas put down the wineglass. "Only when I have more important things to do."

"Perhaps you don't know who you're talking to." There was a noticeable slur to Orestes' words.

"Of course I do."

"Then you should know you could not pos-sibly have had anything more important to do."

"Well, sir, you have my attention now. So, what do you want to tell me?"

"I'm not about to have this discussion over the phone."

"Fine, what if we meet at police headquarters first thing tomorrow morning?"

"*No.* I want to see you *now*. And *HERE.*"

"Sure, anything you say. What's the address?" Andreas marked it down as the phone went dead. He shook his head and smiled. The guy had taken the bait and lost his temper. Orestes sounded drunk and by the time Andreas got there he'd be more so, plus anxious to show Andreas just how big his dick was. No telling what he might say to prove it.

The evening was beginning to look interest-ing. But it wouldn't begin to compare to tomorrow morning, when he'd have to explain to Lila why he'd ended up in Athens' hottest, sexiest nightclub instead of at his mother's.

Chapter Five

Athens' Gazi district sat not far to the northwest of the Acropolis and encircled the city's old natural gasworks, from which the area took its name. Today, the gasworks had transformed into a modern museum and cultural center surrounded by vibrant restaurants and cafes. Greece's free-spending boom years had helped turn the once-blighted area into a primary destination for partiers in a city then ranked number one for the best nightlife in Europe. But things were different now. With less money to spend and Gazi's somewhat dangerous bordering neighborhoods becoming more so, business was off. But you could still find places where no one acted as if they'd heard of the financial crisis and all paid handsomely for the privilege of maintaining the pretension that they'd not been affected by it. At the top of that list was the spot Orestes had picked for their meeting, El Malaga.

Andreas stood on the sidewalk staring at two

massive black doors, one with a florid gold "E," the other with an equally ostentatious "M."

Three six-foot six-inch bodybuilders in matching black suits and white shirts stood behind a red velvet rope administered by a buxom blonde wearing a black, what-you-see-is-what-you-get Hervé Léger minidress. Andreas assumed she was the gatekeeper, the three men her attack dogs. He smiled at the woman and stepped up to the rope.

She smiled back. "May I help you, sir?"

"Yes, I'd like to go inside."

"Do you have a reservation?"

"No, I'm meeting someone already inside."

"May I ask the name of the person you're meeting?"

"Orestes."

"You mean—"

"Yes, that Orestes."

"And your name."

"Just 'guest' will do fine. He's expecting me."

The woman's smile faded. "I need to know your name, sir."

"No, you don't. He asked to see me. If you won't let me in, no problem. I'll just tell him the reason I missed our meeting was that the lovely lady at the door stopped me."

She looked at her three men. One stepped forward. He had four inches on Andreas, forty pounds of muscle, and a scowl. "Petro, please show Mister 'Guest' to Orestes' table."

"Thank you," Andreas smiled.

"And if there is some mistake," she put on a smile, "please show him immediately back outside."

Andreas gave her the thumbs-up. "It's a deal."

Petro opened one door and waved for Andreas to enter a dimly lit vestibule leading to another set of doors. They were alone in the vestibule and Andreas started to reach for the other set of doors when Petro put his hand on Andreas' arm.

"Just a minute, Chief."

Andreas looked at Petro. "Do I know you?"

The scowl turned to a smile. "I'm a cop assigned to headquarters security at GADA."

"Are you working undercover here?"

"No, just trying to make a living. It's a night job."

Andreas smacked him on the shoulder. "Thanks for not giving me away."

"I figured you wanted it that way. Come on, I'll take you to Orestes' table."

Whether Petro was an honest cop earning extra money as a bouncer or something else, Andreas had no way of knowing. But he liked the guy's style. "Stop by my office for a coffee sometime."

"Thanks, I'd like that."

Petro opened the door and a whoosh of sounds

filled the vestibule, followed by the acrid smell of cigarette smoke. Smoking had been outlawed in places like these years ago, but those charged with enforcing the law rarely did. Inside, El Malaga had its share of *de rigueur* low lighting, red and gold flocked wallpaper, faux gilt embellished woodwork, and cigarette burns in its almost-leather uphol-stered banquettes. But what made this place unique were the owner's two primary passions: painting and women. El Malaga earned him the money to sustain and display them both. Stark, Picasso-like images of exaggerated nudes in exotic poses filled the walls, and one of El Malaga's grand parlor games involved trying to guess the women who'd been the models. In some cases it was obvious, because the woman had proudly claimed the portrait as her own by writing her name beneath it. Others simply smiled to themselves as they listened to patrons guess at their identities. But the owner wouldn't name names, for it was his inviolate discretion that kept him in models.

Petro led Andreas through a bar area filled with courting young men and women into a larger room filled with linen-covered tables and an older crowd. A small stage at the far end of the room accommodated everything from intimate cabaret to hardcore urban *rebetiko* performances, depending upon the mood the owner decided to set for the room. Tonight the stage was empty.

They stopped at a table of six men near the stage. Andreas recognized Orestes. He sat huddled in conversation with the men on either side of him while the others laughed in animated conversation with a group of women at the next table. Andreas assumed the women's table was next to the men's for a reason. In these days of ubiquitous smartphone cameras, girlfriends of prudent, married big shots didn't sit at the same table with their patrons.

"Thanks, Petro, I'll take it from here."

Petro nodded and left.

Andreas stood by the table and looked across at Orestes. Orestes ignored him. Andreas cleared his throat. Orestes still ignored him. "Excuse me, sir, my name is Andreas Kaldis."

Orestes acted as if he didn't hear him. Andreas walked up behind him and tapped him on the shoulder. "Excuse me, sir, but I'm Andreas Kaldis—"

Without turning, Orestes said, "I know who you are. I'll speak to you when I'm finished speaking to my friends."

The two men with Orestes smirked.

"But there's no place for me to sit at your table, sir."

"Then you'll have to stand."

The men laughed.

"No problem, sir."

Andreas walked over to an empty chair at the women's table. "Mind if I sit here, ladies?" Without waiting for an answer he sat down and flashed his most charming Cary Grant smile at the blonde to his right and brunette to his left.

"My name is Andreas, what's yours?"

The women looked nervously at the men's table.

"Oh, don't worry about them, I'm here to see Orestes. We're all old friends."

The blonde smiled. "I'm Sasha."

"Hilda," said the brunette.

Both spoke Greek with distinctly Eastern European accents and looked to be less than half, if not a third, the age of Orestes' guests.

"So, how long have you known Orestes?" said Andreas.

"We just met him tonight," said the blonde.

"We're with his friends," said the brunette.

"*Hey you*, get away from that table." It was one of the two men talking with Orestes. He spoke Greek without an accent.

Andreas turned to the man, lifted his hand, and motioned with his forefinger for the man to come to him.

"Fuck you, asshole, I said get away from that table."

Andreas turned away from him, leaned in, and said to the girls, "I hope that one's not yours."

The brunette gestured no.

Andreas smiled. "Lucky you." He turned to the blonde, pressed his lips close to her ear, and said, "I assume that means he's all yours." He kept his lips next to her ear, but out of the corner of his eye watched the man bolt up from his chair and storm toward him. He looked like a small, sixty-year-old bull. In heat.

Without moving from the woman's ear Andreas put up his hand in a sign for the man to stop. Instead the man grabbed Andreas' arm and yanked him out of the chair.

With his free hand Andreas grabbed the man around the waist and laughed as he began quickly spinning them around together. "My, my what would your wife say if she knew about us carrying on like this in public?"

The man let go of Andreas' hand and Andreas abruptly stopped spinning, letting go of the man's waist as he did and sending him stumbling into the women's table. Before the man could regain his balance, Andreas steered him by his shoulders down onto the seat between the blonde and brunette. He tried to stand, but Andreas gripped his shoulders and held him down. "I suggest you stay here. It will be far less a scandal than what will happen if you try to stand up."

Andreas smiled at the people staring at them from the other tables. "Don't be alarmed, folks, just a little lovers' quarrel." He leaned down, kissed the top of the man's head, and whispered. "Like I said, *stay*."

Andreas stepped over to Orestes' table and sat in the now empty chair next to him. "So, what is it you want to tell me? Or would you prefer that I ask you to dance, too?"

Orestes glared but didn't respond. He waved for a waiter. "Please find us a private table for two."

The waiter bowed. "Certainly, please follow me."

He led them to an isolated table in the corner farthest from the front door.

Andreas sat with his back to the wall and stared at Orestes' eyes.

"Do you know who that man you just embarrassed is?" said Orestes, staring back.

"You mean my dance partner?"

"He's the most successful contractor in Greece. His companies build harbors, airports, dams, bridges, power plants."

"I assume you mean the most successful *unindicted* contractor in Greece."

"I don't like you, Kaldis."

"I don't want you to."

"I can have you replaced."

"Try."

Orestes turned his head and motioned to a waiter serving a nearby table. "Bring me my drink." He looked back at Andreas. "You should know better than to turn on your own kind."

"My 'own kind?' What kind is that?"

"Greeks, of course. But not just any Greeks. I'm talking about those of us with the power and ability to achieve great things."

"Not sure I follow you."

The waiter arrived carrying a bottle of scotch and a snifter. He placed the glass in front of Orestes and poured in a ten count of Johnny Walker Blue Label.

"A glass for my friend."

"No thank you, I'll have a Mythos."

"Ahh, despite your champagne bride, you retain your beer roots."

Andreas pointed at the glass in Orestes' hand. "Don't let the courage in that go to your head. You keep talking like that and you'll learn a few more practices I've carried over from my roots."

Orestes raised his free hand. "No offense intended. I simply meant to compliment you on how well you've retained the charm of your origins.

But I do wonder how you would have turned out had you not found your way to Lila."

"And I wonder how you would have turned out had it not been your father's sperm that found its way to your mother."

Orestes' hand shook as he squeezed his glass. Andreas had clearly struck a nerve. This man was the scion of a political family, with a prime minister or two in his ancestry. But on his own, Orestes had achieved no more than what easily came through profiting off the influence of his father's name.

"Easy there, you wouldn't want to break the glass and bloody your own hands."

The waiter returned with a beer and placed a glass in front of Andreas.

"In deference to your social standing, I'll drink this beer out of a glass," said Andreas.

The waiter poured the beer.

Andreas lifted his glass up toward Orestes. "*Yia sas.*"

Orestes jerked his snifter forward, clinked Andreas' glass, and mumbled, "*Yia sas.*"

Andreas took a sip and put down the beer. "As I see it, you need me a lot more than I need you. Your buddies over there don't know it yet, but you're all on the verge of becoming extinct. It's the curse of getting what you wished for. For generations your family and others like it have been turning every government opportunity into personal jackpots. It didn't matter what was involved. Defense, hospitals, public construction, agriculture—anything our government had a hand in, you found a way to squeeze something out of for yourselves. But that was never enough. You wanted to be 'as rich as the Arabs' and along came these Cretan gas fields and you thought they'd be your payday. But *surprise*! Something's happened you never anticipated. You're used to playing in a rigged, small-time game against amateurs. But now the stakes are much larger and mega-rich big boys who play by rules far tougher and dirtier than any you ever imagined are taking over the game. You're scared shitless of losing your money spigot."

Orestes waved his hand. "You don't know what you're talking about."

"Really? Let's see. Greece's finances are under microscopic scrutiny by a host of world financial powers to whom we owe umpteen zillion euros. It has a reputation as one of the most corrupt countries in the world, a disenchanted population heading more into poverty than out, political extremists in Parliament ready, willing, and, God forbid, able to plunge the country into civil war, and you think you can continue to do your little back room 'a bit for me a bit for you' bullshit dance to get anything you want out of our government?

Wake up and smell the coffee, man. But you'd better hurry, for soon it, too, may not be Greek."

"That's just my point."

"What is?"

"Greece should profit Greeks, not foreigners."

"I assume you mean *some* Greeks."

"Does it matter as long as the money stays in our country? If foreigners control our gas, the profits will leave our country. Greece will be nothing more than a colony, exploited to serve other countries."

"Spare me the political rhetoric. Money squirreled away in Swiss bank accounts isn't helping Greece."

"But foreigners won't care what happens to our beloved Greece. They'll destroy our seas, our beaches, our very way of life to profit themselves."

"You're really trying to push every button, aren't you? Trouble is, your facts are wrong. Foreigners have shown more concern than our government at protecting our environment. Greece has been penalized so often by the EU for environmental violations that fines are considered part of the cost of doing business here."

Orestes impatiently waved off Andreas' words. "I'm talking about massive, irreversible ecological disasters on the scale of what happened to America's Gulf Coast in 2010 at the hands of disinterested foreigners. And look what the Russian geologists did to Turkmenistan in 1971. They tapped into a cavern filled with natural gas and started a fire that still burns today. The locals call it their 'gate to hell.' Then there's Chernobyl. No one likes to talk about it anymore, but it still haunts and poisons us every day. If that's the kind of foreign expertise the world has to offer us, I say no thank you."

Andreas knew he was getting Orestes' "Greece is for Greeks" bullshit sales pitch, not a search for truth. It was a lobbyist pitching to get his client what it wanted and damn everything else. But as insincere as Orestes undoubtedly was, the environmental issue was a real one, and it wouldn't be prudent politics to give him an angle on claiming Andreas, and by extension Spiros' ministry. He wasn't concerned with environmental threats.

"I'm not sure environmental issues fall within the domain of my ministry, but I'm willing to look into what you've raised to see if any illegal activity might be compromising environmental safeguards."

Orestes' face lit up like a kid's on Christmas morning. "That's terrific. Come, let's rejoin my party. Tomorrow I will give you the names and details of those you should be investigating."

Before Andreas could respond, Orestes stood up and headed back toward his friends' table. He waved for Andreas to follow. "No need for you to carry my glass and the bottle. The waiter will do that for me."

Asshole.

Andreas stood outside El Malaga, trying to remember where he'd left his car. He'd been inside with Orestes and his crowd until four. Now he had a whole new batch of connected "friends" trying to draw him into their networks. It was age-old, lure-the-fly-to-the-spider style politics. Spiros said Andreas wouldn't like the political game. *Guess he was right about one thing.*

Orestes had announced with a flourish to his table of friends that Special Crimes Chief Inspector Andreas Kaldis has agreed to conduct an investigation into the efforts of certain foreign elements to exploit our nation's resources for their own national interests. That brought on a round of toasts to Greece and to Andreas. It was pure theater, with Orestes cast in the role of noble savior of the nation, having found the "perfect" champion for their cause. Andreas had decided simply to smile. That was all Orestes really wanted anyway—the opportunity to play hero to his guests. Where it all would lead was something for Andreas to sort out with Spiros in the morning.

He remembered he'd parked his car on a sidewalk somewhere around a corner. He waved good night to Petro at the door and headed toward the corner in front of him.

Andreas knew to stay alert to his surroundings. On a scale running from white to red—white being asleep in your mother's arms, red being balls-out raging with an AK-47—on the street he kept perpetually in orange. But with all he'd been drinking, at the moment it felt more like peach, as in Bellini. At the corner he turned left and saw his unmarked police car about a block away. He smiled. *Right where I knew I left it.*

Halfway to the car, two young men came running around the corner in front of him heading straight at him, with a third coming up fast behind them. Andreas backed into a doorway to let them pass. He heard the crack of a gunshot and saw one of the two men in front grab the back of his thigh and fall to the pavement five feet before the doorway. The other kept running. The third man stopped at the man on the ground and shot him three more times. He looked up, saw Andreas in the doorway, aimed his gun at him, and pulled the trigger.

Nothing happened.

Andreas was on him like a wounded grizzly. He'd already snapped the man's trigger finger yanking the gun out of his hand, broken his jaw with a palm thrust under the chin, cracked two ribs with an elbow to the chest, and was kneeling on the man's chest pounding away at his face when someone pulled him away yelling, "*Chief, stop. That's enough.*"

Andreas didn't struggle. He breathed in and out deeply, trying to calm himself.

"Are you, okay?" said Petro.

"Yes, thanks."

"I heard the shots and when I came around the corner I saw that bastard aiming at you."

"He pulled the trigger."

"You're damn lucky his gun jammed or he was out of ammo."

Andreas shut his eyes and nodded. "Tell me about it."

"What happened?"

"No idea, but in this neighborhood at this hour, my guess would be drugs."

"You don't think it was a hit meant for you?"

Andreas gestured no. "Not the way this was done." He fluttered out a long breath. The adrenaline was still there. "I shouldn't have gone ballistic. But I was so angry at myself for not picking up on what was going down, I took it out on him."

"I don't think he'll be expecting an apology."

Andreas laughed and patted Petro on the

shoulder. "There was another guy running away from the shooter."

"Yeah, I got a look at him."

"Do you mind dealing with the blue-and-whites on this? I'd like to get home. If they need anything from me, they can find me in my office."

"Sure, no problem. Besides, I think you're right about this being over drugs." He pointed at the dead man. "He's a dealer from another neighborhood. Locals don't like outsiders cutting in on their territory."

Just like Orestes and his friends.

At 5:17 a.m. Andreas crawled into bed. Lila lay on her belly under the covers.

A millisecond later he heard, "So?"

"I was hoping you'd be asleep."

"So was I."

"It was a long night."

"I can tell."

"No sex," said Andreas.

"Are you asking for some or confessing to none?"

Andreas laughed. "I spent the night at El Malaga being hustled by Orestes and his buddies. Let me sleep and I promise to tell you everything when I wake up." He shut his eyes.

"Are you talking about the Orestes who asked me to marry him before I met you?"

Andreas opened his eyes. "I never heard about that."

"There was never any reason to tell you. It was all before we met. Which Orestes are you talking about?"

Andreas told her.

Lila lifted her hand and patted him on his back. "Yep, same one."

"You're just saying that to wind me up and get me to talk."

"Why would I do that? You said you'd tell me everything when you woke up. I can wait."

Andreas stared into the dark for a moment, sat up, and turned on the light. "But I can't. Tell me about him."

Lila didn't budge or open her eyes. "What do you want to know?"

"Start with the good parts."

"There weren't any. He was an arrogant political opportunist, looking for a socially prominent wife to complement his career."

"With money?"

"For him that wasn't as important as social standing."

"That explains why he kept trying to hook me up with the women at the next table."

Lila opened her eyes. "What women?"

"An assortment of hotties."

"And?"

"And nothing. They were there when I got there. No doubt provided by Orestes as company for his guests."

"That's a nice way to put it."

"He kept trying to pair me up with them. Now I understand why."

"Please share."

"Have you ever heard the expression, 'A husband who cheats on his wife becomes her pimp'?"

"No."

"It means that a man who cheats on his wife gets other men to thinking it's okay to take a shot at her."

Lila laughed.

"What's so funny about that?"

"If you're suggesting Orestes was trying to get you to cheat on me, I can assure you it wouldn't be for the hope of my later having sex with him. Perhaps to get back at me for turning him down. Or even to blackmail you with threats of telling me if you had gone with one of those…what did you call them…'hotties.' But sex, no."

"How can you be so sure?"

"He's gay."

"What?"

"Okay, maybe bisexual, but definitely gay. I can't believe you didn't pick up on that."

"But he wanted to marry you."

"Darling, we were never lovers, and he never admitted to being gay, but the relationship he was interested in with me had nothing to do with the bedroom."

"Bastard."

"Him or me?"

"Tough choice."

"Who else was with him?"

Andreas named five men.

"Ah, a night on the town with his family's longtime financial backers. Their families financed his family's rise to power and, once achieved, Orestes' family used its influence to make them all wildly greater fortunes."

"Last night he was trying to convince them he still had the juice. He made it seem like he'd pressured me into helping them get what they wanted."

"Funny how things turn out. The man who wanted to marry me to complement his image is now looking to my husband to save it."

"Not sure he sees it that way. Besides, even if I wanted to—which I don't—I doubt there's much I can do. That Crete natural gas project is too big. Once it gets rolling no one is going to want to stop it or even slow it down, no matter what I turn up."

"Don't be so pessimistic."

"It comes from sleep deprivation."

She slid her hand across the sheets, up onto his bare belly. "Well, if you can't sleep…"

Having just admitted to spending most of his night surrounded by "hotties," saying no to Lila might lead to the evening's second attempt on his life.

Thirty minutes later a thoroughly spent and exhausted Andreas fell asleep. Smiling and very much alive.

Chapter Six

Kouros watched as his mother lifted the small, twisted shortbread biscuits out of their box and carefully arranged them on a plate. She always served *koulourakia* that way, even when alone. Any suggestion that it would be simpler to put the box on the table drew an immediate lecture on manners. She followed the same sort of ordered procedure in preparing her morning coffee: always strong, sweet, and Greek. If you dared call it Turkish, or worse still, said, "Instant is fine," you risked losing your welcome guest status in *keria* Kouros' home. Tradition meant more to his mother than prayer, and when she moved from the Mani to Athens as a young bride, she carried with her the teachings of her mother much the same as a priest would the lessons of his Bible.

"We are Nyklian," she regularly reminded her son. "Direct descendants of Spartan heroes from the colony of Nikli at Tripoli who came to the Mani more than eight centuries ago, bringing with them order to its wild ways. We are Mani royalty."

In school, Kouros learned that Nyklians also brought with them a feudal, warrior mentality that drove them into ferocious feuds with neighboring Nyklian clans over control of the little available land, and to treat those they considered beneath their class as no better than donkeys. The Mani was a place of chronic anarchy, where the powerful ruled by reason of their force, and a woman's role was to bear male children, called "guns," to carry on the fight. But it was not a closed class structure, for a gifted fighter from the lower class could rise to be Nyklian and a Nyklian boy could properly marry a girl from the lower class. But for a Nyklian girl to marry beneath her class brought immediate disgrace to her family. They were ways reminiscent of the Dark Ages, but in the Mani they persisted well into the nineteenth century, and in some cases, beyond.

Kouros often wondered whether hooking up with a boy beneath her Nyklian class was the sin his slain Great-aunt Calliope had committed in her father's eyes.

His mother placed a cup of coffee on the kitchen table in front of him and another by the chair next to his. She sat down, picked up her coffee, and took a tentative sip. She put down the cup. She'd not said a word all morning, but gone about her routine as if in her own kitchen rather than alone with her son in the house of her now-deceased brother-in-law.

Last night they'd gone directly to the church to join their family sitting with Uncle's body. Despite the late hour, the family sat surrounded by well-wishers, mourners, wailers, shriekers, and even a few tourists drawn in by all the commotion. Mangas did not say a word to Kouros about the circumstances of his father's death. He'd acted as if it were a forbidden topic. Kouros hoped that meant his cousin's anger had passed, but he wouldn't bet on it.

Calliope had insisted they stay with her at Uncle's home, and Kouros insisted she come back with them for at least a few hours of sleep before the funeral. She did but he doubted she'd slept. He'd heard her leaving the house at sunup to resume her vigil next to her father's body.

His mother finished her coffee, stood up, and went up to her bedroom. Kouros took that as her way of letting him know it was time to get dressed for the funeral. The funeral wasn't until eleven, but he knew she wanted to be at the church by nine.

He noticed she'd left her coffee cup and the empty plate on the kitchen table. That wasn't like her, any more than being so quiet and withdrawn.

He picked up the cups and plate, washed them and the coffeepot, and put the box of biscuits away. He hoped she was okay. This was a tough funeral for her. All of her husband's brothers were now gone. She and Uncle's sister were the only two left of their generation. The grave must seem much closer to her today, he thought. Then again, every day brings each of us closer to our own.

"*Whoa*," said Kouros shaking his head and talking to himself. "This somber mood shit is contagious."

"*Yianni. It's time to get dressed.*"

"Yes, Mother." He smiled. She's back.

Kouros parked on the dirt just off the edge of a two-lane road winding up above the tiny hill town of Vathia. Twenty miles to the north the road led to Aeropoli, the city named after the Greek god of war, where Maniots struck the first blow in Greece's War of Independence. Six miles to the south the road ended at the sea near the mythical entrance to Hades.

In the springtime Vathia sat perched on a blanket of wildflowers, laid out across terraced hillside fields dropping down to the sea a mile away. From where Kouros stood it didn't seem real, more like a medieval village of grand, earth-tone towers painted upon a movie backdrop of mountains, sea, and sky. To him, Vathia was the region's most dramatic symbol of the historical essence of the Mani, for the beauty of the scene belied the fierce reputation of its villagers: Upon the walls of those same majestic eighteenth- and nineteenth-century towers once hung the heads of enemies proudly nailed there by those who took them.

Kouros and his mother walked down the road toward the turreted 1750 church of Saint Spyridon sitting with its back flush up against the road just a few paces uphill from the main entrance to the old village. Across the road he saw signs of renovations underway, but not many. Some of the towers and outbuildings in the village had been restored, but plans to do more in hopes of turning Vathia into a tourist draw fell through at the end of the last century. Vathia's battles these days were waged by the half-dozen souls living there year-round, fighting to preserve what they could of its crumbling mystical towers. He wondered if his uncle's plans for creating a resort might have reignited preservation efforts in this part of the Mani.

They reached the church a few minutes past nine. The church and its terra-cotta-tiled roof looked well maintained, in distinct counterpoint to much of the rest of the village. A relatively new flagstone patio abutting the church's main entrance

on its south side sat deserted, but by the time
of Uncle's service the place would be packed. In
the Mani you might miss a wedding, but never a
funeral. Certainly not one of this family.

They took the steep stone steps leading down
from the road to the patio; the same route Uncle's
coffin had taken when brought into the church
through its southern door. Kouros' mother headed
straight for a crowd of black-clad women surrounding the coffin, crying and consoling one another.
Kouros looked for his cousins, but saw only Calliope and her sister. Her brothers weren't here. He
found a seat close by the front door, sat down, and
waited. They would be here soon enough.

He hoped not carrying heads.

Andreas somehow made it into his office by ten.
Before he could ask Maggie for coffee, she burst
though his office door with a pot in one hand and
a cup in the other.

"How did you know?"

"I could say female intuition." She poured
him a cup of coffee. "But a cop named Petro from
headquarters security stopped by with a message
for you. 'Please tell the Chief they caught the guy
who got away last night and he corroborated it was

a drug-related shooting.' He also told me to have the coffee ready for you."

Andreas smiled. "Tell him thanks. Anything else happening?"

"Spiros' office called twice. You're to call him 'the moment' you arrive."

"Oh, God, have mercy. There's not enough coffee in the world to get me up for a call from him this morning."

"Perhaps God considers it your penance for last night." She put the pot down on top of a notepad on his desk. "Call me when you've had enough coffee to speak to Spiros."

"As I said, there will never be enough. I may as well do it now."

Maggie picked up the phone on Andreas' desk and dialed. "Hi, dear, it's me. Is your boss in? Mine would like to speak with him." She handed Andreas the phone just as Spiros came on the line.

"Andreas, where have you been?"

"Morning, Spiros, what can I do for you?"

"I don't know what you did last night but I got a call at home at dawn from Orestes telling me about your behavior last night."

"The guy's a bit of an asshole."

"Maybe, but he thinks you're terrific. Couldn't stop praising you enough or thanking me for finding someone who would 'save our country from ruin.'"

"Make that a 'delusional asshole.'"

"Look, I don't know how you did it, but you got him off my back, and for that I owe you."

"All I said was that I would look into what's happening on Crete to see if something illegal was going on."

Spiros laughed. "On Crete? Something illegal? How could anyone ever think that?"

"It's not smuggling or drug production he's interested in. He just wants to protect his crowd's piece of the gas find. I said I'd look into it. That's all. And I can assure you I do not intend on going to war with the Cretans over anything I find. If our military thinks it's too risky to fight them over drug production in their mountains, I'm not about to start one over gas production in their sea. I'm just going to look around and report. After that, Boss, it's all up to you where you decide to take it."

"Fine, fine, no problem. Just keep me informed. Got to run now. Bye."

The phone went dead. Andreas stared at the receiver. Spiros hadn't changed. As long as his immediate problem is somehow pushed down the road, he's happy. It gave him more time to find someone to blame for whatever might go wrong.

"But not me this time, asshole." Andreas hung up the phone.

By the time Uncle's sons arrived at the church, Kouros' other cousins were already there. The brothers went straight to the coffin. Grim-faced, dressed in black suits and white shirts, they lined its far side staring back toward the door. Mangas locked eyes on Kouros only long enough to nod. Kouros nodded back, tight-lipped, his hands crossed in front of him below his waist.

The priest came out from behind the *iconostasis* separating the main part of the church from the altar area, said a few quiet words to the family, and began the service. Age-old prayers and blessings chanted against a background chorus of crying, moaning, and wailing filled the room. Few others said a word except when called for by the service. This was a time for showing respect to the soul that once lay within the body in the coffin before them.

A half-hour passed, maybe more. Kouros had lost track of time. Memories of his uncle led him to thoughts of his father and how different the two brothers' lives. His father lived as a soldier, guided by a moral code one would think utterly foreign to his brother. Shortly before his father died from lung cancer, Kouros asked him what he thought of his brother and the answer now ran through his mind: "I couldn't live my life as my brother did his, and I wouldn't want you to either, but it's not for me to judge him. Yes, our father was a doctor, but it was our ancestors' success as pirates that paid my father's way. I was lucky and escaped our history. My brother could not."

Before Kouros was born his father had shortened his family name, but never told his son why. Kouros guessed it had to do with his uncle's infamous reputation during the years his father struggled to make a career in the military. His father's gravestone bore both names, and at the funeral his uncle told Kouros, "Your father was a practical man. He did what he had to do to get ahead in this world, as did I. Be proud of the name he chose. I am."

Kouros studied Mangas' face for any sign of what he might be thinking. He saw only calm of the sort you'd expect to find in a flower-filled mountaintop meadow on a peaceful summer day. That's not like my cousin, thought Kouros. He's more the ready-to-explode-at-any-moment volcano type.

Mangas caught Kouros staring and before Kouros could look away he waved for him to come over. It took a second for Kouros to realize what his cousin wanted. The church service had ended and he'd just been chosen as a pallbearer.

◇◇◇

The pallbearers huddled around the coffin, gripped it, and lifted together. It was not as heavy as Kouros thought it would be. Then again, there were six bulls sharing the load. They turned the coffin so that Uncle's body left the church feet first, opposite to how it had entered. The priest led them out through a small, west-facing door and along a stone path toward the village's main entrance, taking care not to retrace the steps the coffin had followed into the church. Behind the coffin walked the family, led by Calliope, followed by a far larger crowd of mourners than had squeezed into the small church for the service.

They slid the coffin into the rear of a black Mercedes hearse. Behind it stood two shiny black pickup trucks filled with flowers. The motorcade slowly pulled away in the direction of Cape Tenaro.

Mourners hurried to their vehicles to join the line driving up the hill to the south. At the crest of the hill the road began a gradual, winding, three-mile cliffside descent to the sea at the area of Marmari, where the Mani's rugged coastline pinched in to form but a mile-wide waist and its mountains dropped to rises. Past Marmari the land spread out and rose up again for a final three-mile, leveling run down to the sea at mainland Europe's southern terminus at Cape Tenaro.

A mile down the hill toward Marmari the hearse pulled off to the side of the road and stopped. The line of vehicles peeled off to park.

Kouros met up with the other pallbearers at the top of a scruffy, brush-covered switchback path. A quarter-mile away, on a rocky clifftop plateau, five shed-like stone structures topped in plain white crosses stood side by side facing west and overlooking the Ionian Sea.

Six men marching in cadence, trailed by a long line of black, carried the coffin across a shadowless, putty color landscape. They trudged in silence toward the largest of the structures, the *tafos* of Uncle's family and final resting place for his earthly remains. Graves could not be dug in this area of the Mani's rocky soil and his coffin would stay within this tomb for at least seven years, perhaps as long as ten, until only his bones remained. They would then be washed with water, followed by vinegar, allowed to dry in the sun, placed in a small wooden box, and put to rest for eternity in a drawer within the walls of this same tomb.

The pallbearers placed the coffin in front of the *tafos*. Wailing came in waves as they removed the lid, subsiding only long enough to hear the priestly blessing and prayer for Uncle's soul. His blessed journey continued as the priest took Uncle's arms crossed snuggly across his chest, drew them apart, and placed them to rest peacefully alongside his body, palms open and facing heaven. Only one tradition from this part of the Mani remained before Uncle's coffin would be sealed and placed within the tomb. The priest picked up a full bottle of red wine and poured its contents over Uncle's body.

Kouros' mother stood among the crowd of women huddled close by the coffin, shrieking and crying as pallbearers sealed and lifted Uncle's remains into the tomb. Such soulful, once-widespread traditions were rarely practiced in Greece these days, even in the Mani, but today all of them were observed, for Calliope had insisted it be so.

Kouros watched Calliope staring at the tomb. She seemed lost in thought. They hadn't spoken today. Nor had she been active among the screaming mourners. But what surprised him most was when he'd heard she'd not participated in last night's *mirologia*. Whatever her thoughts she seemed determined to keep them tightly locked inside. He hoped she was okay.

As if reading his thoughts Calliope looked up, let her eyes run wild across the crowd of mourners, raised her hands above her head, and screamed, "*It is time.*" All eyes turned to her and she began to chant.

It made no sense. This was not the proper time or place for *mirologia*. But no one dared stop her.

She tearfully welcomed and thanked all who'd come to honor her father, taking special care to mention each dignitary by name. Her weeping grew into wailing, a sign to other women mourners to join her. They looked at each other, unsure of what to do. Kouros' mother stepped forward and began chanting alongside Calliope. Others joined her, and soon one emotional outburst fed another as wailing women pulled at their hair, scratched their faces, and shouted blessings for the departed.

The brothers looked down at their feet, as if embarrassed by the scene at their father's grave. But there was nothing they could do. This was their sister's time.

Calliope drew one hand down from pulling at her hair and began pounding on her chest in keeping with the slow rhythmic beat of her *mirologia* to her father:

"He roamed across Mani like the bear,
He was a star guiding a thousand allies,
He was the savior of all his family.
With his firm hand came great new power to
　　our land.
He bound us together through strength found
　　in peace with all clans,
To work as one, not as scatterings of old rivals
Who faced deadly ends at a neighbor's hands.

All those who joined along did for freedom
from murder by Mani known,
And vowed no more profiting in trade off the
blood of Maniots,
But off foreign folk far from our Nyklian
birthplace.
My loving father is now leader to minions on
high
And all Mani and its kinfolk are grieving his
sorry death.
It did happen close-by here, driving homeward
On the road back from Hades and colleagues.
Our patriarch dead alone on the rocks.
Who is convinced he lost direction and died?
This man still vibrant and clear of mind, who
knew the road like his hand.
His eyes may be closed, but mine are not.
What brought his dear family to such grieving,
Mourning a too soon passing life
And his lost warmth and broad smile upon
that day?
Family ran through his heart, his mission to
make us all better,
His goal came from God in heaven, his fierce-
ness from Archangel Michael.
Some treachery leaves us all deep in loss,
For it was a betrayer who sent him to death.

Now his children and our cousins face danger
> here,
At vengeance brought forward against us by
> cowards.
Not by men armed for war, but dogs armed
> with pens.
Who fear no revenge from my dead father
As long as all his sons agree that his death came
> peaceful,
Along a roadway, not from cursed treachery.
Let us pray our Blessed Lord on High and the
> Holy Virgin
That you show us the cowards that we may
> do justice
And turn their children to weeping orphans.
For they'll soon find in our God's wrath
A thirst for vengeance still burns in Mani."

Kouros couldn't believe he'd just heard Calliope stand at her father's gravesite and in front of the entire community call out her brothers to seek vengeance for his death.

Looks like I've been worried about the wrong cousin starting a war.

Chapter Seven

Orestes had promised to give Andreas a list of persons to investigate. What he actually sent him seemed more like a compilation of the world's largest *Fortune 100* companies having anything to do with the exploration, extraction, processing, or delivery of natural gas. It looked like something Orestes' secretary had pulled off the Internet by punching in "world's largest natural gas" in front of each step in the natural gas chain. Not a single individual mentioned by name, just companies and only a few with even an address in Greece.

Andreas threw the list on his desk. Orestes was an idiot. He picked up a pencil and began tapping it on his desk. No, that's one thing he's not. Maybe he's not sure yet which side might be paying him and he doesn't want to risk naming some guy he could later end up with in bed. Andreas smiled at the thought.

He probably wanted police heat put on those

companies so that he could present himself to them as their savior. He'd boast it was his influence with the police that started the investigation and claim only he could stop it. If a company he landed with that line happened to be on the list, it wouldn't be a big deal because the world already thought every multinational corrupt at some level. The trick was not being linked to a corrupt *individual* at a named company. That's what got you hung out to dry.

Andreas twirled the pencil between his fingers.

All you had to do was look at Germany's Siemens. Despite a huge, ongoing bribery scandal over its involvement in Athens' 2004 Summer Olympic Games and dealing with Greece's Defense Ministry, Greece still did business with Siemens. It would be the same this time around. As long as your man on the inside wasn't branded corrupt, you're set. Orestes likely didn't give a damn who won a bid as long as he got his cut. He might even try to make the same deal with competitors for the same contract. Andreas could hear Orestes now: *Give me and my people a piece and I'll get Kaldis off your back. He's in my pocket.*

"Miserable bastard." Andreas squeezed his fist and snapped the pencil in half between his fingers.

He stared at the door to his office. "Maggie, come in. Please."

The door swung open and Maggie's head peeked in. "Yes, Chief, what's up?"

"Where's Tassos?"

"You mean my Tassos?"

"Yes."

"He's on Syros. The police chief there won't let him retire."

Andreas doubted anyone on the force would ever dare mention retirement to Tassos Stamatos, chief homicide investigator for the Cyclades islands. For Greeks obsessed with sightings of the powerful and influential, Tassos Stamatos drew about as much attention as the air they breathed. He had the sort of looks you'd expect to see on a stocky pensioner retired from hard labor that a taverna owner might hire at the last minute to tend bar when the regular guy called in sick. But in a room filled with Greece's movers and shakers, everyone noticed Tassos, for he knew where their secrets were buried and held bushels full of favors for keeping them that way. He'd been a cop since the days of Greece's Junta dictatorship in the late sixties and early seventies, and been making friends on both sides of the bars since his first day on the job at a Junta prison for political dissidents. To Andreas, Tassos was not just a best friend, he was a national treasure.

"I've got to talk with him."

"He's coming back to my place tonight."

"Have you two finally moved in together?" It was Andreas who'd unwittingly introduced his friend and longtime widower to Maggie, not knowing he'd rekindled an old romance.

"Only when he's in Athens. He still considers Syros his home."

"Islanders are like that. Please, get him on the phone."

"Will do." Maggie disappeared behind the closing door.

A couple of minutes passed before Maggie yelled, "He's on."

Andreas picked up the phone. "How are you feeling, my friend?"

"Why is it that everyone asks me the same question?"

"Maybe because they care for you?"

"Yeah, sure."

"Good point. It's probably because you look as old as the Acropolis."

"That's more like it." Tassos laughed. "So what's up? My love said you had to talk to me right away. She pulled me out of a very important meeting."

"Is it already lunchtime on Syros?"

"No, coffee in the harbor."

"I've got a problem developing here that's touchy. How secure is your phone?"

"My cell phone I wouldn't trust as far as I can drop it. Too many people want to know what I know and have connections at the carriers to listen in. But I'm using a landline at the taverna. Maggie thought it might be a 'touchy' subject."

"How does she know these things?"

"I hope that's not what this call is all about because that's a subject only the gods at Delphi might be able to answer."

"No, my problem is with someone who just thinks he's a god." Andreas told him of his meeting with Spiros, run-in with Orestes, and thoughts on what Orestes had in mind.

"Orestes is a chip off the old block. The only time you knew for sure that you could trust what his old man or grandfather had to say was when their lips *weren't* moving. Orestes is running the same routines as those two did in hustling foreign companies to do business through them in Greece. They didn't really need the influence they claimed as long as they got the mark thinking that they did. Once they had the deal with the company, any Greeks they actually needed to make it work fell into line because by then they had money available to spread around."

"Wonderful system."

"It's not just Greece that's like that."

"No, but it's a Greek bastard who's trying to make me look corrupt."

"I suggest you tell him to go fuck himself," said Tassos.

"Frankly, I'd rather do it to him."

"Sounds personal."

Andreas didn't want to mention Orestes' old interest in Lila. It would sound stupid. "No, I just don't like the guy."

"Hell, if we spent our time trying to get back at everyone we didn't like, we wouldn't have time to breathe."

"Since when have you become so Zen?" said Andreas.

"It comes with age. Besides, it's really a waste of time looking into that Crete thing. The fix has been in for years on the gas. Now it's just a matter of reshuffling a few chairs at the dinner table to accommodate the late arrivals."

"Late arrivals?"

"New ones in power who could create problems."

"You're one hell of a cynic."

"You mean a realist born of experience. The louder a politician screams for the rights of the people, the more he wants for himself."

"Spare me the civics lesson. What can you tell me about what Orestes might have in mind?"

"My guess is he's selling himself to the

Russians. The Europeans already have their connections here and the Americans seem more interested in their own gas reserves. It's the new boys on the block who need influence."

"What about the Chinese? They're buying up our port operations."

"And making them profitable. But they already have their contacts. No, my bet is on the Russians, a big energy player with strong national interests in keeping the European energy markets wedded to them. They're just hoping Greece doesn't turn into another Cyprus. The financial catastrophe there threw a lot of light on its gas field discoveries, and drove a lot of serious players involved in exploiting Cyprus' gas scrambling to lower national expectations. After all, if the gas fields are billed as the country's economic salvation, that leaves a lot less cash to bury in Switzerland."

"Are you running for office?" said Andreas.

"No, not crooked enough."

"Jesus, Tassos, what are you saying?"

"I'm saying stay away from Crete. You'll never be able to change what's going on over there."

"How can I do that?"

"Easy. Just don't go. Get a prosecutor to subpoena records on the project from every company on Orestes' list. Their lawyers will inundate you with enough paper to keep every lawyer in Greece busy for years. That's how it would end up anyway, no matter what your investigation turned up. So, give it to a prosecutor and keep yourself out of the line of fire. If Orestes bitches, tell him you did precisely what he'd asked, gone after everyone on his list."

Andreas drew in and let out a breath. "There is another angle to take on this."

"Being?"

"If you want to find the rotten apple in a barrel, follow the worm."

"I never heard that one before."

"Because I just made it up. But that worm Orestes inspired me. I'll just keep an eye on him and see where it leads me."

"Yeah, it sure sounds like it isn't personal."

"I don't like being set up."

"Just be careful. Is Kouros working on this with you?"

"He's down in the Mani. His uncle died."

"That uncle?"

"Yes, 'that uncle.'"

"I knew him."

"Why am I not surprised?"

"Cute, wiseass. It just so happens that back in the late 1800s, when Syros was in its heyday as the shipping capital of Greece, a businessman from Syros with roots in the Mani and a merchant from the Mani teamed up to create a commercial center in the Deep Mani port of Gerolimenas. It thrived for generations. Those days are long gone but many families from both places still remain close."

"Yianni thinks his uncle's death might not be the accident it seemed."

"That should lead to some fun times in the Mani."

"He's worried about that, too."

"If he needs any help, just tell him to give me a holler."

"I'll pass it along."

"Notice I didn't offer to help you," said Tassos.

"The thought did cross my mind."

"It's because Yianni's problem is capable of having a solution. Yours is not."

"I guess that means I won't be seeing you."

"Of course you will. Maggie spoke to Lila while waiting for me to get to this landline and call back. We're all having dinner tonight."

"Why am I always the last to know?"

"I see we're back to questions for the oracle. See you tonight. Bye."

Andreas put down the phone. Tassos was right. He should forget about going after Orestes.

"Maggie, get me the prosecutor on the phone."

Andreas drummed his fingers on the desktop.

"And the personnel file on that cop Petro. I might just have a special assignment for him."

Kouros stood at the entrance of a one-story gray and brown stone taverna built along the road just above the beach at Marmari. Its heavy, dark brown wooden door bore the word "Entrance" in English. Uncle had come to this taverna every morning to meet his friends for coffee and he died on his way home from here. His children thought it only fitting that they host the traditional post-funeral meal of fish soup and fish in the place that had played such a large part in their father's life.

Kouros saw the taverna as something quite different. A crime scene. Here Uncle received a death threat delivered in his morning newspaper and, if his death were not an accident, the most likely spot that led to his end. Kouros turned his head and stared back up the road toward the cemetery and the place of his uncle's crash. But I'm not a cop today, he thought. I'm family.

What better time to start an investigation?

"Yianni, get your ass in here," yelled one of his cousins from the taverna's doorway. "The priest wants to say a blessing and Mangas won't let him start until you're inside."

"Okay, I'm coming."

Kouros jogged the few paces to the front door and down four stone steps into a room the size of a deep, three-car garage filled with empty, well-worn, square-top tables and tattered, lattice-seat taverna chairs. Stone walls and floors made the practically windowless room look much the same as it must have a hundred years before. But no one was in the room.

Directly across from Kouros a wide stone archway opened into a much larger modern room overlooking the sea through broad, wood-framed spaces shielded from the winds by transparent, retractable shades anchored to the floor. Lines of long tables ran parallel to the sea, packed with guests who'd come to pay their respects.

The instant Kouros appeared in the doorway the priest began his prayer and Mangas waved for Kouros to sit beside him at the far end of the row of tables closest to the sea.

"Thanks for coming, Yianni."

Kouros nodded.

"Your mother looks well."

"Puh, puh, puh. Yes, she does."

"You're lucky to still have her."

Kouros nodded again. "I know."

Mangas patted Kouros on the back. "What did you think of Calliope's *mirologia* performance?"

"She's very talented."

Mangas smiled. "I thought you were a cop, not a diplomat."

Kouros shrugged. "What else can I say, it's her father's funeral. She has every right to be emotional."

"What about me? Should I be *emotional* too?" There was no anger in Mangas' voice.

"If it makes you feel better."

"Good. I'll take that as a blessing from you that I should find someone to kill to make my sister happy."

"Since when have you ever listened to your sister?"

Mangas laughed. "Can you stay for a few days? You make me laugh."

"I will if you want me to, but first a question."

Mangas nodded.

"What the hell's going on?"

Mangas rocked his head from side to side. "It's pretty clear Calliope's upset. I don't know what was going through her mind to chant a *mirologia* at the funeral. Especially *that mirologia*, but despite what she said, the mechanic found nothing wrong with our father's car, and according to the coroner who did the autopsy, he died from a massive heart attack."

Kouros shook his head. "A real tragedy."

"I'd like you to take a look at the autopsy report. Just to see if you agree."

"Sure. But if it's technical, I might have to send it on to Athens."

Mangas nodded. "No problem."

"Don't you trust the guy who did the autopsy?" said Kouros.

"I trust him, but he's not a big-time criminal investigator like my cousin, Athens Yianni. And before I go head-to-head with Calliope over her craziness about our father being murdered, I want to make sure she's not right."

"Understood."

Both reached for shot glasses of whiskey sitting in front of them. "*Theos singhorese ton,*" each said before clinking glasses and gulping down the shots.

God forgive his soul indeed, thought Kouros.

The afternoon dragged on slowly for the family. Though many of the guests had left, the family lingered, as if reluctant to return to a world without Uncle's presence. Most sat staring out to sea, adding one story after another to what was fast becoming the legend of Uncle. Not the least of the tales were of Uncle's way with the ladies. Stories his sons took pride in retelling and his daughters feigned to ignore.

At the other end of the same table, five men of about Uncle's age sat drinking, toasting, and laughing. None of them seemed in a hurry to leave.

"Who are they?" said Kouros, nodding in their direction.

"His coffee buddies," said Mangas. "They met for coffee here every morning. Been doing that since long before the new owner took over."

"How long ago did he take over?"

Mangas shrugged. "Six years or so? Why do you ask?"

"Just my natural cop curiosity. I'll be right back." Kouros slid his chair back from the table, stood, and walked over to the five men.

"*Yia sas*. Mind if I sit down?"

A chubby, bald man with a bulbous red nose and fisherman's cap said, "Of course not. Our friend's favorite nephew is always welcome here."

"Even if he's a cop," said a silver-haired, wiry fellow with bright blue eyes.

Kouros smiled as he sat. "I see I don't have to introduce myself."

"We already know all about you, Athens Yianni," said a dark-haired man with a sallow complexion, who looked the youngest of the five. "Your Uncle always talked about you. With pride. You're always welcome here. My name is Stelios." He extended his hand and Kouros shook it.

"I'm Konstantin," waved the bulbous-nosed man from the other side of the table.

"And I'm Panos," said Blue Eyes. "The two silent ones with us are Mihalis and Alexander."

A man wearing a military-style baseball cap atop a weather-beaten face waved. "Mihalis."

The fifth man, the only one in a suit and tie, said, "Alexander."

"In case you don't know, we're all longtime buddies of your uncle," said Panos.

"Yes, Mangas told me. On behalf of my family I want to thank you for coming. Even though I'm sure you were more like family to my uncle than I was."

Panos gestured no. "Yes, we're all very close, and some of us might even know each other better than our own children know us, but we are *not* family. Family is one thing. Everything else is something else."

Kouros nodded. "But I'm certain you know more stories about Uncle than I'll hear anywhere else."

"For sure," said Konstantin. "So, what sort of stories do you want to hear?"

"He's a young guy, Konstantin. He'll want to know about the women," laughed Stelios.

They all laughed and toasted Uncle's memory.

Panos said. "The old bastard used to hit on me for a free room a couple of times a month. He'd always say, 'I only need it for an hour or so. After all, I'm not as young as I used to be.'"

They toasted Uncle again.

"Free room?" asked Kouros.

"Yes," said Panos. "I have a hotel up the coast in Gerolimenas. He'd always be bringing different women around. Amazing how he attracted them."

"And if he wasn't banging them in your hotel, he'd be doing them on my boat," said Mihalis. "He never went to sea. Just did his business right there tied up to the dock."

"Created quite a few tsunamis if you believed him," said Alexander.

More laughter and toasting.

"Hey, Athens Yianni, you're not drinking," said Stelios pouring him a shot of whiskey.

"I was afraid you'd notice. I'm too young to keep up with you." Kouros downed the shot.

"*Theos singhorese ton*," said all six in unison.

"So, what would you like to know, Detective Kouros?" smiled Alexander.

"Nothing more than you want to tell me."

Panos smiled. "He's a better politician than you, Alexander."

"And could probably get elected honestly, too," said Stelios.

Laughter.

"I'll miss him," said Alexander. "We all will. I wouldn't be where I am in government today without him."

"And I'd still have union troubles at my hotel without his help," said Panos.

"On more occasions than I can remember he helped me out of jams with the coast guard over my style of fishing," said Konstantin.

Kouros almost said, "dynamiting?" but caught himself. That undoubtedly was what he meant, and calling Konstantin on it wasn't likely to keep him and the others talking. He wondered if by referring to it as a "style" of fishing meant that at some level he was ashamed to be among those responsible for helping to ruin fishing in Greece. Hopefully not forever.

"He brought peace to my family," said Stelios. "Make that *our* families."

Kouros gave him a puzzled look.

"I'm sure you know of the vendetta started by your great-grandfather. The boy he ordered your grandfather to kill was my father's brother. It was my family who killed some of your own father's siblings. It was your uncle who brought peace to our families."

Alone, Stelios drank a toast to Uncle.

"Did Uncle ever talk of that vendetta?" asked Kouros.

"Not in decades," said Stelios.

"At least not with us," said Mihalis.

The others nodded.

"Would he have if it were on his mind?"

"I'd think so," said Panos.

"We were the unofficial council of elders for the community," said Stelios.

Panos said, "We started meeting decades ago for the purpose of making money. Helping each other make our businesses more profitable. But none of us work anymore, so..."

"I still do," said Alexander.

"You're a politician, you never worked, only took," said Konstantin.

All but Alexander laughed.

"As I was saying, in recent years instead of talking business we'd meet each morning to talk about problems facing our community and try to find solutions."

"What sorts of problems?"

"The kind people told us about or we learned from the news."

"Including newspapers?"

"That was your Uncle's specialty. Every morning he'd have the paper waiting for him at the table, and while we told stories he'd read it. After he finished we'd talk about whatever there was for us to worry about."

"Did my uncle have anything to 'worry about'?"

"Only with what to do with all the money he expected to get from his hotel project," said Panos.

"You knew about that?"

"Of course we did," said Alexander. "Like Panos said, we helped each other. And kept whatever we talked about to ourselves. I promised to set him up with whatever permits he needed, and Panos gave him advice on how to get the best hotel deal."

Kouros looked at Panos. "You weren't worried about the competition?"

"Competition? My son helps runs the hotel now, and we'd love some competition. It would bring in more tourists. Besides, my place is on the sea, your uncle's was in the middle of rocks. I still don't know what was on the mind of the fool who had planned on leasing the place."

"*Had planned?*"

"Yes, your uncle hadn't signed the papers yet. He died the day before the scheduled signing. Rotten luck for the family."

"But don't worry," said Alexander. "I'll make sure the deal still goes through."

"Assuming the goddamned Ukrainian still wants to do the deal," said Konstantin.

And that my uncle's sons and daughters are willing, thought Kouros. "Ukrainian?"

"Yeah, your uncle said the buyer came from the Ukraine. Though he might be Russian," said Konstantin.

"Why wouldn't he want to go through with the deal?" said Alexander.

Konstantin's nose was pulsing. "Because the bastard will probably see some advantage to renegotiating. To drive the price down. Those types are ruthless when it comes to business. Especially the Russians. I've seen them fishing."

"Uh, yeah, but let's not forget who he's dealing with. Mangas ain't exactly an Athenian pansy." Mihalis caught himself. "Sorry, Yianni. No offense intended."

Kouros shook his head. "None taken."

"After all, you and I are both cops. At least I used to be, and I was a childhood friend of your father."

"Mihalis used to be chief of police in these parts," said Alexander.

"I see," said Kouros. "Weren't any of you worried that with so many powerful people meeting every morning in the same place you might be a target?"

"You mean for someone wanting to take out the competition?" smiled Alexander.

"Or just to settle a grudge," said Kouros.

"Is that what you think happened? That someone settled an old grudge with your uncle?" Panos nodded. "It's good to think like that. We were just talking about that same possibility."

The others at the table nodded.

"And?" said Kouros.

"There's absolutely no one out there we can think of with any sensible reason for going after your uncle at this point in his life."

"No one?"

"No one," repeated Panos.

They all nodded.

"What about someone with a nonsensible reason?"

"Good luck on finding that one," said Mihalis.

A light-coffee skinned girl no more than twenty years old came over to their table and said in accented Greek, "Are you okay? Do you need anything else?"

"Just more of your loving," said Konstantin.

The girl laughed and smacked him lightly on the back of his head.

"After all, with our great friend gone, who will there be to pinch your butt?" asked Mihalis slowly extending his hand in the direction of the girl's rear. She smiled as she scooted away from his hand. Her face turned sad. "Yes, I shall miss him."

She turned and walked away, giving Kouros a clear vision of the recent topic of discussion.

"Ah, if I were only twenty years younger," said Konstantin.

"Forty, you mean," said Mihalis.

"Who is she?" said Kouros.

"She works here," said Panos. "She's the girl-friend of the guy who runs the place. He's a Greek from a town in the northwest Peloponnese. Pirgos," said Mihalis.

"She's an Arab. Probably illegal. He brought her here about a year ago. Damn fine addition too," said Konstantin.

"Someone from immigration actually had the balls to walk in here one morning while we were here and ask for her papers," said Mihalis.

"That was quite a morning," laughed Panos. "The poor girl was scared to death and your uncle just sat at our table—we always sit in the front room—and motioned with his index finger for the idiot to come over to our table."

"The stupid son of a bitch didn't even know who your uncle was. He stormed over and demanded your uncle's ID." Alexander burst out laughing.

Panos said, "Your uncle calmly pulled out his wallet and handed him his identity card. The expression on the asshole's face when he realized who he'd just called out was priceless."

Stelios said, "Your uncle calmly said, 'Now leave here and never, ever come back.'"

"I never saw anyone move so fast," said Konstatin. He raised his glass. "To your uncle. There never was and shall never be another like him."

"*Theos singhorese ton.*"

By the time Kouros left the taverna he was as drunk as the rest of the men in the place. How he got back to his uncle's house was a miracle.

If he remembered in the morning all that he'd heard in the taverna it would be an even greater one.

Chapter Eight

Dinner was called for nine at the Kaldises' home. A bit early by Athens standards, but it helped Lila convince Maggie that eating there rather than in a restaurant would not be a bother to her. "I'm not cooking, Marietta is," had Maggie wavering but it took Lila saying "It will give you and Tassos a chance to see Tassaki," to close the deal.

From the moment Maggie entered the apartment, Tassaki was all over her. He loved his "Aunt Maggie," and as a precocious three-year-old, knew to negotiate the terms of his bedtime surrender upfront, while his parents still wanted him around.

"I promise to go to bed if *Theia* Maggie reads me a story," kept Maggie and Lila in his bedroom for almost an hour.

"That kid is a born deal-making politician," said Tassos from a couch in the living room.

"I thought you liked him?" said Andreas sitting next to him.

Tassos laughed and gestured with his wineglass in the direction of the windows lining the wall across from him. "Hard to imagine how he won't aspire to greatness with such a glorious view of the Acropolis every time he looks in that direction."

"I just hope he doesn't take it for granted. That's the downside of all this." Andreas picked up a wine bottle from a silver ice bucket on the coffee table in front of them and poured some into Tassos' glass. "Lila would kill me if she saw me doing this instead of asking Marietta to do it for us."

"Stop complaining. You've got a great family."

"I thought you were on my side?" Andreas smiled.

"I am. That's why I told you to stay away from Orestes."

"And I listened."

"Really?"

"Sort of."

"What's that supposed to mean?"

"I followed your suggestion and told the prosecutor to subpoena the companies on his list."

"And?"

Andreas took a sip of wine. "I'm keeping an eye on him."

"Why?"

"Don't know yet, depends on what he's up to.

I want to know if he has any plans on getting back at me for not playing ball."

"And how do you intend on learning what's in his mind?"

"I have someone from outside the unit keeping an eye on him."

"Why outside the unit? Do you think there's a leak?"

Andreas gestured no. "But Spiros is the big boss and if he finds out, God knows what he might say to Orestes to keep on his good side."

"Who'd you bring in?"

"His name is Petro Dangas. He's a tough kid, who works at GADA but moonlights at a club where Orestes hangs out. I told him to keep track of Orestes' guests and associates. I want to know who's getting his special attention."

"Can you trust the guy?"

"My instincts say yes. He's been on the force less than two years, and six months ago transferred to headquarters' security from a vice unit in the wild-ass western suburbs."

"Why would he leave a wide-open, take-what-you-can money-making assignment like that?" smiled Tassos.

"I thought the same thing, so I spoke to his former precinct commander."

"Surprised he talked to you."

"I promised not to bust his balls if he told me the truth. And to ground them up into powder if he didn't."

"You do know how to make friends in the department."

Andreas shrugged. "He told me the kid 'wouldn't get with the program.'"

"Sounds like a hell of an endorsement."

"I took it the same way. He got the kid transferred to a place where all he'll ever get to do is tell tourists not to take pictures of the building and look tough for photo ops."

"Some career."

"Which is why he jumped at the chance to keep an eye on Orestes. He reports only to me."

"Why do you have such a hard-on for Orestes?"

Andreas smiled. "Interesting choice of words. You can't imagine."

Lila and Maggie swept into the room.

"Your little angel is asleep, Chief."

"Thanks to Maggie. He listens to her," said Lila.

"We all do," said Tassos.

"It's a fear-driven response," said Andreas.

Lila laughed. "On that note, dinner is served."

"Oh, great. Time for more little boys and their stories." Maggie winked at Lila. "At least we begin our fairy tales with 'Once upon a time.'"

◇◇◇

Kouros didn't bother to look at the clock when he woke up. He knew it was morning and that was all he wanted to know. He ran his head under the shower for ten minutes, a real waste of water in parched Mani, and after searching around the bathroom he found some long-expired ibuprofen. He swallowed more than prescribed, stared in the mirror, and made the solemn pledge so many have vowed in similar moments of clarity: "If I survive, never again. I promise."

He dressed in jeans and a polo shirt and followed the smell of coffee out into the kitchen. His mother handed him a cup as he walked into the room. He made a point not to look her in the eyes, just gave her a quick peck on both cheeks, said "*Kali mera*," grabbed two biscuits off the table, and headed out the kitchen door. He didn't need a maternal lecture, his lesson had been learned through on-the-job experience. Again.

Kouros walked five paces from the door, closed his eyes, and for a moment did nothing more than concentrate on breathing in the brisk salt air laced with random whiffs of wild herbs. He opened his eyes and stared out across the plateau toward the bare-as-the-moon Saggias Mountains. It was a typical cloudless, brilliant blue-sky day in the Mani.

He wondered why he always thought of Mani skies as gray. Maybe it had something to do with the bloody history of the landscape beneath them? Not just from battles against Turks, Franks, Bavarians, Venetians, and so many other would-be conquerors, but in neighbor-against-neighbor savagery as merciless as any World War I trench warfare.

He shook his head. Hard to imagine all of this ending up as a golf course. Still, these days nothing seemed to remain the same for long where there was money to be made. And it wasn't as if explorers had come across a lost tribe living a Stone Age existence and, by announcing their find to the world, sealed the doom of their discovery's ancient ways.

No, the modern world had always touched the Mani. It just never held on very long, because the Mani had a tendency to burn a dabbler's fingers. Maybe this time would be different. Kouros sure hoped so. The hard-working strugglers around here could sure use some good luck.

He wondered how his own life might change if he had money coming in regularly without having to work for it. Make that honest money. He'd never thought about anything like that before. His father raised him to expect to work hard for whatever he wanted. Kouros took a sip of coffee. No reason to start daydreaming about that sort of life now, because it didn't seem likely the deal would go through, at least not as his uncle had envisioned it. His uncle's interest in the property had passed to his children, not Kouros. Now it was their call.

He shook his head, thought of his uncle, and remembered he'd promised Mangas to get the autopsy report off to Athens. He'd noticed a scanner in his uncle's office. He'd send it as soon as he finished his coffee.

Coffee. Another memory triggered. The synapses had begun to fire again.

His uncle's everyday coffee crew was a bunch of bad guys, no matter how charming and likable they seemed. And whether truly the "council of elders" they fashioned themselves to be, Kouros knew they hadn't told him anything close to what actually took place in their morning meetings. He might be Uncle's "favorite" nephew, but he was still a cop and, with Uncle gone, they had little reason to treat him much better than any other Maniot prying into their affairs.

Still, he had to try. On the surface several had potential motives, most unmistakably Stelios, whose family—maybe even he—once exchanged vendetta killings with Kouros' family. Yet that seemed too obvious to be likely. But if his uncle had been murdered, everyone was suspect, beginning with those he did business with.

Kouros finished off the biscuits in two bites

and downed his coffee. There would be time for more coffee later, after he'd sent the autopsy report on to Athens and dropped in on his uncle's crew at the taverna for a more sober chat. Why not? After all, they'd told him he was "always welcome."

It was eleven by the time Kouros walked into the taverna. The only one in the front room was the waitress.

"May I help you?" she said.

"Uh, yes, I'm looking for friends of my uncle. They have coffee together here every morning."

"Oh, yes, I remember you. You're the nephew from Athens. They were talking about you this morning."

"You mean they're gone?"

She nodded. "They're here every morning at nine and gone by ten-thirty."

Wow, he thought. Those old guys drank even more than I did. How did they ever make it out of bed for coffee by nine?

"They thought you might show up this morning."

"Did they say why?"

She shrugged. "Said you might have more questions about your uncle."

So much for the element of surprise, thought Kouros.

"They left a message for you if you showed up."

"What's the message?"

"'The trick is to have water in the glass with your whiskey.'"

Kouros burst out laughing.

The girl laughed, too. "Coffee?"

"Yes, please."

He watched her walk toward the kitchen. Tight black jeans, tight white t-shirt, dark hair, dark eyes, great butt. Front not bad either. Kouros' blood started to pulse. Watching her walk seemed likely to sober him up a hell of a lot faster than coffee.

She came out of the kitchen with a coffeepot in one hand and a cup and plate of cookies in the other.

Kouros smiled. "My name's Yianni."

She smiled back. "Stella." She put down the coffeepot, cup, and plate.

He held out his hand. "Pleased to meet you."

She took his hand and he gripped hers. Neither made an effort to let go of the other. They smiled at each other and he withdrew his hand.

"How well did you know my uncle?"

She looked down at the floor. The smile was gone. "Very well. He was a nice man and always kind to me."

"Do you know anyone who might have wanted to harm him?"

"Harm him?" She looked up and seemed surprised. "Do you think it wasn't an accident?"

Kouros shook his head. "No, I'm just used to asking those sorts of questions. It comes from being a cop."

"You're a cop?" She seemed afraid.

"Don't worry. I know about your incident with immigration. I'm not going to hassle you. You were a friend of my uncle, and that's good enough for me." He patted her on her bare forearm.

Stella smiled and touched his shoulder. "Thank you."

"Now will you answer my question?"

She looked down at the floor. "I only knew him from his mornings here. He always sat with his friends and I never heard anyone say a bad word about him."

"Did you ever overhear any talk of threats against him?"

"No, I never listened to their conversations."

Kouros knew she was lying. But, that was to be expected. He was an outsider, and a cop on top of that. She'd be crazy to tell him what her customers talked about, especially those customers.

"How did my uncle get his morning newspaper?"

She looked up. "The man who owns the minimarket at the bottom of the hill on the other side of Vathia always delivered it here."

"When?"

"Around eight."

"Who'd he give it to?"

"He'd put it on the table at the place where your uncle always sat."

"Did he ever give it to him personally?"

She gestured no. "He'd have a quick coffee and leave before they got here."

"Did anyone ever look at my uncle's paper before he arrived?"

She shrugged. "I didn't. Maybe Babis did once or twice, but I don't know for sure."

"Who's Babis?"

"He's my...my boss."

"Where is he?"

"Right here," said a booming voice behind Kouros.

Kouros turned his head and saw a dark, burly Greek of about Kouros' height, but heavier, standing in the doorway between the two dining rooms.

"Hi, I'm Yianni Kouros."

"What do you want?"

Kouros smiled. "We met here yesterday after my uncle's funeral."

"Like I said, what do you want?"

Kouros swung his body around so that he was facing the man head on. "That's a very inhospitable Maniot way to act."

"I'm from Pirgos."

Kouros smiled. "That explains it."

The man stepped toward Kouros. "What's that supposed to mean?"

Kouros now forced a smile. "Ease up there, Babis. It was a joke."

"I don't like jokes about my hometown."

"I have a question for you, Babis. With this hair-up-your-ass attitude how did you ever end up in the hospitality business?"

Babis took another step toward Kouros. "Listen, *malaka*, I don't need your horny sort sniffing around my help. Just have your coffee and get out of here."

Kouros glanced at Stella. She'd brought her right hand across her chest to grip her upper left arm and stood staring at Babis' feet, shaking.

Kouros stood. "I don't know what's with you, but I suggest you get a grip on yourself. I'm just asking questions about my uncle and I'm going to have a few for you, too."

"Fuck you," said Babis, stepping in front of Kouros and grabbing Stella by the arm. "And you, *putana*, into the kitchen." He pulled her forward by her arm then flung her back in the direction of the kitchen.

Kouros stepped between them, his face right up against Babis'. "Hold it right there."

Babis glared at Kouros, but it faded into a smile.

"That's better," said Kouros.

At that instant Babis drew his knee up hard into Kouros' groin, doubling Kouros over, and drove his elbow down onto the back of Kouros' head.

Kouros stumbled forward onto a table. Babis picked up a chair and swung it down at Kouros' back, but Kouros slid off onto the floor and the chair shattered into pieces against the table. Babis grabbed a table leg and swung wildly at Kouros as he struggled to his feet. Kouros ducked and drove forward, delivering a forearm across Babis' face that sent him reeling back onto a table. Kouros kept coming, grabbed Babis by his chest, lifted him off the table, and with a quick, powerful open palm thrust to Babis' jaw, dropped him like rock onto the floor.

Babis was out cold. Kouros bent over and groaned.

"Are you okay?" Stella said.

"No. Definitely not okay."

"What do you want?"

"Ice in a towel."

"Maybe heat would be better?"

"A lot of things would be better, but for now just the ice."

Kouros stayed bent over, struggling not to puke. It could have been a lot worse, he thought. He stared at Babis laid out on the floor. "You miserable cocksucker. I should kick the shit out of you."

Stella returned with the ice in a towel. Kouros put it on the back of his head.

"I thought you wanted it for down there." She pointed at his groin.

"I'd rather not talk about that at the moment." He drew in and let out a deep breath. "Does he always behave this way?"

"Not for a very long time."

"Why now?"

"He's always been jealous. But…"

"But what?"

"He's not hit me since…" She shook her head and stopped talking.

"Look, Stella, your boyfriend, boss, whatever, just kicked me in the nuts for no apparent reason, and if you don't tell me what the hell is going on here, I might just forget what I said before about you and immigration."

She studied Babis' body as if making sure he couldn't hear her. "Not since your uncle warned him not to lay a hand on me."

Kouros stared at Babis. "So he didn't like my uncle?"

"He was afraid of your uncle."

"He's not as dumb as he seems."

Babis started to stir. Kouros picked up the coffeepot and emptied the contents across Babis' face.

Babis smacked at his face, trying to rub off the coffee. "*You burned my face!*"

Kouros put the towel filled with ice on the table and straightened up. "Get up, asshole."

"I can't."

Kouros stomped the heel of his shoe down on one of Babis' hands. "I said get up."

Babis struggled to his feet.

Kouros punched him hard in the stomach, sending him back onto the floor.

"Get up."

"I can't."

Again Kouros stepped on Babis' hand. "I said get up."

Babis pulled himself up, but stayed bent over trying to protect himself from another punch. Kouros feigned a jab at Babis' head, getting him to raise his hands, then faked another to Babis' midsection getting him to bend again and drop his hands, giving Kouros the perfect opportunity for landing two quick slaps across each side of Babis' face.

"Just messing with you, asshole." Kouros grabbed Babis and pulled him down into a chair.

"Let me tell you the new rules, asshole. From now on you'll always be known to me as 'asshole,' so unless you want your customers to hear me calling you that to your face, you better keep your ugly face away from me whenever I'm around. Do you understand rule number one?"

Babis stared at the floor.

Kouros reached down, grabbed Babis' chin, lifted it up, and stared him in the eyes. "I said, 'Do you understand rule number one?'"

"Yes."

"Good." Kouros waved for Stella to come over. She hesitated. He gestured again and she came.

"Asshole, if I ever hear of you laying a hand on her, you better get used to walking without kneecaps." Kouros reached down and squeezed Babis' cheeks between his thumb and index finger. "Understand?"

Babis said nothing.

Kouros shook his head hard from side to side. "I said, 'Understand?'"

Babis mumbled, "Yes, I understand."

"And if you don't see me around here for while, don't think I've forgotten about our little deal. My cousins will be keeping an eye on her for me."

Kouros did a quick thrust of his fist toward

Babis' nose, but stopped just before making contact. It didn't matter, the thought of what was coming had Babis falling backwards off the chair and striking his head on the stone wall. Kouros picked up the ice-filled towel and threw it at him. "Here, you'll need this."

Kouros headed toward the door, but Stella called for him to stop.

"Thank you," she said, tears welling up in her eyes. "You're as kind as your uncle."

Kouros nodded. "My suggestion is that you get yourself another boss. And quick. I don't see much of a future for you here."

Outside, Kouros leaned against the hood of his car. He should have known better than to get in the literal middle of a domestic dispute. The girl's asshole boyfriend had a hell of a bad temper, one likely simmering near the boiling point for a very long time over Uncle telling him how to treat his woman. *Just my luck to remind him I was his nemesis' nephew.*

Kouros shook his head and let out a sigh. If Babis' kick to the nuts had been more effective, the crazed man might have beaten him to death. Kouros' balls hurt, but nowhere nearly as much as they would have if he'd not listened to Andreas' advice and been wearing that American designed holster that fit around his hips, under his pants and held his backup gun flat against his testicles. Kouros reached down and touched what lay sore but protected beneath the holster.

"Thanks, Chief. You saved them again."

Chapter Nine

Kouros drove from the taverna up toward Vathia. He doubted the minimarket owner would know anything about the message written in Uncle's newspaper, but he still had to talk to him. Besides, in a small town gossip was currency, and where better to exchange it than at the place where you came for news about the rest of the world?

He'd just passed the path leading to the cemetery when his mobile rang.

"Hi, Maggie. Did you get the autopsy materials I sent you?"

"Yes. That's why I'm calling. I sent it all off to our techies, but they just called to say they needed more information. They need the raw info. Photos, recorded media, blood and tissue samples, etcetera."

"If we start asking for that, the whole of the Mani will be saying GADA thinks it wasn't an accident."

"Don't worry, I told the techies to call the

coroner and tell him new procedures required that a copy of all material relating to any official autopsy be stored centrally in Athens."

"You're a genius, Maggie."

"I know. But thank you, anyway."

"Is the chief around?"

"I'll get him for you."

Kouros pulled off the road just above a reno-vated, centuries-old, four-story tower. A large, modern wooden deck at the rear of the stone tower overlooked the sea. Traditionalists must have gone wild, but whoever built the place had obviously turned a wreck into a home, and brought new blood—and money—to the Mani. That's what things were all about these days. He turned off the motor and waited.

"Yianni, how are you?"

"Alive, but barely."

"What's up?"

Yianni told Andreas about his cousin's request for a second look at the autopsy, the cast of charac-ters he'd met yesterday, and his run-in with Babis.

"Aren't you the lucky bastard to be in the wrong place at the right time?" said Andreas. "I sure hope your little flirtation was worth it."

"I'll let you know when I can feel my balls again."

Andreas laughed. "Do you still think your uncle was murdered?"

"Don't know yet. If the autopsy doesn't find something, I'll be heading home. No reason to stir up my cousins on a hunch."

"What about the death threats in his newspaper and that phone text?"

Kouros shook his head. "I know it's hard to believe it was all coincidence, but without any proof of foul play, what else could it be?"

"Mani voodoo? What about the guy you just tangled with? Sounds like he had a motive."

"I have the feeling I'm not the first guy in the taverna to hold hands with his girlfriend. He could be angry with a whole lot of people. I'll have Maggie run him through the computer and see what she comes up with."

"Well, do what you have to do. No need to hurry back on my account. That Crete thing with Orestes is now on wait-and-see status."

"What happened?"

Andreas told him.

"He's going to be pissed when he finds out about the subpoenas."

"I certainly hope so. All that thought and effort deserves some reward."

Kouros laughed. "Could you patch me back to Maggie? I want to give her that guy's name."

"Just tell me, and I'll get her to cut through all the red tape for you."

"Thanks, Chief."

"No problem. Your balls have been busted enough for one day."

Andreas personally passed along Kouros' request for a STAT criminal background check on the taverna owner. He also called GADA's techies and pressed them to expedite their review of Uncle's autopsy, though he knew Maggie's calls likely carried more weight. Certainly more fear. If you crossed Maggie, her network of strategically placed support staff would make your life miserable. Pathologically disorganized desk jockeys found their haystacks of paper scrupulously organized into neat piles impossible for them to fathom, and the neat found clutter mysteriously accumulating in every corner. And that was just for starters.

"Chief?"

Andreas pressed the intercom button. "Yes, Maggie?"

"Your friend, Petro, stopped by. He said to tell you that Orestes never showed up at the club last night."

He paused. "The next time Petro stops by, send him in to see me."

"Do you want me to find him?"

"No. Not necessary." At least not yet, he thought. But if Orestes starts making himself scarce, it would call for new tactics. Andreas needed to know what the bastard was up to.

Especially after it started raining subpoenas on Crete.

Kouros' conversation with the minimarket owner was akin to having one with a radio. All Kouros got to say was, "Hello," and the owner was off and running. He said he recognized Kouros from the funeral and spent the next fifteen minutes raving about how much he'd admired his uncle and considered it his honor to drop off Uncle's newspaper each morning at the taverna "fresh out of the stack of papers" he picked up each morning from the distributor. At least that nailed down one point for Kouros: The death threat must have been put into the paper at the taverna. No one up to that point knew which paper in the stack would end up in front of Uncle. Yes, it was possible the minimarket guy did it, but that seemed even more unlikely than someone putting the same message into every newspaper in the stack.

Kouros tried thinking of some gracious way to escape the owner's clutches when a message came through on his mobile from Maggie: CHIEF TOLD ME WHAT HAPPENED. HERE'S BALL BUSTER'S RAP SHEET. HOPE YOU'RE FEELING BETTER…OR AT LEAST FEELING SOMETHING :-)

I'll never hear the end of this, Kouros thought. As he waited for the document to download, he pointed at the phone, smiled at the owner, and said, "Sorry, I have to take this."

The man nodded and quickly pounced on another customer.

Kouros wandered over to his car. It took a minute for the document to show up on his screen. It was a three-page report dealing with crimes of the sort that gave Babis' hometown a bad name throughout the rest of Greece. From childhood, he'd been in trouble. First for breaking into tourists' hotel rooms, and later for robbing them face-to-face. By the time he was old enough to qualify for adult jail time, he'd gone into a different line of work, capitalizing on his hometown area's fertile cropland. Not as an agricultural laborer, but as a supervisor, or more appropriately for how he was expected to treat those under his watch, slave overseer.

Immigrants worked for slave wages harvesting by hand backbreaking crops like strawberries, and when a supervisor could steal from them he would. Babis' job in that line of work made his rap sheet because he'd been one of several supervisors suspected—but never proven—to have shotgunned a group of Pakistani laborers protesting over six months of unpaid back wages.

In his personal life, twice he'd been arrested for badly beating up a Polish girlfriend who'd left him. The first time, she refused to press charges. The second time she did but never appeared at his trial to testify. And no one had seen her since.

Nice guy, thought Kouros. *I should have kicked the shit out of him when I had the chance.*

The last entry was an arrest six years ago for growing marijuana hidden among rows of spinach-like *horta*. In that part of Greece and a few other places, that sort of cash crop farming practice wasn't uncommon, and viewed much like "moonshining" in the United States. Babis' drug charges were dropped and from that point on he had a clean record.

Not so much as a parking ticket since he'd relocated to the Mani.

Kouros walked through the front door of the taverna, past a startled Stella, and stopped just outside the kitchen. "Babis, come out here. Don't worry, all is forgiven. I'm not even calling you 'asshole.'"

There wasn't a sound in the kitchen. Kouros turned to Stella and mouthed, "Is he in there?"

She nodded.

"Babis come out. I only want to talk. Now play nice."

He heard metal against metal, and saw Babis wiping his hands on an apron as he walked toward him. "I have cooking to do."

"It won't take long." He turned to Stella. "Would you excuse us, please?"

Babis jerked his head in the direction of the front door. "Outside." He sat down.

Kouros sat across from him. "I've seen your rap sheet—"

"That's all in the past. I'm clean."

Kouros nodded. "I know, but I want to know how you found religion?"

"What are you talking about?"

"You went from bad boy to model citizen overnight. Why?"

"I grew up."

"I think you mean you were scared shitless."

Babis shifted in his chair.

"You faced a long stretch in prison on your last arrest. Yet you walked. Must have been divine intervention that saved your ass."

Babis shrugged. "Think what you want."

"I checked. You walked on your last arrest, but the owner of the property didn't. He got six years."

Babis shrugged again. "He deserved it."

Kouros shook his finger at him. "I'm not so sure about that, my friend. You see, that property owner was a very prominent piece of garbage in your hometown. He had his finger in just about every illegal scheme in the northwest Peloponnese. His farms were used to launder money, not make it. Everybody knew that, but no one could prove it. He was too smart and too cagey."

Babis looked at the floor.

"Hard to imagine that this same guy would be growing hash in the middle of a field owned in his real name. The DEA would have had to be blind not to find it in a flyover. He was practically inviting the DEA to catch him."

Kouros leaned in to within six inches of Babis' face. "You know what I think? I think there's no way an operator like that would ever be stupid enough to grow that shit on his own property." Kouros paused. "*No way.*"

Babis shrugged.

Kouros sat back in his chair. "My guess is he was set up. I doubt he even knew there was grass growing out in the middle of all that *horta*. But you did. Probably even planted it. And when DEA found it, you made a deal to give them the owner.

They got to nail a bad guy they'd wanted for years, and you got to walk away clean. Everyone's happy, except of course for the guy who went to prison. Does he still call you on your name day?"

"He's dead. Died of a heart attack, two years ago in prison."

Kouros nodded. "Convenient. What about his family? Have they forgotten about what you did to their father?"

Babis stared at the floor.

"Somehow I don't see you hanging around this place because you think they don't know you're here. If I'd crossed someone as powerful as that guy, I'd have moved to some place like China long ago." Kouros shook his head. "So, tell me, Babis, what keeps you here?"

"Why should I tell you?"

"Because I'm pretty sure I already know the answer to that question. I just want to know why. And if you don't tell me, I might just have to visit your old stomping grounds and start poking around for answers. I'd hate to open old wounds, but you're leaving me no choice."

Babis started running his hands through his hair, but abruptly switched to rubbing them furiously on his thighs. The textbook example of a suspect about to turn violent.

"Uh, uh," said Kouros. "Don't go there. Just

answer my question so we can end this interview and you can get back to going about your business. But if you go crazy on me again, I promise you'll be back in jail. After you get out of the hospital."

Babis took his hands off his thighs to hold his head, elbows on the table. "The DEA guys gave me no choice. They had me cold on the drug charge and a whole lot of other things that could put me away for twenty years." He got up, went over to a cooler, pulled out a beer, and snapped it open.

"What choice did I have?"

"What happened?"

Babis chugged the beer, took another from the cooler, and came back to the table. "I testified, the DEA got its conviction, the owner went away, and I moved here. End of story."

"So why are you still breathing?"

"You already guessed it. Your uncle had me under his protection."

"Which leads to my 'why' question."

"He felt he owed me."

"Owed you?"

Babis popped opened the second beer. "I was growing the grass for him."

Son of a bitch, thought Kouros. *Uncle was lying when he said he was out of the business.*

"You can't grow grass around here and your

uncle offered me a lot of money to do it for him up there."

"But why did you pick that guy's property?"

Babis' took a sip of the beer. "That's where your uncle told me to grow it. I told him there were a lot safer places to do it, but he insisted I grow it there."

"Any idea why he made you do it there?"

"Not when he asked me, but I pretty much figured all that out later. He had a hard-on for the guy. The owner double-crossed your uncle in some business deal years before and your uncle never forgave him. I don't think your uncle ever intended to take delivery of the grass. He just wanted to fuck the landowner. And did he ever. I'm sure he's the one who tipped off the DEA, too."

Son of a bitch, thought Kouros suppressing a smile. Uncle was just settling a score. *Never cross a Maniot.* "But he fucked you, too."

Babis shrugged. "He paid me what he promised, and protected me ever since. Even set me up in this business. I'm very grateful for all your uncle did for me."

"I come back to what I said before, now that my uncle's dead, what's to prevent the landowner's family from coming after you?"

"They're not vendetta-crazy like you people from the Mani. Your uncle's dead. He's the one who set everybody up. That should end it."

"Sounds like you're praying."

Babis drained the rest of the beer. "I have to prepare for my lunch customers. Are we done?"

"For now." Kouros stood and headed toward the door, passing Stella coming back inside.

"Hurry back," she whispered.

He sensed she was right about that.

Something's not right. Kouros left the taverna and drove south toward Cape Tenaro along a winding mountain road filled with hundreds of domesticated goats herded by a single dog, all of them acting as if the road were theirs alone. But his mind wasn't on the goats, the dog, or the scenery. He had to think. Kouros squeezed the steering wheel and gritted his teeth. "*He's the one who set everybody up,*" kept running through his mind.

That didn't sound like someone "grateful" for what Uncle had done for him. It was more like a man bearing a deep grudge. For six years Babis had run a taverna on the ass end of the Peloponnese, far away from the action he was used to up north. And every day of those six years he'd had to serve coffee to the guy who put him there. Babis would have been better off serving his time in prison. With prison overcrowding what it was, he'd probably be out by now, even with a twenty-year sentence.

Babis certainly had reason for a grudge. But was it a big enough one to risk murdering his protector? Babis was full of shit about Uncle's death ending the Pirgos family's desire to come after him for their father's death. They'd go after him the moment they knew he'd lost Uncle' s protection. Maybe Babis was banking on Mangas' protection? Could be. He'd likely honor his father's commitments. But if the autopsy showed Uncle was murdered, that family up north would be the least of Babis' problems. He'd spend the rest of his days looking over his shoulder worrying whether one of Uncle's children might someday think Babis had something to do with their father's murder. And why the death threat notes? Kouros smacked the steering wheel.

Something's *definitely* not right.

Chapter Ten

Maggie opened the door to Andreas' office. "Chief?"

Andreas looked at his watch. "Why are you still here?"

"Curiosity."

"Okay, I'll bite. Curious about what?"

She walked over to his desk and handed him a large flat envelope. "It's our techies' take on the autopsy of Yianni's uncle. They called to tell me it was on the way, so I waited."

"That was fast."

She smiled. "Someone lit a fire under them and they did the same to the local guy who performed the autopsy."

"So, what's it say?"

"Chief, I don't open your mail."

"Right. I forgot. It arrives that way from the mail room."

Maggie shrugged.

Andreas unwound a string holding the cover

flap closed, slid out a document, leaned back in his chair, and began to read.

Maggie sat across from him.

The first page recited all the customary exculpatory language to the effect that the author's conclusions were based solely upon data provided by someone else so that if the data were in error the conclusions might change.

He slid the first page across the desk to Maggie and started reading the second. Halfway down the page he sat up in his chair. "Jesus."

"What is it?"

Andreas held up the page and pointed with a pencil to four words. CONCLUSION: DEATH BY POISON.

"My God. Yianni was right. His uncle *was* murdered."

Andreas went back to reading the report. He finished and slid the pages across the desk to Maggie.

"This technical stuff is all Chinese to me, Chief. What does it mean?"

Andreas tapped his pencil on his desk. "If the report is correct, his uncle died from exposure to an exotic poison lethal to the touch that rapidly brings on a massive heart attack in an otherwise healthy individual. According to the victim's medical history, his heart was sound and asymptomatic for heart disease or any other suspect cause for such a natural death."

Andreas leaned forward and with the eraser end of the pencil drew the report back to him. He looked at the second page. "According to a blood analysis done by the local coroner, there were traces of markers to the poison. Not of the poison itself, because it breaks down rapidly, but of the byproducts of its disintegration. We got a break with a quick autopsy, otherwise all evidence of the poison would have disappeared."

"Doesn't sound like the local coroner was involved in a cover-up."

Andreas nodded. "My guess is once he found signs of a massive heart attack, he took that for the cause and didn't bother to look any further. But even if he had, picking up on this poison would require sophisticated forensics skills I doubt he had. Even our guys couldn't tell how the poison was administered."

"So, how can they say it was death by poison?"

"It's the old 'within a reasonable degree of medical certainty' routine. In other words, they're pretty sure he was murdered, but it's up to us to find out how."

"Was it something he swallowed at the taverna?"

Andreas gestured no. "That would have killed him on the spot," said Andreas.

"What about a needle?"

"Not as far as they could tell. It's possible bruises and cuts sustained in the crash covered up a needle mark, but that would mean whoever planned it to look like an accident left to blind luck whether the injection site would be discovered on an autopsy. I don't see whoever's behind this as being the sort to take that kind of risk. This was planned as a 'no comebacks murder.'" Andreas emphasized "no comebacks" with finger quotes. "A simple, obvious heart attack with no links back to the killer."

"So, how do we figure out how he was poisoned?"

He smiled. "Push the techies harder. That's your job. Starting first thing tomorrow morning."

Andreas resumed tapping his pencil on the desk. "The big question for me is, why did they work so hard to make it look like an accident?"

"They didn't want to trigger a war in the Mani?"

"Death threats tied to an old vendetta don't make sense if you're trying to make a murder look like an accident so as *not* to start a war."

"So, which of us passes the news on to Yianni?"

"I'll do it," said Andreas. "And let's keep this to ourselves for now. The last thing we need is a bunch of crazy Maniots running around the Peloponnese chasing after suspects. That sort of paranoia runs up the body count pretty quickly."

Andreas picked up the phone. "I sure wish Yianni had been wrong."

"Poison!"

"Yes, a rare sophisticated one. Not something you'd find in a gardening shed or local pharmacy." Andreas picked up the report. "It says here that 'depending on the method of administration, the onset of a heart attack would be in two to ten minutes.'"

"That meant he was poisoned just before leaving the taverna," said Kouros.

"Or inside his car."

"But that would require some way of administering the poison inside the car. A needle, gas canister, or some other device, and that sort of thing should have turned up in the examination of the car after the accident."

"Maggie will push the techies to take a closer look for needle marks and ask them if the poison could have been administered as a gas. You better check out the car just to make sure no one missed something."

"I hear the taverna's pretty busy in the mornings, so anyone tampering with his car there would have been taking a hell of a risk. But if it happened inside the car, it could have been set up somewhere else and rigged to go off when he drove away from the taverna."

"Just to be sure, you ought to verify how busy that taverna actually is in the mornings."

"I'm beginning to become a regular there."

"Look at it as your chance to bond with your sparring partner from this morning."

"You mean my *numero uno* choice as my uncle's killer?" Kouros told him of his afternoon conversation with Babis.

"Sure sounds like he had a reason for disliking your uncle. Just not sure it's enough of one to murder him. And why now? From the threats your uncle received, his murder seems more likely related to his hotel project, and I don't see anything linking Babis to that."

"I was wondering the same thing."

"What about the girl? She might know something. Ask around, but be careful. We don't want your kinfolk thinking we suspect murder."

"The one I'm worried about thinking that way is Mangas. Once he gets that into his head, there will be no stopping him."

"Isn't he who asked you to make sure it was an accident?"

"Yes, to get his sister off his back. That's my explanation for why I'm asking all these questions. But he's pressing me for my take on the autopsy report and I don't want him thinking I'm hiding something."

"How much longer can you stall him?"

"I told him I'd send the report on to Athens this morning but that they needed additional information from the coroner. Between that and what I assume he shares with the rest of Greeks as a universally low opinion of the work habits of our public employees, I should be able to stall him for another two days, three at most."

"I hope we have our killer by them."

"I don't want to think about it if we don't. I wish I could lie and tell him it was an accident. Not telling him what we know is as far as I'm prepared to go. After all, he is family."

"Sounds like the priorities on your moral compass are still in working order."

"Yeah, but I'm beginning to worry about my other parts."

Andreas laughed. "Just be careful. Bye."

Andreas put his feet up on his desk and stared out the window. Kouros' cousin should lose his patience with the Greek police's official investigation into his father's death at just about the same time subpoenas started flying all over Crete, Orestes started flying all over Spiros, and Spiros all over Andreas. The elements of a pro-verbial perfect shit storm massing in Greece's two most violent-tempered parts just waiting for the perfect moment to come together in the middle of Andreas' desk.

Andreas decided to follow his own moral compass. He took his feet off his desk and went home to his family.

It started out innocently enough. Andreas returned home at a reasonable hour, something quite unreasonable for him, but he'd forgotten Lila was at a charity event with her mother. He toyed with the idea of catching a movie, *souvlaki*, and beer at the open-air theater in the park just across the street from their apartment but decided instead on what he thought a much better idea: a "whatever you want to do" good time with his son.

"Finger painting" was not among the answers Andreas expected, but a deal was a deal, especially with a three-year-old. So, after changing into jeans and a white t-shirt, and covering the laundry room floor-to-ceiling in plastic, Andreas plopped Tassaki amid a sea of glossy finger paint paper and surrounded him with an array of brightly colored paint jars.

Andreas looked down at his handiwork and said, "Let's do it!"

It was a peaceful beginning. Tassaki carefully

opened one jar, dipped in one finger, brought it out, and showed a blood red fingertip to his father.

"Terrific start. Now rub it on the paper to make a picture."

Andreas watched with a smile as his son carefully selected and began rubbing his finger on one particular piece of paper.

Tassaki looked at his father and held up his finger. "It's all gone."

"That's okay. Dip your finger into the jar to get more."

Tassaki dipped his finger and with studied care went back to his painting. Five minutes later, Andreas smiling through every second of it, Tassaki held up the paper. It was a circle, with dots inside and out, and three relatively straight lines roughly intersecting the circle.

"It's beautiful," smiled Andreas.

"It's you."

"Me?"

Tassaki nodded.

Andreas leaned over and kissed him. "Thank you. Now, I think you should make one of Mommy."

"But I need more colors."

Andreas wasn't quite sure how to take that, so he just said, "Fine," and opened two more jars of paint.

"All of them."

"You want all of them open?"

"Yes, it's for Mommy."

Andreas had started down this road, so there was no going back.

Andreas opened the remaining jars one by one and placed all ten in front of his son.

Tassaki pulled a clean sheet of paper in front of him. Very carefully he dipped a separate finger into each jar before proudly holding up ten different colored fingertips to his father.

"Now what?" smiled Andreas.

Tassaki placed his fingertips at the top edge of the paper and carefully brought each hand out, down, and around to form two five-ring, rainbow semicircles roughly joined together at the top and bottom. He finished by pulling his fingers straight down and off the paper in ten nearly parallel lines.

All Andreas could think of to say was, "Wow."

"Mommy."

Andreas pulled Tassaki to his chest, hugged, and kissed him. "Yes, your mommy is very beautiful."

Tassaki pulled back and pointed at the front of Andreas' t-shirt, now bearing the handprints of a three-year-old Picasso. "You're shirt is dirty, Daddy."

Andreas nodded and dipped his fingertip into a jar of blue paint. He stared at it for a moment, considering the ramifications of his intended act. "And so is your nose," drawing a blue line straight down the center of it.

Ten minutes later Lila returned home to the sounds of giggles and laughter in her laundry room. Inside she found her husband and son rolling around on the floor in what looked to be a psychedelic Jackson Pollock painting come to life.

When the two rainbow bodies rolling around on the floor realized Lila was standing in the doorway, the room went suddenly quiet.

Lila cleared her throat. "Darling, remind me to make a point of sending a drum set to the child whose parents gave Tassaki those finger paints for his birthday."

Chapter Eleven

By 8:45 the next morning, Kouros sat parked on the road to Cape Tenaro looking down on the taverna about a quarter-mile away. From here he had an unobstructed view of the front of the taverna and for the next hour and a half watched a seemingly endless flow of fishermen, farmers, tradesmen, retirees, and local business types flow in and out of the taverna. Just before ten-thirty he put down his binoculars and drove to the taverna. Anyone hoping to tinker unnoticed with a car parked in front of that place during its morning hours had a far better chance of winning the lottery.

He got out and went inside. The moment he stepped through the door, his uncle's hotelier friend Panos yelled out from a table, "Ahh, finally, you decided to join us. We've been wondering how long it would take you."

"Practically everyone walking in here since we got here wanted to know who's the guy sitting up there on the hill watching us," smiled Stelios.

Make that the mega-millions lottery, thought Kouros.

"I told them not to worry, he'll come inside," said Panos.

"You cost me fifty euros," said Konstantin. "I bet Mihalis you were just waiting for us to leave so you'd have Stella all to yourself."

Everyone in the place laughed.

Babis came out of the kitchen, glanced at Kouros but said nothing. Instead he began bantering with a table full of farmers and fishermen, making them laugh.

"Come, sit with us," said Konstantin to Kouros.

"Aren't you missing one of your crew?"

Panos nodded. "Alexander had business in Athens yesterday and won't be back for a couple of days."

"Yeah, monkey business," said Mihalis. "Our political friend is getting laid."

"Better he's busy screwing his girlfriend than our country," said Panos.

"Even his wife would agree with that," said Stelios.

Panos poured Kouros a cup of coffee from a pot on the table. "So, tell us why you were sitting out there for so long?"

"I wanted to get an idea of how busy the place is."

"To see if anyone had the opportunity to screw around with your uncle's car?" said Mihalis.

"What makes you think that?"

Stella came out of the kitchen, saw Kouros, and smiled.

"I was an ex-cop, remember. As I see it, you had one of two reasons. You're either the good nephew making sure your uncle's death was an accident, or you really are here because of Stella. But since alternative two would get my friend his fifty euros back, I'm all for number one." Mihalis waved at Stella, "*Svenaki* for all."

"It's a bit early for me for shots of whiskey," said Kouros.

"Not to toast your uncle it isn't."

Stella went around to the other tables setting down trays of shot glasses filled with a clear liquid, but at Kouros' table she handed each man a separate shot glass.

Kouros braced himself for what it might be: *ouzo*, *tsipouro*, vodka, or tequila. He needed a clear head and this definitely was not in keeping with that program. But he had no choice, so he shouted, "*Theos singhorese ton,*" and downed the toast in a gulp. The taste startled him. It wasn't anything close to what he expected: it was water.

He looked at Stella and she smiled.

He laughed.

"Mihalis, I want my fifty back. Or at least half of it," said Konstantin. "Look at those two."

Stelios said, "Another round."

"Not for me, thanks. One's enough." Having downed one, no one pressed Kouros to do another.

After two more *svenaki* shots, Panos leaned over to Kouros and said, "We could have told you no one could get to your uncle's car while he was in here. Nobody had balls that big. Besides, he was careful where he parked. Always at the same spot right in front, locked, with the alarm on."

"Was he always that careful?"

"With his car, sure. He used to say he'd done so much to other people's cars in his time that he wasn't about to make it easy for anyone to get at him. And everybody knew it. No one even leaned on your uncle's car."

Kouros nodded. Another likely dead end. He caught himself staring at Stella and stopped. No reason to piss Babis off any more than he already had. He might just take it out on her despite Kouros' warning.

Besides, all Kouros saw in starting something up with Stella were a few "slam, bam, thank you ma'am" moments. And even those were getting complicated these days. Everybody's looking for a way out to a better place. No telling what's on a woman's mind these days. He looked at Babis. Or a man's.

Babis stood with his back to Kouros, holding court at another table, telling jokes, patting men on the back, lightly smacking the backs of their heads, and pinching the backs of their necks. He was playing the quintessential Greek taverna owner, as if lifted straight out of a Greek National Tourist Office promotional film.

Whatever else Kouros thought about Babis, he had to give him credit. The man knew his customers.

The question was, did he know them well enough to kill them and make it look like an accident?

Uncle's buddies kept Kouros penned up inside the taverna until nearly noon. They had far too many stories to share of their friend's exploits to stick to their out-by-ten-thirty routine. Kouros actually enjoyed the stories; though most seemed more the fantasies of old men living vicariously through another's imagined talent with the ladies than real life. Still, if only a tenth of the tales were true, Kouros' aunt truly must have had the qualities of a saint.

Finally, Kouros left the taverna and drove north through Vathia. Five miles later he passed the turnoff to Gerolimenas. Fifteen miles ahead, along a two-lane road winding through the heart of ancient Mani, lay Aeropoli. Twenty-five miles further north sat the seaside village of Kardamyli, home to famed British travel writer Patrick Leigh Fermor. Beyond the Mani, another twenty-five miles would have brought Kouros to the bustling port city of Kalamata. Famous for plump, pungent olives of the same name, Kalamata stood second in population on the Peloponnese only to Patras.

But Kouros stopped in Aeropoli. Mangas had shipped Uncle's car there, to the only body shop in the region with a chance of repairing it. Luckily, work hadn't started on it. Unluckily, Kouros found nothing suspicious. No hidden needles, gas canisters, or evidence of any tinkering with the air-conditioning, heating, or any other part of the ventilation system. Everything checked out just as in the original report.

Kouros left the body shop and started walking to his car. But he paused and looked back toward Aeropoli's town square a few blocks away. "Why not?" he said to himself and headed for it.

A statue of the Mani's most famous citizen, Petros Mavromichalis, legendary Nyklian hero of Greece's War of Independence and the Mani's last Ottoman-appointed chieftain, dominated the marble and limestone square. Sadly, the immediately surrounding area had lost much of the charm Kouros remembered from his childhood, succumbing to the ill-fated belief of so many tourist-driven communities that tourism must be served, no matter what the cost. But just off the square, in the old town proper, a different sort of civic wisdom had prevailed and classic two-story, honey and gray fieldstone homes lined meandering flagstone streets in testament to preservation meticulously executed with care and good taste.

Kouros bought a *souvlaki* and bottle of water, sat down on a bench under a mulberry tree next to the statue, pulled out his mobile, and called Andreas.

The first words he heard were, "Any luck?"

"Everything checked out. No surprises."

"Between that and what you told me on the drive up about your morning in the taverna, I'd say your uncle was poisoned in the taverna."

"Everyone with him at the table that morning had a possible motive, but my money's on Babis," said Kouros.

"Aren't you forgetting someone?"

"Who?"

"The girl."

"But he helped her."

"I know, and it doesn't seem likely, but what do we know about her?"

"Not much. And the only person who would

know about Stella is Babis. I doubt he'll talk to me about her."

"What about that immigration guy, the one who threatened to arrest her but your uncle chased away? He might know something."

"How the hell am I going to find him?"

"You're in Aeropoli, aren't you?"

"Yes."

"Try the port police in Gytheio. That office covers your uncle's part of the Mani and they deal with immigration all the time. Maybe they know something about her or who might have come looking for her in the taverna. After all, the story about him being run off by your uncle is funny. It's the kind cops like to repeat."

"Not when it's about themselves. If I were that guy, I'd never breathe a word of it to anyone."

"What the hell, you're already there."

"Already there? Gytheio's all the way over on the Mani's east coast."

"Stop complaining. It's only a half-hour drive and think of all that beautiful mountain scenery you'll get to see."

"Fine, but the gas is going on my expense report."

"Good luck with that. Let me know what happens. Got to run." The line went dead.

Kouros shut off his phone, ate his *souvlaki*,

and walked back to his car. It seemed a long shot, but Andreas was right about the drive. Gytheio lay across the mountains, a picture perfect harbor town nestled up against the Laconian Gulf in the northeast corner of the Mani. It was the largest town in the Mani, the municipal seat of East Mani, the seaport of ancient Sparta, and a thriving export center during Roman times. A massive earthquake had leveled the place in the fourth century, and it remained a small village until the early nineteenth century when refugees escaping from Greece's War of Independence got the population growing again. Gytheio returned to glory in the 1960s with its new port.

But Kouros wasn't going on holiday. He somehow had to find the guy run off by his uncle. As a general rule the best chance at getting dicey information from another service was to put the request on a cop-to-cop, off-the-record basis. Then again, from his experience with cops in this part of the country, he suspected he'd get a warmer reception introducing himself as his uncle's nephew.

Chapter Twelve

Port police headquarters in Gytheio sat almost directly across from the causeway entrance to the tiny island of Kranae on which mythology had Paris spending his first night with the abducted Helen before spiriting her off to Troy. Kouros pulled into a spot marked RESERVED FOR HCG VEHICLES. A port policeman dressed in a black t-shirt, black military fatigues, and matching baseball cap told him to move along. Kouros showed him his badge and said he was there to see his boss, the Coast Guard harbormaster. In peacetime Greece, the Hellenic Coast Guard also served as its port police.

The man pointed at a two-story, ochre with Greek-blue trim building behind him. "Top floor, second door on the left."

A second-floor balcony enclosed by a blue metal railing ran across the front of the building. But no one seemed to be taking advantage of the sea view, for dark brown shutters tightly covered every window.

Kouros found the harbormaster's door open but knocked on it anyway.

A man about Kouros' age, with close-cropped, jet-black hair and a deep suntan looked up from behind a cluttered desk. "May I help you?"

"I'm Detective Yianni Kouros of GADA. I'm hoping you might be able to help me with a matter I'm looking into in your jurisdiction."

The man stood and extended his hand. "The name's Pavlos. Please, sit and tell me how I may help you."

Taller than Andreas, slim, and wearing a starched white uniform with gold trim, Pavlos looked like a proverbial movie star. Kouros couldn't help but think it was no wonder these port police guys get all the girls.

They shook hands and Kouros sat down across from Pavlos.

"It's a delicate matter, and somewhat personal, so I hope I can trust your discretion."

Pavlos nodded and flashed a George Clooney smile. "You sure do know how to capture my interest."

Kouros smiled back. "It's about my uncle."

Pavlos nodded.

Kouros said his uncle's name.

Pavlos blinked twice. "He's your uncle?"

Kouros nodded, "Yes, my name's been shortened a bit from his."

Pavlos' lips went taut.

"As I'm certain you know, my uncle died a few days ago, and at my family's request I'm making sure nothing's been missed."

"Missed?"

"Yes. My uncle's past left a lot of, shall we say, 'unsettled grudges' and the family just wants to make sure none of that played any part in his passing."

"Which side are you on?" said Pavlos.

"What do you mean?"

"The side that anticipates a new war on the Mani or the side that doesn't."

"Let me rephrase my question," said Kouros. "What the fuck are you talking about?"

The harbormaster shrugged. "You know the routine. We gather intelligence on what's happening in our port from locals. Dockworkers, fishermen, taverna owners, marine suppliers. They know better than anyone what's going on. And once in a while we pick up information from someone we arrest. A couple weeks back we picked up a rumor from a guy trying to make a deal to stay out of prison."

"What sort of rumor?"

"He called it a 'big project' involving your

uncle that had 'people up north' seriously concerned a 'war' might break out 'down in the Mani.'"
Pavlos emphasized the words with finger quotes.

"Over a hotel project?"

Pavlos shrugged. "I don't know what kind of
project. All I heard was that it involved your uncle."

"Who are the 'people up north'?"

"Don't know. It came from a smuggler trying
to trade what he said was 'hard' information against
jail time. Turned out all he knew was that there was
something big 'out there' involving your uncle and
that he'd rather go to jail than name the guys up
north." Pavlos smiled. "And so he did."

"Drug smugglers would lie to God on their
deathbeds."

Pavlos nodded. "But this guy wasn't a drug
smuggler. His deal was arms. We caught him on a
freighter bound for North Africa."

"So 'north' to him meant what?'"

"We took it to be the Balkans. The freighter
was out of the Balkans and most arms smuggling
into that part of Africa runs through the Balkans
or the Ukraine."

"Have you heard of anyone else with an interest in going after my uncle?"

"No. He was pretty much retired as far as I
could tell. That's why I took the smuggler's talk for
the bullshit it was."

Kouros paused. "There's one other matter you might be able to help me with. It involves a girl who works in a taverna just south of Vathia. Her name is Stella—"

Before Kouros could say her last name, Pavlos burst out laughing. "Please don't tell me you've heard that story, too."

"From the way you're laughing, I think I have."

"Your uncle was quite a character, God bless his soul. Especially where women were concerned."

"So I've heard."

"About six months ago he showed up in my office and asked me to help a girl working at a taverna he owned—"

"That 'he owned'?"

"Yes. At least that's what he said. He wanted to get her a residency card. I asked why he was going through me, and he said it was delicate. It had to be done without her knowing."

"How did you manage that?"

"I didn't. He said everything had been arranged except for her personal interview with the police. He wanted me to sign off on it."

"What did you say?"

"That I couldn't possibly do that without meeting her."

"And?"

"He said that was fine as long as I didn't tell

her the true purpose of my meeting her or of his involvement." Pavlos burst out laughing again.

"I loved your uncle's style. He told me to come into the taverna any morning he was there to satisfy myself that the girl actually existed and spoke Greek." Pavlos shook his head and smiled. "Then he added that he'd really appreciate it if I made him look 'good' in the girl's eyes."

"You're kidding me."

"Nope. He sat right there in the same chair you're in and told me how to play it. I took it to mean he wanted to screw her." Pavlos shrugged. "I decided what the hell, someday maybe I'd need the same sort of help with a woman."

Kouros doubted those days were anywhere close for a guy with Pavlos' looks. "But why go through all that if he was getting her a residency permit? If you wanted to impress an illegal immigrant girl into bed, I can't imagine anything better than letting her know you're making her legal."

"I told him just about the same thing, but he said she wasn't like that. She'd feel like a hooker if she knew. Besides, he said even if he never got into her pants he wanted to help her out. Her boyfriend was always threatening to turn her in to immigration if she didn't do what he told her. Your uncle wanted to end all that."

"Did the boyfriend know?"

"Don't see how. I've told some of my buddies on the force a made-up story about when I was stationed on Mykonos and how an old guy once asked me to play an immigration bad guy to win the heart of a fair maiden. I never mentioned real names or places, and certainly not the residency card shenanigans. Just in case the real story ever got out, I didn't want to seem more involved than I was, because, even though your uncle's heart was in the right place, it's pretty obvious everything wasn't kosher with her application."

"Kosher?"

"It's a Jewish word. Means 'legit.' And I'd appreciate it if you didn't spread that part of the story around."

Kouros nodded. "So what's the status of her residency permit?"

Pavlos shrugged. "She should have it any day."

"Did my uncle ever sleep with her?"

Pavlos gestured he didn't know. "Personally, I think she'd have done him even without our little performance. Your uncle was a charmer, good to her, and both of them thought her boyfriend an asshole."

It seemed his uncle and he agreed on a lot of things. "Any idea why my uncle kept the boyfriend running a place he owned if he thought him an 'asshole'?"

"Because he was 'his' asshole?"

"What's that supposed to mean?'"

"It's no secret the boyfriend put his former boss away to die in prison and that your uncle likely set the whole thing up. The boyfriend had no place to run but to your uncle, and my guess is your uncle wanted to keep it that way. Better to have him inside the boat pissing out, than outside pissing in."

Kouros smiled.

"Those guys up north still haven't forgiven your uncle or his asshole."

"Guys up north?"

"By Pirgos, not the Balkans."

Kouros paused. "That arms smuggler on the Balkan freighter who mentioned 'people up north.' What was his nationality?"

"Greek. From Crete."

"If you're from Crete, both the Balkans *and* Pirgos are 'up north.'"

Pavlos nodded. "And both places have 'people' capable of bringing 'war' to the Mani."

Kouros thought but didn't say, *if they haven't already.*

"Maggie, it's Yianni. Is the chief free?"

"He's in a meeting but I can pull him out if you need him."

"No, not necessary. Just tell him I spoke to the port police in Gytheio about the girl, Stella, and it looks like my uncle was involved with her in a way that if her boyfriend knew, would definitely make him our likely guy."

"You make it sound like one of those Turkish soap operas."

"This one is all Greek. Tell the chief I'll call back. Any more word on the autopsy?"

"They're working on it. Hope to have something definitive this afternoon."

"Terrific. Catch you later."

"Bye-bye and be careful, my boy."

As he drove away from the port, a sign for a hotel caught his eye. It incorporated an ancient Mani tower into its design and bore the name of an old, well-respected Mani warrior clan. Maybe his uncle had the right idea and hotels were the way to go. Which gave Kouros an idea.

An hour later he turned right off the main road at a sign to Gerolimenas and wound down a narrow, well-paved road for a half-mile into a tiny harborside village just beyond a broad beach of white pebbles. At the far end of the beach, behind a row of centuries-old homes in need of various levels of attention, gray and terra cotta sheaves of limestone cliffs shot five hundred feet into the sky and ran straight out to sea for almost a mile, offering natural shelter to the harbor from harsh north winds and a perfect haunt for pirate ghosts.

The harbor-front road hosted five tavernas, two rooming houses, a hotel, three private residences, a tiny supermarket, and a hodgepodge of tables, chairs, and umbrellas perched upon a stone apron wider in some spots than the narrow road it abutted. All but one taverna sat across the road from the sea, and all were built of gray and honey color limestone—in recognition, perhaps, of this tiny port town's survival depending upon a single word: picturesque.

At the other end of the harbor the road turned abruptly west, narrowed by half, and ran between a ramshackle array of melancholy stone huts, homes, and workshops, some teetering on the edge of eroding into rubble. Once tied to lives at sea, their futures now hinged on preservation whims of the sort that had saved the stone buildings just beyond them, the target of Kouros' journey.

An elegant hotel stood at the southwestern tip of the harbor, offering new life for a long ago bustling dock and warehouse complex. Merchant ships once flocked here to the region's thriving mercantile center, but now the village depended on tourists looking to spend seaside holidays in quiet seclusion amid memories of a bygone era.

Kouros parked in a tiny courtyard close by

a flagstone patio spanned by a stone archway. He found the hotel lobby under the archway to the left, a former nineteenth-century warehouse office appointed with preserved wide plank and stone floors, fieldstone walls, and massive ceiling beams.

He asked the young woman behind the reception desk to please tell her boss, "The new guy from his morning coffee crew would like to see him."

She relayed the message into a walkie-talkie, paused, and smiled at Kouros. "Mr. Panos would like you to join him for lunch. He's in the dining room." She pointed behind him. "It's in our former warehouse, through those doors on the other side of the patio."

Like the lobby, the dining room reflected considerable effort at leaving no doubt that this now-elegant space owed its origins to a place of hard, difficult work.

Panos stood by a table at the far end of the room shaking hands with a man in a suit and tie who looked to be in his late thirties. The man had left by the time Kouros reached the table.

"I'm sorry. Did I interrupt something?" asked Kouros.

Panos waved his hand in the direction of the departing man. "More liked saved me. He's a lawyer from Athens. He came to pitch me with an offer from one of his clients to buy my hotel. Every son of a bitch who got his money out of Greece before the crisis is now running around the country trying to buy the best properties on the cheap. You spared me telling him to go to hell. Nicely, of course."

"I'm surprised he left so quickly."

Panos smiled. "I told him an investigator from the tax office was here to see me. I invited him to stay and I'd introduce him. Suddenly he remembered another appointment and bolted."

Kouros smiled. "Why did you agree to see him?"

"I'm in the hospitality business, and on the high-end side of it. Guys like him, and more importantly, his clients, are my bread and butter. I just listen and graciously decline their offers to steal my business. Even offer to treat them to lunch while they try to screw me. By the way, I hope you like lobster and linguini. It's what that *malaka* ordered. Those types always order the same thing, even when they're paying for it. It's the most expensive dish on the menu and they think it's impressive to order. Someday they'll learn the only thing it impresses is my cash register."

"Remind me to drop him a thank you. I'd be embarrassed to order more than a chicken *souvlaki*."

Panos leaned forward and planted a finger squarely in the middle of Kouros' chest. "Which is precisely why your uncle thought so highly of you. You're real."

Kouros nodded. "Yeah, and by the time this conversation is over you'll probably be calling me a *real* pain in the ass."

Panos laughed. "Just tell me what you want to know."

Kouros stared straight into Panos' eyes. "Was my uncle screwing Stella?"

Panos smiled. "I sure as hell hope so."

"That's not a helpful answer."

"How about, 'With all that he did for her I sure hope she at least gave him a hand-job.'"

"You're still not helping. Let's go at this a different way. Just what did he do for her?"

"Scared off the immigration guy."

Kouros shook his head. "Time for me to become that pain in the ass I promised. We both know that was a full of shit hustle he ran on her just to get in her pants."

Panos looked away. "I wouldn't know anything about that."

"Why do I get the impression you're fucking with me?"

Kouros watched Panos' face redden. "Be careful what you say."

"Then be honest in what you say."

"Are you calling me a liar?"

Kouros leaned in, "Since I'm not in the hospitality business, in a word, *yes*."

Panos glared at Kouros. Then smiled. "So you know about the port police cop from Gytheio?"

Kouros nodded. "And?"

"And what?"

"Stop making me pull teeth here, Panos."

"The residency card?"

"Bingo, we have a winner."

"I go back to my original question, 'Was my uncle screwing, Stella?'"

"Only a few times. That I know of."

"How would you know?"

"He used my hotel. He'd bring her here when Babis was away."

"Away?"

"Athens, wherever."

"How often was he away?"

"Not enough for your uncle." Panos smiled. "Maybe once, twice a month."

"How did you find out about the port police cop and the residency card?"

"Your uncle told me. He knew I'd find out about him and Stella using my hotel and didn't want me talking to the guys about it. So, on the condition I'd keep it just between us, he told me about the song and dance he'd arranged to put on at the taverna to get Stella her card."

"And now for the big question. Did Babis have any idea my uncle was screwing her?"

"Why? Do you think his death wasn't an accident?"

"The rules are that I ask the questions and you give the answers."

Panos bit at his lower lip. "I don't know."

"Does that mean maybe?"

Panos shrugged.

"Aside from my uncle, Stella, and you, who else knew they were screwing?"

"No one, unless somebody saw them going into a room together. Or coming out."

Again Kouros leaned in. "Or maybe you told somebody?"

Panos' eyes fixed on Kouros'. "I told no one. I kept my word to your uncle."

Kouros shook his head. "Sure sounds to me that if Babis found out about them screwing around in your hotel, it likely came through you."

Panos glared.

"You know, maybe you drank a bit too much one morning in the taverna, decided to tease my uncle, said something about Stella that Babis overheard?"

"As I said before, I never said a word to anyone, including your uncle, about the two of them. It was forbidden to talk about, let alone joke."

"So you tried?"

"No. I knew your uncle all my life. I knew what I could joke about and what I couldn't. This definitely wasn't a subject to raise with him. And so I didn't. Period. End of story, *Detective*."

If only it were.

Chapter Thirteen

Kouros left his car at the hotel and walked into the port. He hadn't been in Gerolimenos in years and wondered if that crazy priest with the long black hair, jeans, and dirty cowboy boots still hung around the harbor. Kouros was never actually sure he was a priest, even though he wore the cassock. And considering the colorful history of priests fighting alongside the Mani's bandits and pirates, he wouldn't be surprised at anything.

He stopped at the southern edge of the harbor next to a lone pay phone. It had no handset, the same as the last time he'd been here. In this day of mobile phones no one probably noticed. Certainly never complained. This village always struck him as a combination of traditional Greece and the American Wild West. The harbor scene was quintessential, old-time, tiny Greek fishing village taken to perfection. But behind the busy row of harbor-front buildings stood a single row of open spaces and tired, nondescript two-story homes bearing no resemblance whatsoever to the quaint images portrayed one street over. It made him think of the false-front towns used in making old-time American cowboy movies.

His phone rang. "Yes, Chief."

"I thought you were going to call me back?" said Andreas.

"Just finished an interview with the owner of the hotel where my uncle was screwing Babis' Stella."

"Then you'll love what I have for you. I just read our tech guys' final take on the autopsy report. Your uncle definitely was poisoned, but they're still not sure how. The only new information they thought might be relevant was a bruise on your uncle's body containing traces of wax."

"Wax? What's wax got to do with anything?"

"For that I have to thank Tassaki."

"Huh?"

"The other night we were playing with finger paints and I remembered Tassaki kept coating his fingertips with paints. That got me to thinking. If you're a killer looking to administer a poison lethal to the touch in front of a lot of people, you have two primary concerns. One, doing it in a way that doesn't get you noticed, and two, not killing yourself in the process. Since this hit happened in a taverna, it wouldn't be a big deal to melt some wax in the kitchen and dip your finger in it before touching the poison. Especially if it's your kitchen."

"Sounds like something out of a BBC mystery."

"I know. But I went online and you'll never guess what I came up with. Applying wax to a fingertip was an ancient ninja method used for administering poison through a finger thrust to a penetration point. The question is, how was our killer able to get to your uncle and apply that sort of force in a crowded taverna without anyone noticing?"

"Where was the bruise with the wax?" said Kouros.

"On the side of his neck by the carotid artery."

"Jesus, Chief. Babis must be our man. This morning I saw him slapping backs and squeezing necks as his customers were leaving. It was his style. No one would have noticed."

"But the jealousy angle doesn't tie in to your uncle's death threats."

"Yeah, I know. But Babis is all we've got, and maybe once we start squeezing him we'll get an answer that makes sense of it all."

"Okay. Bring him in."

"I'll be there in ten minutes."

"Be careful. I don't want you going after him without backup. If he's our killer, he'll know he's facing prison."

"If he did it, once my cousins find out, he's a dead man. In or out of prison."

"Not our problem. We just solve the cases and let the justice system run its course."

"That's comforting."

"No, it's Greece."

The lights flashing, siren blaring, the blue-and-white police car streaking through Vathia on its way to the taverna created precisely the sort of bravado entrance Kouros told the local cops to avoid. He'd hoped to get Babis safely away from the Mani before his cousins learned of Babis' arrest. No way they'd think he'd been busted for overcooking the *spanakopita*. Kouros' hopes on that score vanished when Mangas pulled up to the taverna seconds behind the police car.

Kouros stared at a pair of Laurel and Hardy look-alike cops walking toward him, followed by Mangas. "Why didn't you two *malakas* offer to give Mangas a ride when you told him I needed help with an arrest?"

The fat cop shrugged. "We're family here. We take care of each other."

"Forget about them," said Mangas. "What did you find out?"

"I want to take Babis in for questioning."

Mangas stared at Kouros. "I'll take care of the questioning."

Kouros stared back. "No, you won't."

Mangas clenched and unclenched his fists. "I'm not going to let him get away with murdering my father."

"Nor am I. If he did. But we don't know that. We just have questions." Lying seemed appropriate under these circumstances, as the truth would lead to Babis' immediate demise.

"If you're lying to me..." Mangas let his words trail off.

Kouros nodded. "Let me handle this. With the help of Mani's finest."

The two cops looked at Mangas. He nodded. "But I'll be out here just hoping the son of a bitch makes a run for it."

Kouros nodded. "If he runs he's all yours." That sounded like a perfect argument for convincing Babis it would be in his decided best interest to come quietly.

Kouros didn't expect many customers at this hour and the lone motorbike parked outside the kitchen entrance had him hoping they'd be alone for the arrest. Kouros held his gun in his hand as the three cops walked through the front door, Kouros first. He stood in the front room and listened. Not a sound. He walked toward the kitchen, and stood in the doorway. Still no sound. He motioned toward a door at the rear of the kitchen and the three cops spread out and crept toward the door. As soon as the two cops were in position on either side of the door, in one swift move Kouros grabbed the doorknob, turned it, and pushed the door open into the room.

The room smelled of onions and dill, and a bit of light from a tiny window shined down on an array of vegetables and a half-naked body on a cot. A female body.

Stella jumped up, her bare breasts moving slightly slower than the rest of her body, but catching up in time for Kouros and the two cops to realize her butt was not her only perfect quality. "*What are you doing here?*" she screamed, not making any attempt to cover up.

"Sorry, Stella," said Kouros, moving his eyes with a struggle up to meet hers. "We're looking for Babis."

"With those?" She pointed at the guns.

The fat cop made no effort to take his eyes off her breasts. "Just tell us where he is."

"I don't know."

Kouros shook his head. "Get dressed. You're coming with us."

"But I've done nothing."

"Sorry, but you still have to come with us."

"Maybe he's at Cape Tenaro," she said.

"Why would he be there?" said Kouros.

"He goes fishing there sometimes in the afternoons."

"In a boat?"

She took her time putting on her bra. Something every male eye in the room followed with exacting attention to detail. "No. He fishes off the shore."

Kouros said to the two cops, "Take her back to the station. And hold her until I get there."

The thin guy grabbed Stella's arm before she could put on the rest of her clothes and started dragging her out the door in her bra and panties.

Kouros grabbed the man's arm and squeezed. "Don't even think what you're thinking. That is unless you and your fat fuck of a partner want to know how vengeful this Maniot can be."

He looked at Stella. "Now get dressed. And fast." He walked back into the kitchen and through the kitchen door leading to the outside. His cousin stood leaning against the hood of his car, talking on his mobile. He gestured for Kouros to come closer as he shouted into the phone, "And don't hurt him, I promised my cousin." He hung up.

Kouros shook his head. "Does that mean what I think it means?"

"If you mean did I find him, no. But I told

my friends to search every inch of Cape Tenaro until they do."

"How did…?"

Mangas smiled. "I said I'd stay out here, but nothing about not listening in. I heard everything through that." He pointed at the tiny storeroom window.

"I hope you meant what you said about not hurting him."

Mangas smiled. "I would no more lie to you, cousin, than you would to me." He patted Kouros on the back. "Smile, you will soon have your answers." Mangas dropped his hand, and the smile left his face.

"And when you do, I shall have my vengeance. So help me, God."

The phenomenon known as Cape Tenaro drew both locals and tourists to its shores, the former for its fishing and coves, the latter for what the merger of the Ionian and Aegean Seas represented to the civilized world. Those two great bodies of water once stood as stages for antiquity's greatest dramas, upon which ancient gods came to be and battled, loved, and died, and Homer's Odysseus spent much of his odyssey. More than seas, today they serve as living links to modern civilization's classic past, joined together at a desolate spot two hundred miles across open seas from the cradle of man's existence, Africa.

Kouros followed along behind his cousin's car as they drove toward Cape Tenaro. Kouros looked at his watch. Sunset was closing in but it made no sense for him to join in the search, and the likelihood of getting any timely help out of Athens on a hunt of this sort was virtually nil. Kouros knew his best bet was to stay close to his cousin, prepared to remind him of his promise to bring Babis in alive should one of Mangas' dozens of "friends" scouring the coastline happen to find him. He looked left, down to the Gulf of Laconia and the lapis and emerald seas running up against the white sands of the Greek mainland's southernmost natural harbor. Porto Kayio was named after the once limitless flocks of quail passing through the Deep Mani each September.

Kouros' daydreaming abruptly ended when Mangas slammed on his brakes, forcing Kouros to swerve around him and nearly launch an airborne entrance onto the beach he'd been so fondly admiring below. Mangas pulled off the road. Kouros drew up next to him, rolled down his passenger side window, and yelled, "What the fuck's wrong with you?"

Mangas jumped out of his car and leaned in through the passenger window holding his phone up to Kouros' face. "I want you to hear this straight from the source."

Mangas pressed a button. "You're on speakerphone. Repeat exactly what you told me to my cousin."

A voice came over the phone. "Like I said, we found him on the way out to the entrance to Hades. The son of a bitch sure was headed in the right direction." The voice laughed.

"You're not to harm him," said Kouros.

"Little late for that," said Mangas.

The voice over the phone said, "He was dead when we got here. He'd tied one end of a rope around his neck, the other around a boulder, and when the boulder went into the water he went in behind it. It's not that deep where we found him, but deep enough to do it if you have a rock tied around your neck."

"I don't want them touching a thing," said Kouros.

"Did you hear that?" said Mangas.

"Yes."

"Good, then don't. We'll be right there and whatever my cousin says goes. Understand?"

"Yes."

Mangas turned off the phone. "I hope you realize I had nothing to do with this."

"Somehow I think that if you were involved,

Babis wouldn't be floating around in shallow water complicating your life. And he certainly wouldn't have been discovered by one of your friends."

"Or by anyone. At least not in recognizable pieces."

Kouros shook his head. "Who do you think did it?"

"I know this sounds crazy, but it sounds like suicide. More people than you'd think who live by the sea and want to end it use the 'rock and rope' method."

"But why would he kill himself?"

"You were all over him. He had to know it. And if you were all over him, that meant I wouldn't be far behind. And I can assure you he knew that if I got ahold of him his death would not be a quick and peaceful drowning."

Kouros nodded. "Could be that you're right."

"Let's hope so."

"What does that mean?"

"Because the dying will end with him. I'm really not all that different from my father. I see no need for vendetta once the problem is solved. If he killed my father and did it alone it will end with him. His family is spared." He smiled. "Including his young lady."

"Stella?"

"Who else? Hope she decides to hang around

and run the taverna. She'll draw a hell of a lot more business than that nasty-minded motherfucker of a boyfriend ever did. She might even get you back here to visit more often." Mangas smacked Kouros on the arm.

Kouros reached for his phone. "I've got to get police out to where your friends found Babis' body."

Mangas smiled. "Don't worry. That's who you were talking to, our local chief of police."

"Fuck," said Kouros.

This time Mangas reached over and patted Kouros on the shoulder. "Don't worry, cuz. You'll see. He did it to himself."

Don't we all, thought Kouros.

Kouros found Babis' car parked along a ridge over-looking the sea a hundred yards from the remains of a Spartan temple to the god Poseidon, and a mile away from the lighthouse marking the literal end of mainland Europe. A police van sat behind Babis' car. A small crowd had gathered but the local police kept them away from the immediate vicinity of the car. Obviously, the police chief took Mangas' instructions seriously. Kouros' check of the car showed no signs of a struggle or anything suspicious.

"Are you ready?" said Mangas.

"For what?"

Mangas nodded. "The cave's that way." He pointed at a sign and the bay beyond the temple.

Kouros followed his cousin down a narrow rocky path through prickly brush to a small cove, across a beach, and up onto a similar path leading south. Halfway to the entrance to Hades they saw two cops and two men with a stretcher on rocks down by the sea.

They left the path and began making their way down to the others.

"Someday, I want you to tell me how you figured out it wasn't an accident, and that Babis killed my father."

"I never said anything like that."

Mangas waved his right hand in the air. "Yeah, yeah, I know. I just want to know how you figured it all out…as a matter of professional curiosity."

"Professional curiosity?"

"Yeah, I don't ever want to make the same mistakes that dead dumb bastard Babis did." Mangas laughed.

Kouros shook his head. "Let's talk about something else."

"His girlfriend, Stella?"

"Something else."

"Great ass."

"Like I said, something else."

Mangas laughed again. "Well, cousin, here we are."

Kouros stared for several minutes at the body floating facedown in the water. Its hands and feet were free. On the shore he saw nothing but gear of the sort you'd expect to find with someone fishing from land. Kouros used his camera to photograph the body and every inch of the scene he could reach within a thirty-yard radius of the body. Fish had started nibbling at the corpse. No way they could leave the body in the sea until the coroner got there in the morning. He called Andreas who suggested they take the body to the coroner's office in Sparta, about a two-hour drive away.

It took a bit of acrobatics and the strength of three men to pull the boulder, rope, and body out of the sea and onto the stretcher in the same con-figuration as they'd gone in, and all six men shared turns lugging the stretcher back to the police van. The answers to who, how, when, where, and why about his uncle's murder might lay with that body, and Kouros wasn't about to let it out of his sight. After arranging for his cousin to get his mother back to Athens, and for a uniformed cop to follow in his car, Kouros jumped in the van taking Babis' body to Sparta.

If this were truly the suicide it appeared to be, and his cousin meant what he'd said, the risk of vendetta ended with Babis' death and there would be no war in the Mani.

That was the good news.

Actually, as Kouros saw it there really wasn't any bad news, just disappointment on his part that he never had the chance to ask Babis one question: Why did you send my uncle such a weird death threat?

Chapter Fourteen

Andreas usually got to work each morning by eight, a bit before Maggie and way before Kouros. Today he found company sound asleep on his office couch. He slammed the door shut. "Rise and shine."

Kouros shifted slightly on the couch. "Humans aren't meant to be up this early."

"Maybe, but you don't fit the profile. You look like shit."

"Nice to see you too, Chief."

Andreas sat behind his desk, picked up the phone and dialed. "Morning, it's Kaldis....Yes, the usual, but double the order, I've got company." He hung up.

"What's for breakfast?"

"Enough coffee to make you bear a closer resemblance to those 'humans' you're rambling about."

Kouros swung his legs off the couch, sat up, and stretched out his arms. "By the time I got back to Athens from Sparta it was almost sunrise and I figured if I went home I might oversleep."

Andreas nodded. "And being the dedicated public servant that you are you decided to crash on my couch."

Kouros nodded. "Precisely."

"In other words, no clean laundry at home."

Kouros yawned and waved an open palm in Andreas' direction.

"You did some good work, Detective. Your family should be proud."

"Thanks, Chief. My cousin Mangas actually sounded relieved when I told him the coroner concluded there was no question Babis had killed himself. He said it would make it easier to convince his sister."

"What's there to convince? The local cops found candle wax in the kitchen and a vial of the poison that killed your uncle hidden in the storeroom. Open and shut that he did it."

Kouros nodded. "I know. But Mani women with their instincts can be quite difficult to convince with just facts. Especially my cousin Calliope."

"Trust me. It's not just Mani women."

Kouros smiled. "And she doesn't even know about the death threat on the back of my uncle's newspaper. I still can't figure out why Babis wrote something like that if he was pissed off at my uncle for screwing his girlfriend."

"Yeah, it bothered me, too. Remind me what the note said."

"'Your father took his sister's and her lover's lives to preserve our ways. We shall take yours to save our Mani. You have one week to change your plans or die.'"

"Sounds like the sort of radical bullshit notes we get from Molotov cocktail-tossing anarchists around Parliament. I didn't know they were active in the Mani. Thought that was royalist country."

"Maybe Babis did it to give himself a cover story if after the murder it came out that my uncle had been sleeping with Stella. Without that note and the follow up SMS, he'd be a prime suspect."

"Too bad for Babis your uncle kept the note and SMS to himself."

"And I'm not about to tell anybody about them now."

"It all fits. With you breathing down Babis' neck and the vendetta story nowhere to be found, he checked out rather than risk your cousins doing it for him."

"But what still doesn't fit is that Babis needed my uncle's protection from the crew he'd crossed up in Pirgos. So why would he kill him and risk losing that protection?"

Andreas shrugged. "Maybe he thought they'd given up on going after him or jealousy overran good judgment. Happens all the time, especially where a woman's involved."

Kouros nodded. "It just bothers me."

"Would an all-out war in the Mani bother you less? Everyone's satisfied we have the killer. Let's leave it at that."

Kouros stared at Andreas. "This doesn't sound like you."

"Of course it does. You're just too close to the situation."

Kouros' stare turned into a glare.

"Is there any doubt in your mind that Babis killed your uncle?"

"No."

"Do you have even a hint that anyone else was involved?"

Kouros looked away. "No."

"Because if you did, I'd be right beside you looking to cut off any other responsible bastard's balls.

"But while we're on the subject of frank talk, let's be realistic. This wasn't the murder of an ordinary, law-abiding Greek citizen, where further investigation would be welcomed by the victim's family as police thoroughness. He was the head of a major criminal enterprise whose family would take it as a sign of more bad guys out there. More who should die.

"And, yes, before you say it, it's possible Babis

did not kill out of jealousy. Perhaps it was a hit getting back at your uncle for who knows what sort of grievous sin he'd committed. But the bottom line is we'll never know. Accept that, consider the case closed, and take solace in knowing your family will be spared further bloodshed and that the lowlife who killed your uncle is dead. Which is far more justice than your family would ever get out of his hide under Greek law."

Kouros raised his eyes and stared at Andreas. "Yes?"

"So, where's breakfast already?"

The remains of breakfast sat on paper plates and cups atop Andreas' desk and Kouros lay asleep on the couch when Maggie popped her head in the doorway. "You have a visitor."

"Who?"

"Your friend, Petro."

"Send him in."

Maggie stepped into the office, closed the door, and began gathering up the plates and cups. "No reason to let the poor boy think you're just as big a slob as every other cop. And what's with Sleeping Beauty over there?" She tossed the rubbish in a wastebasket in a corner of the office behind Andreas' desk.

Andreas picked up a tiny replica soccer ball from his desk and lobbed it at the back of Kouros' head. "Mama says it's time to get up."

"I don't have school today."

"Let's go boys," said Maggie, "you have to make a good impression."

Kouros rolled over and sat up. "On who?"

"The kid from headquarters security I told you about. The one who's keeping an eye on Orestes for me."

Maggie opened the door to the office. "Come in, son."

As Petro entered, Maggie stepped out, closing the door behind her.

"Good morning, Chief."

"Morning, Petro. Do you know Detective Yianni Kouros?"

"Only by reputation. We've never actually met." Petro put out his hand to Kouros.

Kouros shook it. "Pleased to meet you."

"Sit, please." Andreas gestured to one of the chairs in front of his desk. "So, what news do you have for me?"

"Last night, at about one in the morning, Orestes came into the club with three men I'd never seen before. One Balkan type, one likely from the Ukraine, and a Greek."

"How could you tell?"

"From their Greek accents. I heard them talking in front of the club before they went inside."

"What did they say?"

"Just bullshit about how they were hoping to find some 'hot pussy.'"

Andreas frowned. "That's it?

Petro smiled. "That's all I heard. But I knew there was no way I could ever get close enough to Orestes' table to hear what they were saying. So I had a friend do it for me."

"How'd you do that?" asked Kouros.

Petro turned his head to face Kouros. "A working girl. Reminds everyone of the American actress Sofia Vergara. She owes me. I look out for her when she's inside so that no one gets rough with her. All she had to do was walk by Orestes' table once, smile at the ugliest guy with him, and she had a place of honor on his lap for the rest of the night."

"They let a hooker sit with them while they talked business?" said Andreas.

"The ugly guy wouldn't let her leave. Even tried to get her to fly back with him to Kiev on his private jet."

"Did she go?"

Petro gestured no. "She's smart enough to know that too many pretty girls in the Ukraine end up as slaves in the sex trade."

"Was he a bad guy?"

"Not sure about the Ukrainian, but the Balkan guy with him had bodyguard written all over him and was a certified, grade-A hard-ass. The type with hands covered in prison tattoo tears, one for each of his kills."

"Braggart," said Kouros.

Petro laughed. "Don't know how many were real, but he sure looked the part and acted like a pro. Later, I had to stop him from dragging the girl into Ugly Guy's limo and Bodyguard didn't give me any lip, just his best 'I'd kill you if I had the chance' glare. Lucky for me there was a crowd in front of the club or he might have tried."

"What did she tell you?" said Andreas

"That it was hard to follow their conversation. They sounded like characters in a gangster movie talking about things they all knew and didn't want or need to use specifics. Lines like, 'About that thing down there, the one with the problem. We got to make it work before the other guys kill our deal.'"

"That could mean a lot of things," said Kouros.

"Or nothing," said Andreas. He picked up a pencil and began tapping it on his desk. "What about Orestes? What did he say?"

"He didn't seem to know the foreigners and spent most of his time trying to impress Ugly Guy with his political clout. The other Greek guy seemed to know Ugly Guy and be more in tune with whatever was going on. This looked to be Orestes' introduction to Ugly Guy. Greek Guy kept saying how Orestes was the person Ugly Guy needed to 'make things work' in 'building their first step' toward monopolizing a business 'guaranteed' to make them all 'fortunes.'"

"What kind of business?" said Andreas.

"Didn't say, but they all seemed to know what it was. When she sensed they were about to get into specifics, Ugly Guy sent her off with Bodyguard to 'powder her nose for the trip.' That's when Bodyguard tried forcing her into the limo and I had to explain to him the available long-term housing provided courtesy of the Greek state for those who tried to abduct its citizens. He let her go and she took off. She called me later to tell me what happened."

"That's it?" said Andreas.

"She thought the other Greek guy might be a politician, because he 'kept kissing ass.'"

Andreas studied Petro's face. "So we have some presumed Greek politico trying to convince a monied Balkan type that Orestes had the necessary political contacts to make them all a hell of a lot of money. Sounds like business as usual for Orestes. It's what he does for a living."

He's given me nothing, thought Andreas. *Could Orestes have reached him, turned him to find out what I'm up to?* A bit of a coincidence that those subpoenas to companies on Orestes' list went out late yesterday afternoon, and Petro was in his office this morning with news.

Andreas leaned forward. "Did anyone mention anything about subpoenas?"

"What subpoenas?"

"The ones tied into that crew from last night's plans for Crete."

Petro blinked. "Crete? Who said anything about Crete?"

"Isn't that what this is all about? Orestes' interest in making money from Crete's gas discoveries."

Petro shrugged. "Maybe, but the girl never said anything to me about anyone mentioning Crete. There was a mention of the Peloponnese, but that was it on naming places."

Kouros suppressed a yawn. "What about the Peloponnese?"

"The Greek guy told Ugly Guy that he and Orestes could help him with his plans on building something down there."

"What sort of plans?" said Andreas.

"Don't know. All she heard was that they'd fallen through when the property owner died a few days ago in a car accident."

◇◇◇

Petro left Andreas' office with instructions to return ASAP with photographs of Orestes' three companions taken off a security camera mounted outside the front of the club.

Andreas told Petro to tell the club owner that if he refused to cooperate, Andreas would personally arrange for a half-dozen uniforms plus a representative of Greece's special tax squad to be at his club every night, photographing every customer until either they found the three they were looking for or the place ran out of clients.

Petro suggested it might be easier if he didn't bother the owner, but simply used his key for the club to get inside and copy the photos himself.

"Clever kid," said Kouros.

"Kid? You're not much older than he is."

"My time in this unit has aged me far beyond my years."

Andreas waved his hand in the air at Kouros. "So, what do you think? Is the 'kid' shooting straight with us?"

"I wasn't sure until he dropped the bomb about the accident," said Kouros.

"Hell of a coincidence if it's your uncle's accident."

"More like a miracle if it's not."

Andreas nodded. "I'm a big believer in not trusting coincidences, but how the hell could it be anything else?"

"We'll know the answer to that when he gets back from the club."

"My instincts are he's legit."

Kouros nodded. "Mine too. Any idea on how to ID the mystery guys with Orestes?"

"There's always a shot with Europol or even our own records department. But maybe we'll get lucky and recognize them, at least the Greek." Andreas paused. "Just to increase our chances… *Maggie.*"

The door swung open. "Yes?"

"Is Tassos in Athens?"

"He's at my place cooking and cleaning while I slave away at police work."

"Please ask him to get over here as soon as he can. We need his help."

"Can it wait until he's finished doing the windows?"

Andreas waved her off. "The two of you deserve each other."

Maggie smiled. "By the way, what should I tell Petro's boss from headquarters security who just called to ask—and I quote—'Who the fuck does your boss think he is assigning my men to do work for him without my permission?' End quote."

"What did you tell him?"

"That I'd pass along the message."

"Good. Tell him, quote, 'The same guy who two years ago caught you with your literal fucking pants down in the middle of a vice bust on a low-end whorehouse on Filis Street and let you walk away.' End quote."

Maggie smiled. "That should do it." She closed the door.

"Did you really?"

"The idiot didn't even know he was on top of a hooker on the top floor of an Albanian drug-cutting operation. He was still pounding away on her when we broke down the door."

"You're kidding."

"You can't make this stuff up." Andreas leaned across his desk toward Kouros. "Which brings me back to our little coincidence of last night."

"Meaning?"

Andreas sat back in his chair. "Meaning it looks like it's time to get back to work on your uncle' s case."

Tassos came through the door into Andreas' office without knocking, dressed precisely as always: dark suit, dark tie, and white shirt. "I worked hard to be entitled to dress this way," was his only explanation to any tieless, jacketless cop who asked why he dressed so formally no matter what the weather or occasion.

Tassos plopped down on the couch next to Kouros, grabbed Kouros' thigh, and squeezed. "Nice job you did down on the Mani. Your uncle would be proud."

"Thanks."

Tassos looked at Andreas sitting behind his desk. "So, what's so important that you dragged me away from doing my beloved's windows?"

Andreas stared at him. "She told you to say that, didn't she?"

"Who am I to question the ways of my beloved?"

Andreas dropped his head and shook it. "Okay, let me tell you where we are."

It took about fifteen minutes to bring Tassos up to speed, and just as he was explaining his potential concerns about Petro, Maggie opened the door and popped in her head.

"Petro is back."

Andreas said to Tassos, "Any questions?"

"No, I get the picture. Send him in."

Andreas nodded to Maggie, the door opened, and Petro walked in.

Andreas introduced him to Tassos and motioned that he sit in the same chair as he had the last time, directly across from Andreas. "Do you have the photographs?"

Petro gestured no. "I couldn't pull them off the recording."

Andreas kept his eyes fixed on Petro but out the corner of one he saw Kouros grimace.

"So, I brought the whole thing. It's on this." Petro handed Andreas a DVD.

Kouros smiled.

"Let's see what we have here." Andreas slid the disc into his computer as the other cops came behind his desk and crowded around the screen.

"It covers everyone coming into the club last night," said Petro.

Andreas stood up. "Sit here, Petro, and get us to where the three guys we're interested in show up."

Andreas, Tassos, and Kouros huddled around Petro as he scanned through the recording. A minute or so into the search he froze the video. "Here's where they got out of the limo."

The first one out looked the size of a giant. "That's the bodyguard."

"Anyone recognize him?" said Andreas.

"No," said Tassos and Kouros together.

"Probably not from around here. I'll get Maggie to pull a photo off the DVD and see what our records boys and Europol can come up with."

Petro pointed to the screen. "This one's 'Ugly Guy.' He's the boss."

"Sort of built like you, Tassos," said Kouros.

Tassos gently smacked Kouros on the back of his head. "Thank God he has your looks. Otherwise the ladies would never leave him alone."

"Enough already. Does anyone recognize him?" said Andreas.

"No," said Kouros.

Tassos leaned in and studied the image. "There's something about this guy that seems vaguely familiar, but I can't quite put my finger on it."

"Another one for Maggie and Europol. So who's next?"

"It's the Greek. He's getting out of the limo now." Petro froze the image.

"Nope," said Tassos.

"Me either," said Andreas.

Kouros didn't speak.

"Yianni?" said Andreas.

Kouros leaned in closer to the screen, leaned back, and nodded. "Yes, I know him. He was one of my uncle's morning coffee buddies. His name is Alexander, he's a politician."

"Holy shit," said Tassos.

"No, more like 'holy war' if any of this ties into my uncle's murder and my cousins find out about it," said Kouros.

"But the girl didn't hear anything to suggest that any of the people at Orestes' table had something to do with murdering your uncle." Tassos looked at Petro. "Or did she?"

"No."

"Just the opposite," said Andreas. "It sounded to me like they were hustling to hold things together *because* of his death."

"So, where do we go from here?" said Kouros.

Andreas pointed at the screen. "If anyone knows whether someone other than the dead taverna owner was involved in your uncle's murder, it's likely one of these guys."

"I guess that means it's time to pay Alexander a visit," said Kouros.

Andreas gestured no. "Not yet. He's not going anywhere. Especially if he doesn't know we're on to him. I want IDs on the other two guys first, because as soon as they know we're interested in them they'll disappear from Greece."

"I assume asking Orestes for his buddies' names is out of the question for the same reason?" said Tassos.

Andreas nodded. "Let's get photos of the two we don't know out for a priority ID and see what comes back."

"Make a copy of Ugly Guy for me," said Tassos. "It might help jog my memory."

"While doing windows?" smiled Kouros.

Tassos shrugged. "One must do whatever it takes to make things clearer."

Kouros smacked his forehead and shook his head.

Tassos patted Kouros on the shoulder. "No need to say it, my boy. I know. You've missed me."

Chapter Fifteen

Tassos left Andreas' office with Ugly Guy's photograph and an idea. If Ugly Guy had a criminal record, sooner or later Europol would identify him. But Tassos had another, more expeditious sort of international information clearinghouse in mind.

The Kolonaki area of downtown Athens was as chic as you'd find in Greece. Just west of the main boulevard leading north toward the city's more affluent northern suburbs, its fancy shops, restaurants, and residences lay at the heart of official Athens. Parliament, its members, and anyone dependent upon government largesse knew it well, for in Kolonaki much of the government's business—both official and otherwise—took place. Some met in offices, but it was in tavernas and cafés alongside park-like Kolonaki Square that a grand measure of the country's past had come to be.

Tassos parked in a no-parking zone and walked along the northern border of the small park surrounding an ancient column from which the area drew its name. He stopped in front of a large taverna at the intersection of Tsakalof and Patriarchou Ioakeim streets. Customers at its sidewalk tables sat checking out every passerby as if hoping to spot a celebrity, but it was well past morning coffee time for Greece's movers and shakers. By now they sat in their offices doing whatever the important and powerful did.

No matter, Tassos was hunting different game: old lions who still came out for early morning coffee, but lingered on into the afternoon talking among themselves of the good old days when they ruled the universe. He crossed the street toward a storefront of broad glass, polished natural wood, green marble, and Parisian green trim. A long row of green-top café tables and matching beige and green chairs sat next to the building and continued on alongside an awning-covered abutting patio, all part of the same self-service *cafenion*.

He walked into the shop though a break in the line of sidewalk tables and stopped in front of a row of glass display cases filled with pastries, assorted sandwiches, and brioches. An array of liquor bottles adorned the wall behind the counter, and brightly polished chrome and brass coffee machines dominated the space between.

Tassos placed his order, and while waiting,

looked out at the patio. In its prime only tourists stared out at passersby from this place, for regulars knew that anyone who mattered already sat inside. This was Dal Segno Caffe, the once inner sanctum to all things Greek politics. But that was back in the days when sitting members of Parliament dared venture out in public. These days Greek politicians rarely appeared in the wild, no doubt fearing who might be hunting for their heads.

Tassos studied the faces at the tables. Mostly tourists, plus a few local businessmen out on a coffee break. Off to the right, away from the main street and tucked away at a corner table partially hidden behind the trunk of the patio's lone tree, a stocky, pasty, bald Greek sat engrossed in conversation with tall, trim, tanned silver-haired foreigner. The men looked at least a decade apart in age, but Tassos knew each was in his early eighties. He carried his coffee over to their table.

"Do you mind if I join you?"

Neither man looked up.

Tassos put his coffee down on their table. "What's the matter, have you two old farts lost your hearing?"

"We were hoping you wouldn't see us," said the bald guy.

"Not with old Strip over here still working so hard at dazzling all the broads with his tan."

The tanned guy smiled. "Nice to see you, too, Tassos."

"What has you in town, Strip? I thought you'd lost interest in this part of the world once the Balkans settled down. Went back to America, I heard."

"I'm out of that business. Left it to the young guys. The world's too nuts these days for a legitimate businessman."

"In the arms business?" said Tassos.

Strip smiled. "In any business."

"So what has you in Athens?"

He nodded toward the bald man. "Dimitri's granddaughter is getting married this weekend. I'm in for the wedding."

Tassos picked up his cup and took a sip of coffee. "How nice that our former minister of defense has kept up with his old friends from the arms industry even after all these years."

"Some things never change," said Dimitri.

Tassos smiled and put down his coffee. "For sure. Congratulations on your granddaughter's wedding, Dimitri."

Dimitri nodded. "Thank you. So what brings you to Dal Segno?"

Tassos laughed. "Don't worry, it isn't you. I'm trying to get a line on a businessman from the Balkans and I was hoping to bump into someone here who might know him."

"Why here?" said Dimitri.

"He's dealing with our government."

Dimitri nodded. "So, how can I help?"

Tassos pulled the photo of Ugly Guy out of his jacket pocket and handed it to Dimitri. Dimitri stared at it and handed it back to Tassos.

"Sorry, I don't recognize him."

Tassos handed the photo to Strip. "What about you?"

Strip took the photo and squinted at it.

Dimitri smiled. "If you're really going to look at it, Strip, put on your glasses. Don't worry, there aren't any women watching."

"Asshole." Strip pulled a pair of gold-rimmed reading glasses out of the inside jacket pocket of his very expensive blue blazer.

"So, where's the wedding, Dimitri?" said Tassos.

"Grande Bretagne."

"The best place in Athens for a wedding. On the roof I assume?"

"No, weather's too iffy. Using the hotel's main ballroom."

"Hey," said Strip. "I know this guy. A real lowlife. Mean, dark, dirty, and ruthless. Which is probably why he's so rich."

"What's he do?"

"Whatever makes him money. Big money.

Drugs, arms smuggling, probably human trafficking, too. I knew him from the arms business. He's the sort that made me realize it was time to get out."

"Does he have a name?"

"It's one of those all-consonants Ukrainian ones."

"Is that your way of saying you don't remember it? Come on, Strip, you haven't forgotten the name on your first baby bottle," said Tassos.

"With age there are some things you forget. And some things you better forget. My friend, I've spent a decade getting my name off of 'we don't want him around anymore' lists. I'm not about to do anything to get myself back on one. Especially this guy's."

Tassos nodded. "Okay, but what can you tell me about him?"

"He works out of the Balkans. That's where most gunrunners operate these days. North Africa is the big market."

"Where in North Africa?"

"You name it. Sudan, Somalia, Mauritania, Algeria, Morocco, Libya, Tunisia, possibly even Yemen."

"Why would he be interested in doing business in Greece?"

"No idea, and before you say it…no, I'm not going to ask around."

"How about a guess?"

"Ask Dimitri. He knows more about that sort of thing in Greece."

Dimitri shook his head. "If this guy's a big-time illegal arms smuggler, he's probably interested in running ships out of ports like Piraeus and Patras. Boats are what arms and drug smugglers prefer these days. They're harder to detect than planes, as long as your paperwork is in order."

Strip shook his head. "This guy runs his business primarily through the air. At least he always did."

"Well, that sort doesn't operate in Greece," said Dimitri. "They need an airstrip. And airstrips get noticed in the parts of Greece they'd be interested in."

"What 'parts' would that be?"

"Places closer to Africa than their operations in the Balkans. A location that increases their range."

"For a quick in and out with less time in the air to attract attention," said Strip. "Crete would be perfect for them."

"Yes, but Crete comes with several serious downside factors," said Dimitri.

"Such as?" said Tassos.

"A NATO airbase, missile-testing range, gunnery range, and bombing range. Plus, the United States Navy provisions its Sixth Fleet out of there. Air traffic in and out of Crete is closely monitored."

"That makes Crete a no go?" asked Tassos.

Strip smiled. "Except for those who'd like an up-close and personal firsthand experience as a target."

"So where else might he be looking?"

"Somewhere customs can be greased not to look too closely at the cargo. And with a runway long enough to accommodate the planes they'd need," said Strip.

"How long would that be?" asked Tassos.

"Seven thousand feet," said Dimitri.

Strip gestured no. "You're thinking of a C-5. That sort of runway attracts way too much attention for an arms smuggler. Guys like this use Ukrainian-made Antonov birds that can land on short, uneven runways. An AN-70 can land on two thousand feet and the bigger ones on five thousand."

"So where would he want his runway?"

"As close to his customers as possible," said Strip. "It's the same principle small-time smugglers on the Peloponnese follow with their gunrunning boats."

"What are you talking about?"

"They run boats out of Kalamata with enough range to reach Africa. Can't get to every market they'd like, but it's still profitable."

"Why don't they use planes?"

"Because they'd need an airstrip, and the only ones in the southern Peloponnese capable of handling even short-runway Anatovs are Kalamata International, a military base in Sparta, and a closed airport at Triodos. No way they could operate out of any of those without being noticed."

"What if they built their own runway?" asked Tassos.

"It would cost a fortune," said Dimitri.

"Depends," said Strip, "if they wanted to build a half-mile runway the right way, using big name contractors, it would cost five or six million. But if the land doesn't require much preparation and you don't have to worry about complying with environmental and other legal niceties, you could build one in six months for around a million. And arms dealers can make that much on one delivery to the right buyer.

"But even assuming money's not a problem, building a private runway of that size screams, 'Arms smugglers here.'"

Dimitri nodded. "Even in Greece, one can't just build an airstrip in the middle of nowhere and expect it to go unnoticed."

"Hard to imagine the cover story they'd need to come up with to mask that sort of operation," said Strip.

"Hard to imagine indeed," said Tassos. He couldn't wait to get back to Andreas' office.

◇◇◇

Twenty minutes after making a hasty good-bye to his coffee mates, Tassos burst into Andreas' office.

"I've got news." Tassos looked around the office. "Where's Yianni?"

Andreas leaned back in his chair. "For the sake of appearances we maintain separate offices. Though you might not think that. Shall I call him?"

Tassos nodded.

"Mag—"

The door swung open and in walked Kouros. "Maggie said you wanted to see me ASAP."

"How the hell did she know that?"

"She said if you asked that question it's because her boyfriend didn't even say hello to her, just rushed right into your office. She figured it must be important."

"I'm in trouble," said Tassos.

"She also said, 'Tell Tassos flowers will work.'" Kouros dropped onto the couch. "'Roses.'"

"I'm glad she's on our side," said Andreas.

"'Two dozen.'"

"Enough with the flowers. I caught up with an old friend who knows just about everything nasty that's gone on in our part of the world since Vietnam, and he recognized Ugly Guy."

"You got a name?" said Andreas.

"He wouldn't say, but from all the deep shit he's involved in, we shouldn't have any trouble getting an ID from Europol. But that's not the big story."

Tassos turned to Kouros. "That hotel project you mentioned your uncle was setting up...Did I hear you right about it including an airstrip?"

Kouros nodded. "Yes. Without direct air access, the developer didn't think he could lure high-roller Russian and Middle Eastern tourists into the Mani. It's too hard for them to get there any other way."

"What's the land like for the project?"

"A relatively level plateau set back away from the mountains."

Tassos nodded. "What if I told you the *only* reason for the deal was that airstrip? I bet the plans called for the runway to be built first. The hotel and golf course later."

"I wouldn't know. But what are you getting at?"

Tassos sat down in a chair in front of Andreas' desk. "The Ukrainian is an arms and drug dealer, possibly into human trafficking, too. He needs the airstrip to expand his operations. Or maybe as a hedge against things getting worse with the Russians in the Ukraine than they already have."

"How the hell did you come up with that?" said Andreas.

Tassos repeated the substance of his conversation with Strip and Dimitri. "It all fits."

"But why the hell is Orestes involved?" said Andreas.

"My guess is Yianni's uncle's death cost the Ukrainian not only the deal, but the political grease he needed to make certain things happen."

"Like cooperative customs folk?" said Kouros.

"Precisely. And until he knew for sure that he had the political cover he needed, he wasn't about to try and resurrect the deal."

Kouros sat up. "That might explain why my uncle's friend is involved. Alexander is trying to make the right political connections to keep the Ukrainian interested, and if he still is, try and sell the deal to the family. My cousins probably don't even know what Alexander's doing. I sure as hell didn't."

Andreas picked up a pencil. "But that means Alexander must know the true purpose behind the deal."

"Which means my uncle did, too. But he never mentioned any of that to me."

"Does that surprise you?" said Tassos. "Let's not forget what he was. In fact, this might be one of the cleaner deals he'd ever done. He sells off his property—"

"Rents," growled Kouros.

"And has nothing further to do with the dark side of the transaction."

"Aside from bribing government officials," added Andreas.

"No, he'd only be doing introductions. The rest would be between the Ukrainian and bad guys with badges."

Kouros shook his head. "And I'd have been profiting off it all. Son of a bitch."

"Not your fault your inheritance comes with a history," said Andreas.

Tassos nodded. "As Balzac wrote, 'Behind every great fortune lies a great crime.'"

"I want no part of it."

Tassos smiled at Andreas.

"But why would the Ukrainian be involved in the murder of my uncle if he needed him for the deal?"

Tassos shrugged. "Maybe your uncle reneged? Wanted more than the Ukrainian was willing to pay. Or maybe someone came to the Ukrainian with a better offer than your uncle's, with guarantees the deal would still go through."

"Who? Alexander? I don't see him having the balls to cross my uncle," said Kouros.

"Well, one thing's for sure. Alexander *is*

involved. The only question is on whose behalf?" said Tassos.

"Are you suggesting one of my cousins?"

Tassos shrugged. "Who knows? Family members cutting each other's throats over property isn't unheard of. Not in Greece and certainly not in the Mani."

Kouros sat back on the couch. "I just can't believe…" His voice trailed off.

"There is another possibility," said Andreas tapping his pencil on the desk.

"What's that?" said Tassos.

"That it's someone we haven't thought of yet. Someone with a real motive."

"And who would that be?" said Tassos.

"Don't know yet. But so far we have anonymous death threats tied to a stale generations-old vendetta, a jealous lover who killed himself, and a Balkan arms dealer in search of a home for his birds."

"Sounds like the perfect cover for the Ukrainian. Whether it's pinned on an old vendetta or an angry lover, he couldn't care less as long as he doesn't end up with Yianni's cousins coming after him."

"Anybody involved in his uncle's murder, not just the Ukrainian, would want to avoid that," said Andreas. "What bothers me is that if Yianni's uncle were the target of either a vendetta *or* a jealous lover's rage that would make sense. But not both."

"Like I said, it sounds like whoever was behind this didn't give a damn about consistency just as long as whatever story played didn't point back at him."

"What bothers me is that with all the money the Ukrainian stood to make once that airstrip was operational, why take the risk of killing my uncle even if it meant a better deal for him? It wasn't as if he'd be getting rid of a problem once and for all. He planned on setting up shop in my cousins' literal backyard. They'd destroy his operation in a heartbeat if they ever came to suspect he'd played a part in their father's murder."

"And nail his head to their tower," said Tassos.

Andreas began tapping the pencil on his desk. "I think it's time we pay a visit on your uncle's friend, Alexander. Yianni, find out if he's still in Athens. I want to make it a surprise, something we can't do in the Mani."

Kouros nodded. "Do you really think my uncle was betrayed?"

Andreas shrugged. "I don't know. But I wouldn't bet against it."

"Me either," said Tassos.

Kouros shook his head. "Jesus."

Tassos nodded. "Yep, happened to him, too."

Chapter Sixteen

Alexander never drew attention to his extramarital affairs. He kept a nondescript studio apartment in a low-profile Athens neighborhood, and unlike his buddies back in the Mani, never talked about his conquests, though he'd had many. He saw discretion as the key to success in every aspect of his life, be it public or pubic.

At the moment he was enjoying his newest lover, a lithe young thing, barely seventeen. His hands squeezed the smooth, taunt cheeks of his lover's bottom as he thrashed on the edge of orgasm with each new deep thrust of hard flesh between arching, open buttocks. He'd never expected it to remain this exciting with each new lover.

Nor did he expect what happened next.

Alexander didn't hear the deadbolt lock on the front door click open. Nor did he see the doorknob turn. But he did hear the exploding kick that tore the security chain away from the doorjamb and the two men coming straight at him.

Alexander tried twisting himself out from under his lover, but he got his legs tangled in the boy's and they both rolled off the bed onto the floor at the feet of the two men.

"My, my, what do we have here?" said Andreas.

"Looks like *buttfuckus interruptus* to me," said Tassos.

Alexander pushed himself off the floor and grabbed a pillow to cover his genitals. "How dare you break into my home? Do you have any idea who I am?"

Andreas nodded. "A one-time member of Parliament and full-time, full-of-shit crooked politician."

"If you're blackmailers, you're wasting your time. Get out of here now or I'll call the police."

"That won't be necessary," said Kouros, stepping through the doorway. "We're already here."

Alexander's mouth dropped. "What are you doing here?"

"I missed you at coffee the other day, just thought I'd drop in for a quiet chat about my uncle's murder. Sorry about the door, but I guess your neighbors are used to noise in here."

Alexander leaned back against the edge of the bed, still clutching the pillow.

"By the way, your building owner asked me to tell you that he apologized but it was either opening your door for us or his books for a tax audit."

The boy cowered on the floor by the end of the bed. "I've got nothing to do with whatever shit this old queen's got himself into with you. I just took his money to fuck him."

Andreas crouched down next to the boy. "I bet." He looked at his watch. "You've got thirty seconds to get out of here before I change my mind."

The boy jumped up, grabbed his clothes off a chair, and ran out of the apartment without bothering to dress. Kouros closed the door behind him.

Alexander looked at Kouros. "Are these your cousin's friends?" He gestured with his head at Andreas and Tassos.

"Does it matter? We're all family. If you screw with one of us, you screw with us all."

"What do you want from me?"

"Answers, a lot of them." Kouros stepped between Andreas and Tassos and sat next to Alexander on the edge of the bed. "And frankly, I don't give a damn who or how you fuck. Unless it's me or my family."

Alexander pulled the pillow closer.

Andreas made a fist and stuck it in Alexander's face. "Let me at the old *pusti*. I'll get him to tell us what he's up to with Orestes."

"Orestes? How do you know…?" He stopped himself.

Kouros shook his head. "The question isn't

how we know, it's why you didn't tell me. Or better yet, why you didn't tell my cousin Mangas."

"There's nothing to tell. Just business."

Kouros patted Alexander on the knee. "Come now, Alexander. I'm giving you a chance to explain. Something you'll never get from Mangas." He made a tsk-tsk sound. "Especially if you make it necessary for me to tell him that you were involved in his father's murder."

Alexander's right eye started twitching. "I had nothing to do with your uncle's death."

Kouros shrugged. "But I promised Mangas I'd let him know if I found anyone I thought might have played a part in it." He spread his arms apart, hands facing up. "And after your meeting last night with Orestes and your big, ugly Ukrainian buddy, how can I not think of you as a suspect?"

Now both of Alexander's eyes were twitching. "I don't know how you know about that, but you're fishing. You have nothing to tell Mangas. That meeting had nothing to do with his family. Now, why don't you get out of here and leave me alone?"

Kouros laughed. "Leave you alone? My friend, we're way past that. Your meeting was all about the hotel project the Ukrainian planned on doing with Mangas' father. Good luck on selling your 'nothing to do with his family' bullshit to him once he hears the tape."

Kouros grabbed Alexander's thigh and squeezed hard. "Knowing him as we both do, there's no upside in this for you but to tell me what I want to know." He released his grip. "Otherwise, my friend over there beats the shit out of you until you tell us, or, if by some miracle you don't talk, I tell Mangas what I know and he slices and dices you until either he believes you or you die."

Kouros patted Alexander on the shoulder. "Your choice."

Alexander brought his hands up to his face and rubbed at his eyes. The pillow didn't move. He talked between his hands, his fingers pressing hard against his eyes. "Your uncle asked me to help get whatever approvals were necessary to build the resort project. I told him no problem. He introduced me to the Ukrainian. Told me to deal with him directly. Never said why. But once I realized who the Ukrainian was, I knew this involved a lot more than just a hotel. And I also understood your uncle wanted nothing to do with any of that. He left the political maneuvering to me."

"You mean the bribes," said Kouros.

Alexander dropped his hands to the pillow. "Yes. At least he didn't want to think he was involved. But all I had to do was mention I was acting on your uncle's behalf and any favor I wanted was a done deal. Everybody owed your uncle."

"And now what?"

"Now nothing. When your uncle died, his influence and the deal died with him."

"Then what the fuck were you doing playing footsies with Orestes and the Ukrainian?" asked Tassos.

Alexander studied Tassos' face and shrugged. "Trying to resurrect it."

"For yourself?" said Kouros.

"How could I? The property isn't mine."

"Maybe you were looking to sell him another property?" said Andreas.

He gestured no. "That property was the only one the Ukrainian was interested in."

"So you did try to sell him something else?" said Kouros.

"I made suggestions. But only after your uncle died. Never before."

"How did you plan on making money out of the deal since it wasn't your property?"

"I figured your cousins would cut me in for a share of the deal if I saved it. That's what your uncle had promised to do for me on the original deal."

"Add another piece from the Ukrainian, plus more from your new political patron, Orestes, and you have a pretty sweet arrangement."

Alexander shrugged. "Why not? I'd have

earned it if the deal went through. That's the way business is done."

"Sounds to me like you had a lot to gain from the uncle's death," said Andreas.

Alexander raised his right hand as if swearing on a Bible. "As I said, no way I had anything to do with his death. I loved Yianni's uncle."

"Yeah sure," said Tassos.

"Okay, so don't believe me. But check the proposed contracts for the deal and you'll see that I was in for a piece of it." He looked at Kouros. "Your uncle believed in paying people for their services. That's why he was so successful. I stood to make a lot of money if the project went through. And whether or not I might make more now, killing your uncle put everything at risk. It made no sense for me. On any level."

"One last question," said Kouros. "Why would the Ukrainian have wanted my uncle dead?"

"The Ukrainian? He was the last guy who wanted your uncle out of the picture. Your uncle was the only one who could keep the family in line and get everyone to agree on the terms."

"My guess is Mangas could still achieve that," said Kouros.

"And with the way the economy's in free-fall, at a better price for the Ukrainian," said Andreas

"I think the same way," said Alexander. "But

the Ukrainian doesn't. He's ready to walk away from the deal. That's why I brought in Orestes. If this deal happens for the family it'll be because of me."

"Who would have wanted him dead if not the Ukrainian?" said Andreas.

"A lot of people. But I'm not one of them." Alexander stood up, still holding the pillow in front of him, and walked over to where his clothes were neatly laid out on the dresser. He put on his shorts.

"I hope you'll believe now, gentlemen, that I have nothing to hide."

Tassos nodded toward Alexander's shorts. "That's for sure."

Traffic heading in the direction of GADA ignored the police siren, and the several side streets Kouros tried offered no better route.

Andreas drummed his right hand's fingers on the passenger side dashboard. "Relax, Yianni, we'll get there when we get there."

"You did a great job, kid," said Tassos leaning over from the backseat to smack Kouros on the back of his head. "I particularly liked the part about the 'tape.'"

Kouros smiled. "Me, too. It was an easy bluff with nothing to lose. If he'd called it I'd have told him he'd get to hear it soon enough."

"You mean like when you played it for your cousin?" Tassos smacked him on the back of the head again. "Did he even realize Andreas and I were cops? He acted as if we worked for your cousin."

"In his part of Greece there's not much of a difference. And the chief's imitation of a kick-ass, bad-cop act didn't do anything to disabuse him of that notion."

"What do you mean imitation?" said Andreas.

"I personally thought you showed just the right combination of John Wayne and Rambo."

Andreas lifted his right hand from the dash and flashed an open palm at Tassos. "I agree with the *malaka* in the backseat. You were the only one of us who had a shot at making him talk. Alexander's not afraid of cops, but he's scared to death of your influence with your cousin."

"Kicking in doors is easier for me."

"And a damn good job you did on Alexander's," said Tassos.

"Surprised the shit out of the landlord."

"Not our problem. He's who insisted on being there in case any of his tenants got curious."

"Not one of them bothered to check on who'd just kicked in their neighbor's front door," said Tassos.

"My guess is the only curious one in the building is the landlord," said Andreas. "And he just wanted to get a peek at what his 'quiet' tenant's been doing with all those boys he'd been bringing up there for years."

"As if he didn't know," said Tassos.

"If he didn't before, he sure as hell does now," said Andreas.

"Not sure who looked more surprised when I kicked in the door. Alexander or the landlord. You'd think guys like him would know better than to bring their mobile phones to places they don't want to be found."

"He probably thought only the Americans have GPS," smiled Andreas.

"What do you think is Alexander's next move?" said Tassos.

"Find another apartment," said Andreas.

"Cute," said Tassos.

"I doubt he'll tell anyone about our little get-together this afternoon. There's no upside in it for him unless he thinks we might say something to someone first. But Yianni made it crystal clear that everything Alexander said would stay just between us, as long as he didn't have anything to do with his uncle's murder."

"There's another reason for him not saying anything to my uncle's friends about our visit. It risks they'll find out we caught him playing Juliet to the boy's Romeo and those old-time *macho* types aren't very open-minded on the subject."

"When you told him that what we found going on in his apartment would stay 'just between us,' I thought he'd kiss your feet," said Tassos.

Kouros smiled. "At least."

Andreas rolled his eyes. "Up until that comment I was about to compliment you on how much you've matured. You actually seemed to have meant it when you said, 'I don't give a damn who or how you fuck.'"

"Thank you, I did, and I don't. It's just hard acting mature with you two dragging me down."

Andreas laughed. "My guess is Alexander's already distancing himself from the Ukrainian. He knows we'll keep squeezing him for information if he doesn't, and the odds are that sooner or later someone in the deal will figure out he's been talking to cops. Alexander is the sort of political hustler who has survived by knowing when to cut his losses and move on."

"If neither Alexander nor the Ukrainian had anything to do with my uncle's murder, then who did?"

Tassos shook his head. "It's back to looking like the only one with both motive *and* opportunity is one very dead taverna operator."

"Maybe," said Andreas. "Or maybe we're looking at this the wrong way."

"Meaning?" said Kouros.

"Perhaps we should stop looking for someone who wanted your uncle dead, and start looking for someone who wanted the *project* dead?"

"That narrows down the field of potential suspects," said Tassos.

"And fits with the death threat to my uncle if he didn't change his 'plans.'"

Andreas stopped drumming his fingers. "Another hotel owner? Jealous neighbors who wanted the project for themselves?" He paused. "Or, perhaps, one of your cousins who didn't like your uncle's plans for sharing the inheritance with the other cousins?"

Kouros squeezed the steering wheel for an instant. "I get your point."

"Good. But whoever we're looking for has to be someone with *real* leverage on that taverna owner. Enough to get him to kill his protector and ultimately himself."

"An even smaller universe of suspects," said Tassos.

"And it gives us a place to start," said Andreas.

"Namely?" said Tassos.

"Orestes."

"Orestes?" said Kouros.

"He's another political hustler. But unlike Alexander, he knows all the players behind the scenes in every transaction he's involved with." Andreas smiled. "And he's too arrogant to cut his losses when he should."

"May I help you?"

"Yes, *keria*. I'm here to see the man whose office is behind that door." Andreas pointed at a dark, raised-panel, tall wooden door six feet behind the receptionist.

"I beg your pardon, sir?"

Andreas handed her his card. "Please, just give Orestes this."

She took the card, picked up her phone, pressed a button, waited, and said, "Chief Inspector Andreas Kaldis is here to see you."

She paused, looked up, and smiled. "He said to tell you to go to hell."

"You're too kind. I'm sure he really said to say, 'Go fuck yourself.'"

She smiled again. "Whatever interpretation works for you, works for me."

Andreas leaned in. "Just tell him his daddy might cut off his allowance when he wakes up tomorrow morning to find his pride and joy described in the press as the new butt boy for a certain Ukrainian arms smuggler, drug trader, and sex-slaver planning to set up operations in Greece. In the southern Peloponnese to be exact. And, please, my love, in your message, make sure to emphasize 'butt boy.'"

The woman's smile disappeared.

Andreas pointed at the phone. "Butt boy has two t's, just in case you're afraid to call his royal highness and prefer to email him instead."

She jumped up, shuffled quickly to Orestes' door, knocked, went inside, and closed the door.

Andreas heard muffled shouting from inside the office. Fifteen seconds later the door opened and the woman stepped out. She said nothing, but nodded for Andreas to go inside. He waved and smiled as he walked by her into the office. She slammed the door behind him.

"Touchy help," said Andreas looking around the office. The walls were plastered with photographs of what looked to be every powerful person Orestes had ever met.

"Take your time. Take a good look. As you can see, I know everyone. Figure out for yourself how many ways I can bury you."

Andreas kept looking at the walls, ignoring Orestes. The space was three times the size of Andreas' office. "As far as I can tell, a lot of your pinup pals are in or headed to prison. You ought to be more careful whom you're photographed with. Could ruin your reputation."

From behind his ornate, Louis XIV desk, Orestes pointed at a lone straight-back chair in front of and facing him.

Andreas walked to the chair and without breaking stride lifted it with one hand above his head and continued around Orestes' desk.

Orestes' arms shot up in front of his face, "What are doing?"

Andreas dropped the chair inches from Orestes' feet. "Rearranging the furniture." He sat down. "Now, isn't this cozier?"

"Get out of my office, *now.*"

"First, a few questions."

Orestes played with his tie. "After screwing me in Crete, you expect me to help you?"

Andreas pointed at his own chest. "Me? I did precisely what you asked." He pointed at Orestes and back at himself. "You and I, working together at protecting Greece from foreign predators. What more could you ask for? But don't worry, I didn't steal your credit. The prosecutor knows the list of suspects came from you."

Orestes glared.

"I told him to do his best not to reveal you as the source. After all, we wouldn't want potential clients on that list learning of your indiscretion.

Might hurt business." Andreas reached inside his jacket pocket and pulled out a print of a photograph captured from the DVD obtained by Petro. "Speaking of your business, what can you tell me about this?" He handed the photo to Orestes.

Orestes shrugged. "What's there to tell?"

Andreas locked eyes with Orestes. "Short version or long?"

"Whatever version you think is going to mean more than a rat's ass to me."

"Fair enough. I'll go short and let your imagination fill in the details. You and Alexander," Andreas pointed at a face in the photograph, "saw the chance of making a lot of money by helping this dude," he pointed at another face, "set up operations in Greece. The fact he's high up on NATO's shit list didn't matter in the least to you or," he pointed at an oversized portrait of Orestes' father on the wall behind his desk, "Daddy."

Orestes smiled. "You're right."

"Nor do you care what the Americans might think."

Orestes smiled again. "You're very well informed."

"Too bad you weren't, before you jumped into bed with Alexander and his Ukrainian mate." He paused. "Figuratively speaking, of course."

Anger flashed across Orestes' face but he said nothing.

"You see, if certain folks in the Mani learn you've been working with those two, you'd better be sure your life insurance premiums are paid up. And his." Andreas pointed at the painting again.

"I assume you're talking about your colleague Kouros' cousins."

Andreas nodded. "You, too, are very well informed."

"I had absolutely nothing to do with their father's murder."

Andreas shook his head from side to side. "You're missing the point, my dear friend. Whether or not you were involved in the murder isn't the issue. It's how hard you're working at the cover-up that's going to get you killed."

"What are you talking about?"

"You and I know that either the Ukrainian killed their father or knows who did. And if I know that," he smiled, "and Detective Kouros knows that, how long until the sons know? And when they find out…" Andreas shook his head, "I don't have to tell you how seriously those Maniots take their vendettas." He nodded toward the portrait, "It's practically biblical, as in 'An eye for an eye.'"

"You're bluffing. All you have linking me to

your bullshit story is a photograph taken at a club where every sort on Earth says hello to each other."

"If you're betting on Alexander riding in on his white horse to cover your ass when they start twisting his nuts, good luck." Andreas shook his head. "I wouldn't be surprised if he's down there right now putting as much distance as he can between you, the Ukrainian, the deal, and him." Andreas smiled, "And oh yes, let's not forget the Ukrainian's plans for the airstrip."

Orestes bit at his lip.

"Personally, I'd rather have NATO and the U.S. gunning for me than *that* dead man's sons."

"Where are you headed with this?"

"Perhaps it's time to consider taking out insurance. The kind which promises that when the sons start looking into your role in their father's murder, a certain detective cousin of theirs tells them how you fully cooperated from the moment you realized you might know something about their father's murder."

Orestes bit harder at his lip. "Why should I trust you?"

Sold, thought Andreas. He patted Orestes' knee. "Because I'm not like you." He leaned back and yawned. "Besides, what choice do you have?"

Orestes got up out of his chair and walked

around the side of his desk away from Andreas. "I really don't like you."

"Old news."

"Or the nephew."

"I'm sure Detective Kouros would be hurt by that."

"What do you want from me?"

"Names of anyone you think might have been involved in the murder."

"I don't have names."

"Too bad, because I have yours."

"You're pretty stupid if you had to ask me that question."

"I'll live with that. Just tell me."

"The competitors of the Ukrainian."

"Competitors?"

"Local gunrunners operating on the Peloponnese. The kind that wouldn't take kindly to a big player moving in on their territory."

"But the locals use boats, the Ukrainian is into planes."

"For now. But competition is competition, and if the Ukrainian gained a foothold in the Mani through a strong business alliance with the father, his expansion into their highly profitable sea routes would be inevitable. He presented an unacceptable risk they'd prefer to nip in the bud."

"What makes you think that?"

"Because that's what the Ukrainian told me. In private, when that old queen wasn't around."

"What did he say?"

"His best guess was that the local boys somehow found out about his interest in the Mani and thought if they took out Mangas' father, the project would die with him."

"But how did they get the taverna owner to kill him?"

"The Ukrainian had no idea. But he doubted it was a coincidence."

Funny how cops and crooks so often think alike, thought Andreas. "Okay, which locals?"

"He didn't say, and I don't know."

"For your sake, you'd better not be holding out on me."

"No reason to. I'm too busy to take on this project anyway. The Ukrainian will just have to find someone else to assist him or drop it."

"Hope he's not disappointed."

"Not as disappointed as when he finds out that the reason his deal is dead is because the girlfriend who spent the night sitting on his lap spent the morning talking to cops." His lip had curled into a snarl.

"I've no idea what you're talking about."

"The Ukrainian will."

"Big mistake."

"Why? Are you protecting hookers now, too?"

"No, except it wasn't his girlfriend who talked." Andreas winked, stood, and walked toward the door. "It was yours."

Andreas didn't bother to say good-bye to the receptionist. Nor did he wait for the elevator. He double-timed it down four flights of stairs out to the street, and jumped into the front passenger seat of a marked blue-and-white police car parked with all but its driver side wheels on the sidewalk.

"How'd it go?" said Kouros.

Andreas reached for his mobile, and hit a speed dial number. "Like charming a snake. Just drive. I'll tell you after I speak to—Maggie, get Petro to call me ASAP in the car. It's urgent."

Andreas put down the phone and waited until Kouros had edged into the Formula One-style traffic on Vassilis Sofias, one of Athens' busiest roads. "That bastard threatened to tell the Ukrainian that the girl on his lap was working with us."

"How'd he figure that out?"

"He's smart. But he'd do something like that even if he knew it wasn't true, just to make us squirm."

"What did you tell him?"

"That it wasn't she; it was Alexander."

"Jesus, I promised him we wouldn't name him."

"Yeah, I know, but Alexander can protect himself, the girl can't. Besides, I didn't exactly name Alexander, and that might make Orestes think twice about blaming him."

"What did you say?"

"That it was Orestes' 'girlfriend' who talked."

"You really do like pouring gasoline on the flames, don't you?"

"He deserves it. Besides, I wouldn't be surprised if Orestes and Alexander had balled each other."

"Some hard-on you have for that guy."

Andreas turned his head and studied a smiling Kouros. "I'll let that one pass. Orestes said the Ukrainian's best guess was that local arms smugglers had your uncle killed. They'd figure murdering your uncle would kill the deal, too, and keep the competition from moving in."

"Ever think that maybe Orestes told you that story in hopes it would get back to my cousins and they'd wipe out the *Ukrainian's* competition?"

Andreas looked out the windshield. "That's possible, but a very risky play by Orestes. And the Ukrainian. Pointing a finger means three others on the same hand point back at you."

"So, which locals are involved?"

"No idea. Tassos might have one, but it's way outside his stomping grounds, or maybe he can get his arms-dealing buddy to give us some names once he hears he's not being asked to cross the Ukrainian."

"Any idea on how they got Babis to kill my uncle?"

"Nope. We'll just have to keep following the string. Sooner or later it will end somewhere."

"Hopefully not back at the Minotaur."

Andreas looked again at Kouros. "My literate friend, you've just given me an idea."

"What kind of idea?"

"Theseus had his Ariadne to save him when all seemed bleakest. And you have your Stella."

"The taverna owner's girlfriend?"

"Yep. If anyone is likely to know what drove him to kill your uncle and then himself, it's the girlfriend. Before we go anywhere else with this I want you to find out everything she knows, even things she doesn't know that she knows. We have to make sure Orestes isn't running *us* instead of the other way around."

"You're just pissed about what I said about your having—how shall I say it this time?—an uncommon interest in giving Orestes *agita*."

"I like that better, but my thinking's the same. I want you down in the Mani first thing tomorrow morning. And don't come back until you're sure who was running her boyfriend."

The car's speaker squawked their car number.

Andreas reached for the handset. "Now, if you'll excuse me, it's time for me to dispatch another brave knight to save a fair damsel."

"Yeah, but all he has to do is spend five minutes warning her to be careful and lay low for a while. I could end up spending a month with Stella and still not know any more than we already do."

"Care for a suggestion?" Andreas smiled. "Bring flowers."

Chapter Seventeen

Kouros remembered once hearing a Navy psychiatrist say that for most of us getting through life each day was pretty much like flying a plane: takeoffs and landings presented the greatest challenges, the rest generally involved hours of routine separated by moments of sheer panic; though for some, panic might be no more than "Where's my phone?"

If that shrink was right, Stella probably felt her plane had just been hijacked by Martian terrorists. Her man was dead, and despite the price she paid for his company, he'd provided her with food, shelter, and work. Gone, too, was the other man in her life, the one who protected her from deportation. She was back to being a stranger in a strange land.

Kouros pulled up in front of the taverna just before noon. The only other vehicle in sight was a beat-up motorbike by the door to the kitchen. She must be scared shitless, he thought. What do I say to her? I'm never good at talking to girls I like. *Like?* What am I thinking? She could be involved in two murders.

A handwritten sign on the front door to the taverna said CLOSED. Hardly a surprise. He tried the doorknob but it didn't budge. He walked over to the kitchen door and knocked. No answer. He turned the doorknob and as he did the door pulled away from him.

"Hi," said Stella with a brilliant smile. "I heard someone at the front door, but by the time I got there you were gone. Then I heard a knock at this door. You're the impatient sort, aren't you?"

"Uh, sorry, I wasn't sure you'd still be here."

"Then I'm happy I am." Another smile.

Kouros fought off the urge to blush.

She wore cutoff jeans and one of those t-shirts that looked as if it had been ripped from the jaws of a Rottweiler. No shoes, no makeup.

Kouros didn't know where to look. He decided to aim for her eyes. Those deep, dark, brown ones.

She cocked her head slightly to the side and fixed her gaze on him. "Nothing to say?" She paused. "I wouldn't have taken you for the shy sort. Come, I'll make us some coffee." She stepped back and waved him inside.

"I thought the place was closed."

"It is. But I remember how to make coffee.

And your uncle's friends still show up every morning like clockwork. They bring their own pastries.
I make the coffee."

He followed her through the kitchen out to
the small dining room.

"Sit wherever you want. I'll be right back."

He wanted to go with her, but did as she said.
Everything was neat and clean. Nothing out of
place. He saw a bucket and mop over by the door
leading to the larger dining room. A pair of sandals
at the entrance.

He yelled, "You were mopping the big room
when I tried the front door?"

Stella came out of the kitchen with two cups
and a pot of coffee. "Yes, I felt I should clean the
place before I left."

"You're leaving?"

"Yes, for Athens. Tomorrow. I have a cousin I
can stay with there."

That was the smart move for illegal immigrants. Athens still offered the best opportunities
for those willing to work hard, and a place to lose
yourself among the hundreds of thousands of other
illegals hiding in plain sight from immigration
authorities.

He glanced around the room while Stella
leaned over to pour the coffee. At least he tried to
convince himself he was looking around the room

and not struggling to ignore the breasts inches from his face as she filled his cup. "Have you ever thought of staying here?"

"What's here for me? A horny local guy. Or an even hornier passing tourist? No, I have no future here."

Kouros wondered if he should tell her the truth. But the truth took away a lot of leverage if he wanted her to talk. "You're worried about your immigration status, aren't you?" he asked.

She looked up at him, anger flushing her face. "What are you getting at?"

"Nothing."

"*Nothing?* You're an Athens cop who shows up out of nowhere at the place where I sleep, you can't keep your eyes off my tits, and just happen to raise the subject of my immigration status when you already knows it's illegal. What's the matter, Detective? Are you the type of predator who prefers your victims to beg you to fuck them so you won't turn them in? You think that makes you any better than a fuck-me-or-I'll-beat-you-to-death rapist?" She stood up. "I thought you were different. You want to fuck me? Here, fuck me." She had already pulled off her t-shirt and was working on her shorts when Kouros grabbed her hands.

"You've got it all wrong."

She twisted away from his hands and turned away from him.

Kouros stayed where he was. "Put on your top and come back here."

She didn't move. He could hear her crying.

"Like I said, you have it all wrong."

A minute passed. She reached down, picked up her t-shirt, put it on, and turned around, eyes red and nose running.

He handed her a napkin.

She took it, blew her nose, and sat down across the table from him. "I'm sorry. It's just that since Babis' death practically every man through that front door has tried getting in my pants. I can't stand it."

"I can imagine. I'm sorry."

"I've always had guys hitting on me. But it's sickening to have to face a line of Babis' supposed friends coming by to see if they can be the first to console me with their dicks."

"I can't believe everyone who's come to see you was like that?"

"No, but enough to make me sick of them all."

"Who for instance?"

"I don't want to talk about them."

Kouros nodded. "Locals?"

"I said I don't want to talk about them."

"Anybody I know?"

"You're not going to stop, are you?"

He smiled. "No. Because I can help you."

She shut her eyes, drew in and let out a deep breath. "His friends from Pirgos."

"What friends?"

"Three guys stopped by yesterday. Real nasty bastards. They said they hadn't seen Babis in a very long time and drove down from Pirgos to pay Babis' 'widow' their respects."

"They thought you were his wife?"

"They said the words, but I didn't believe anything they said."

"Why's that?"

"Because I saw one of them with Babis a little more than a week before your uncle died."

"Where?"

She pointed at the front door. "He came in after lunch, spoke to Babis at the door, and left. I thought Babis had told him we were closed, and when I said I didn't mind waiting on the guy he told me, 'Mind your own fucking business,' and left. I guess to meet him."

"Why do you think that?"

"Because I heard Babis yelling at someone outside. I couldn't make out what he said, but I could tell he was angry."

"You're sure it was one of the same guys who came by to see you yesterday?"

"Positive. He had jet-black hair with a white streak running straight down the middle, front to back. Like a skunk."

"What did they want?"

"It certainly wasn't to make me comfortable. One looked and smelled like a bear, another kept licking his lips and staring at my breasts."

"So we've got a skunk, a bear, and a...uh," Kouros stared at Stella's breasts.

"Whatever you're thinking, don't say it."

Kouros smiled. "But he needs a name."

"Fine. *Malaka*."

"Too common."

She shut her eyes. "He had a big mole on the back of his right hand."

"Terrific. A skunk, a bear, and a mole walk into a taverna."

"Are you trying to be cute, Detective?" She smiled.

Again Kouros almost blushed. "What *did* they want from you?"

"From their looks, to the extent it involved me it had nothing to do with my mind. But their questions were all about your family's reaction to Babis killing your uncle."

"What sort of questions?"

"The kind designed to learn who, besides Babis, that Mangas and your family might be blaming for the murder. They said they were concerned the family might somehow be blaming me as Babis' wife, but I knew they didn't give a damn about how the family felt about me."

"What did you say?"

"As far as I could tell everything was fine and no one was blaming me for what Babis had done."

"Did you tell them anything else?"

"Yes."

"What?"

Her face turned very serious. "That I wasn't Babis' wife, but engaged to one of your uncle's nephews."

"You what?"

She smiled. "I was alone in here with them. I had to come up with something to make them think twice before trying anything."

"Smart."

"Aren't you going to ask which nephew?" She smiled.

Kouros felt himself flush. He swallowed before speaking. "Did Babis ever mention anything to you about a Ukrainian?"

Stella's smile vanished. "I don't believe you asked that question."

"Why?"

"They asked me the same thing."

"What did you tell them?"

"The truth—no—but the bear kept pressing me on it. Scared me a bit. The skunk had to tell him to cool it. Then they left."

"That's it?"

She nodded. "But their visit made up my mind for me. That's when I called your cousin Mangas and told him I'd be leaving tomorrow."

"What did he say?"

"'No hurry, take your time.'"

"I agree with him."

"Between immigration and those guys from Pirgos, there's no upside to my staying here."

"I wouldn't worry about the boys from Pirgos. As for immigration, well, I think that's going to work itself out."

She leaned across the table and stared into Kouros' eyes. "If telling me that you'll cure my immigration worries is your revised technique for getting into my pants, I have two words for you."

"No, you're wrong again. My uncle made all the arrangements before he died. He wanted to surprise you. You'll have your ID card any day now."

She put her finger to Kouros' lips. "Like I said, I have two words for you." She paused. "Not necessary." She leaned farther across the table. "I've wanted to make love to you since the moment we met."

Kouros blinked.

Stella stood up, came around, and took his hand. "Come along with me, Detective Kouros."

And he did.

Brown, chestnut, soft, flowers, light, dark, smooth, touch, taste, hold, press, grasp, turn, bury, release, cling, stroke, kiss. Straddle, lift, fall, reach, touch, squeeze, race, harder, finish. Caress. Sleep. Awake. Watch. Speak.

"I'm glad you came back."

"I'm glad you didn't leave."

Stella kissed Kouros on his shoulder.

He lay on his belly, his arm across her chest. Neither spoke a word.

"Do you know about me and your uncle?"

Kouros opened his eyes and stared at the side of her head. "I don't even want to think about what possessed you to ask me that question at this moment."

"But you do know?"

"Yes."

"Good."

"Okay, I'll bite. Why 'good'?"

"Because now I have nothing left to hide from you." She brushed her lips against his shoulder and reached one hand under his body to hold him.

But Kouros' mind was elsewhere. "Did you hide it from Babis?"

"I didn't have to. He knew."

"How did he know?"

She pressed her head back against the pillow and sighed. "Why are you asking that?"

"Because I'm a cop and you started it."

She pulled her hand away. "Someone gave him a picture of us coming out of a hotel room."

"Who gave it to him?"

"I don't know, but it was taken at Panos' hotel."

"How do you know about the photo?"

"He showed it to me."

"When?"

"About a week ago."

"That would be a couple of days before my uncle died."

"Yes."

"Why did he show it to you?"

"He said he wanted me to know that he knew. And that the moment your uncle 'was out of the picture' he'd start turning some 'real money' by *peddling my ass as his whore*." She spit at the words.

"Nice guy."

"He was angry." Again she sighed and turned her head away. "But in his own way he loved me."

Why do the abused always say that? "I'm sure." Kouros sat up and almost fell onto the floor. He'd forgotten they were on a cot in a storeroom. The smell of onions and disinfectant hit him. He preferred the scent of Stella's hair, the taste of her body, but this conversation was headed in the wrong direction and he did have a job to do.

"If he loved you why did he kill himself?"

"I don't know."

"Did he ever threaten to kill himself?"

"Himself, no." She raised her arms in the air. "Me, yes." She slammed her arms down onto the cot.

"Anyone else?"

"All the time. It was his way of expressing anger."

"Did he ever kill anyone?"

"Why don't you stop with the questions and come back down here next to me?"

Kouros turned and placed his hand on her belly. "I need these answers."

She shut her eyes and put her hands on top of his hand. "Not while I knew him, but I wouldn't be surprised if he had before. From what he told me he ran with a rough crowd."

"Like the crew that paid you a visit yesterday?"

She nodded. "Sometimes he'd threaten me with how easy it would be for a body to disappear in the sea. As if he knew how to do it."

"Such as by tying a rock around your neck?"

"I heard the ancient Greeks used that as a method for committing suicide, but for Babis to do that…" She opened her eyes again. "That's not how I would have expected him to kill himself. He'd almost drowned as a child and once told me he'd rather shoot himself in the head—several times, if necessary—than drown in the water."

"So why did he do it that way?"

"No idea. But I guess when you decide to kill yourself, how you do it is the least of your concerns."

Just the opposite, thought Kouros. If someone starts talking in detail about how he plans on killing himself, that's when you know it's serious. Suicides tended to be planned final acts, not done on a whim.

She reached out and touched his side. "So, are you done with the questions?"

He smiled. "For now, yes."

"Good," she spread wide her arms. "Come. Make me forget all my other lovers."

Kouros rolled his eyes. "Sounds like quite a challenge."

She laughed and grabbed his cock. "I think you're up to it."

◇◇◇

Andreas felt the vibration in his pants pocket. He

adjusted his position in the chair and reached in without taking his eyes off the television. The riots in Syntagma threatened to turn more violent and tear gas-saturated than usual. Another peaceful demonstration in Parliament Square successfully hijacked by masked anarchists and mobsters. The former sought any excuse to battle police with Molotov cocktails and rocks; the latter were happy to vandalize and rob neighborhood shops under cover of whatever government action triggered the current massing of angry protestors.

He put the phone to his ear. "Yes."

"It's Yianni."

"What's up?" said Andreas

"You sound busy."

"Just watching the latest episode of Greek democracy in action."

"Is it bad?"

"Not yet, but heading there. Not sure how much longer our guys on the front lines are going to take this shit without someone losing it and seriously busting a few heads."

"Too bad it's always the wrong heads."

"On both sides."

"Isn't that just the way it is? Big bastards making decisions that have little bastards taking all the risks."

Andreas shifted his look from the television to

his office windows. "Why do I sense there's something you want to tell me?"

"I spoke to the girl Stella. Yesterday she had a visit from three very nasty characters out of Pirgos."

"Her late boyfriend's hometown."

"Precisely. They were particularly interested in whether my cousins thought anyone other than Babis might have been involved in the murder."

"How thoughtful of them."

"And whether Babis ever spoke to her about a Ukrainian."

Andreas leaned forward in his chair. "Sounds like some folks are nervous."

"With reason. Stella said one of them paid a visit to Babis about a week before my uncle's murder, putting him in a bad mood."

Andreas thought for a moment. "That would have been around the time of your uncle's first death threat."

"Orestes might actually have been telling you the truth about Peloponnese gunrunners wanting my uncle dead. And it fits with what the Gytheio harbormaster told me of rumors about 'people up north' worried about a 'war' breaking out on the Mani over a 'project' involving my uncle."

"Well, if the girl is telling the truth, for sure they had something to do with her boyfriend."

"And his suicide."

"They'd need a hell of a lot of leverage to get him to kill himself. Maybe they threatened to kill the girlfriend if he didn't do himself?"

"I don't think that would have done it."

Andreas heard Kouros draw in and let out a breath.

"He'd seen a photograph of my uncle and Stella coming out of a hotel together."

"How do you know that?"

"Stella told me he'd shown it to her a couple of days before my uncle's murder, and threatened to pimp her out like a whore once my uncle was out of the picture."

"He actually said, 'out of the picture'?"

"According to her."

"Who took the photograph?"

"No idea. But I guess the Pirgos boys gave it to him."

"I wonder if Babis planned on killing your uncle when he showed Stella the photo?"

"From my run-in with him, I'd say his temper controlled his tongue. And he definitely lacked a sense of humor on the subject of messing with his girlfriend. I've no doubt that photo would have fired him up big-time."

"Fine, but if what drove him was love triangle rage, that's usually a murder-murder-suicide scenario, not something like this where the angry one kills the third party and himself but lets the girl live."

"There's more. She said Babis was afraid of drowning and she couldn't believe he'd kill himself that way."

"Sort of makes you wonder."

"Especially since he still had the vial of poison he'd used to kill my uncle hidden away in the taverna. But what's really bothering me is, after all those years of my uncle's protection, what made the Pirgos boys think they could get Babis to turn on my uncle now?"

"From what you're telling me, the likely answer has to do with your uncle screwing Babis' girlfriend."

"But how would the Pirgos guys know about that? Who would have told them?"

"Sounds like you've got some more interesting questions to ask."

"There's no one in the Mani who's going to admit to turning on my uncle. It would be suicide."

"Start with the photograph."

"Like I said, Chief, who's going to admit to taking it?"

"If you find who took it, my guess is you'll get an answer to why Babis killed your uncle."

"The only ones who knew about my uncle and Stella were his morning coffee buddy Panos and the chief of Gytheio's port police. And at the moment they're both dead ends, motive-wise."

"What about someone at the hotel?"

"Possible. I'll see what I can find out, but how would a chambermaid or porter know what to do with the photograph unless someone put them up to taking it? My uncle and Stella weren't exactly a *paparazzi* quality couple."

"Since it ended up in Babis' hands, likely via Pirgos, it had to be someone who knew she was Babis' girlfriend and of Babis' past link to the Pirgos mob."

"How are we ever going to get a lead on that?" said Kouros.

"Start at the end. The three guys from Pirgos would know who gave them the photo."

"Can't imagine how we'll ever get them to talk."

"Let's begin with their names and see where that takes us."

"Don't have any. Just descriptions. A bear, a skunk, and a mole."

"Come again?"

"'A bear, a skunk, and a mole.'"

"I'll pass it along to Tassos to see what he can do with it. He'd said that without something more specific than what Orestes called 'local guys,' his friend wouldn't be volunteering names, but maybe, with Stella's description, we'll get lucky and find ourselves an arms dealer among them. To me, though, they sound more like something out of Winnie-the-Pooh."

"I see you've been watching television with Tassaki."

Andreas looked back at the television screen. "It beats real life."

Chapter Eighteen

Kouros' afternoon of asking questions at Panos' hotel yielded nothing. No one had seen his uncle at the hotel with any woman other than his daughter Calliope for lunch. If nothing else, Uncle knew how to be discreet. Or Panos' employees knew how to keep their mouths shut.

Kouros sat alone at a seaside table in Gerolimenas, sipping coffee and staring out across the harbor toward Panos' hotel. No way to take that picture of Uncle and Stella from here. He looked north at the high cliff face running out to sea. A goatherd's shed at the base of the cliff offered a clear sight line to the front door of the hotel room in the photo. But you had to know how to get out there, and you'd be visible to anyone looking in your direction for practically the entire time.

Maybe someone took it from inside the hotel complex? Without some fix on at least the approximate date of the photo, from the number of camera-armed tourists passing through Gerolime-nas each season, potential photographers numbered in the tens of thousands.

The lanky priest he'd been thinking about the other day kept pacing the thirty-foot stretch of pavement between Kouros' table and the tav-erna across the road. Long, dark, unwashed hair, a dark scruffy beard, dusty cowboy boots, and a priest's black cassock loosely buttoned at the top and bottom over a faded, red plaid shirt and worn blue jeans served as his form of priestly dress. Then again, this was the Mani.

Every few seconds the priest stole a quick glance at Kouros without breaking stride.

Kouros decided to end the priest's curiosity and waved for him to join him.

"Me?" said the priest pointing at his chest without slowing his pace.

Kouros nodded. "Yes."

The priest stopped and turned his hands palms up in a pleading gesture. "Why?"

"I need the company of a holy man."

He nodded and walked quickly toward Kouros. The passing waiter muttered loud enough for Kouros to hear, "I see he's caught another one."

The priest dropped into the chair across from Kouros, flashed a quick nervous smile, and said,

"My name is Father Carlos. How can I be of service, my son?"

"What would you like to drink?" said Kouros.

"That's most kind of you, but I never drink coffee. It is a stimulant born out of the labor of oppressed workers."

"Tea?"

"Even worse."

Kouros smiled. "Orange juice."

"Only in the mornings."

Without being asked, the waiter came by and set a half-full bottle of bar scotch on the table together with a single glass. "He doesn't believe in sharing, just in *not* paying," he stage-whispered to Kouros before walking away.

Carlos ignored the waiter's words, twisted off the bottle top, and poured four fingers of scotch. He lifted the glass. "To your health, most kind stranger."

Kouros tipped his coffee cup against Carlos' glass. "*Yia sas.*" He watched him drain a third of the glass before putting it down.

"Bless you, my son."

"Why were you looking at me?"

"What do you mean?" said Carlos.

"Like I said, why were you looking at me?"

"I thought I recognized you."

"From where?"

"Your uncle's funeral."

"So you know who I am?"

Carlos nodded and took a more measured gulp from his glass. "You're the nephew from Athens, the one who became a cop."

"Since you have the advantage on me, who are you?"

"Just a humble man serving God."

"Yeah, but God's not paying for your drinks, and neither am I if you don't start giving me answers."

"I have served my Lord in many ways, official and otherwise. At present I am between ecclesiastical engagements and so I returned home to the place of my roots."

"You're from the Mani?"

"From this very village." He pointed at Panos' hotel across the harbor. "My grandfather and great grandfather both worked there when it was a place of trade. Now it is a place of sin. Where the unwed run to cohabitate. Where sodomites practice their evil ways. Where—"

"I get the picture," interrupted Kouros. "Anybody I know among those sinners?"

Carlos shrugged. "My vows forbid me from disclosing their names anywhere but in my prayers for their forgiveness and redemption."

"Do you ever pray aloud?" Kouros struggled to maintain a straight face.

"When in the right state of mind."

"And how far away from that are you at the moment?"

Carlos picked up the bottle. "About another liter and a half."

Kouros picked up the bottle, used it to catch the waiter's eye, and said, "Another one."

The waiter rolled his eyes and crossed the street to the taverna.

"So, start praying," said Kouros.

Carlos took another drink. "The one you're interested in was your uncle?"

"Why do you think I'm interested in him?"

"If not, who?"

"Tell me about my uncle."

"I live here," he pointed at the taverna, "above that notable establishment. The property belongs to my dear mother, may she live another thousand years."

"And?" said Kouros.

"Your uncle often came here with women. I'd see them driving by. No one ever notices me. They think of me as part of the place. You didn't notice me at the funeral did you?"

"No, I didn't."

"But I wasn't dressed like this. Mother said I

could not wear my cassock since I wasn't officiating at the service."

"Did you recognize any of my uncle's women?"

Carlos picked up his glass and smiled. "I assume you mean with him here, not at his funeral."

Kouros simply stared.

"Just trying to lighten the moment."

Kouros kept staring.

Carlos averted his eyes. "Most were the kind of women whose company one pays for."

"Mostly?"

"A few divorced locals."

"Ones with jealous boyfriends or ex-husbands?"

"Not that I knew of."

"Are you sure?"

Carlos hesitated as the waiter arrived and placed the bottle on the table. Carlos reached for the bottle, but Kouros grabbed it first.

"Like I said, are you sure?"

Carlos bit at his lower lip. "That girl from the taverna. The one whose boyfriend committed suicide." He crossed himself three times.

"Did you ever tell anyone about them?"

Carlos vigorously nodded no. "Never." He crossed himself again.

"Did you ever happen to pray for their souls?"

"I may drink too much, but I wasn't insane enough to risk making your uncle my mortal enemy by talking about things he'd know could only have come from me. Besides, I went to school with your cousin, Calliope. She is a friend and I would never do anything to harm her or her family."

"Was there anyone else who knew?"

"I can't say. With the others he'd come in broad daylight in the middle of the afternoon, almost as a macho demonstration."

So much for getting truthful answers out of Panos' hotel staff, thought Kouros.

"But with this one he came late at night," Carlos continued.

"And you saw them?"

"God's work permits little sleep. I was meditating along the beach by the turn at the end of the harbor when they drove in, and they were gone when I awoke at God's brilliant light." He took another gulp of scotch.

"When was that?"

"Several weeks ago."

"Did you ever see them here again?"

He gestured no.

"Did you ever see someone take a photograph of them together?"

Again he gestured no.

"Did you ever tell Calliope you saw them?"

With one hand still on his partially full glass

he reached for the bottle with his other. "As I said, no. I would never do anything to upset her."

Kouros let go of the bottle.

"You heard her *mirologia* at the funeral?"

Carlos nodded yes.

"Why do you think she thought someone murdered her father?"

"I have no idea." Carlos drained the glass. "Why don't you ask her?"

Kouros found Calliope dressed head-to-toe in black, her hair drawn back in a tight bun, sitting on a straight-back taverna chair at the edge of the hardscrabble garden thirty feet or so outside the kitchen door. At her feet sat a large basket filled nearly to the top with potatoes. She balanced a brown ceramic bowl on her lap, deftly stripping the skin off a potato in a continuous strand with a short-blade knife gripped in her right hand. A small basket partially filled with peelings lay on the ground to her right.

"Hi, Calliope."

She didn't look up from her peeling. "I see you're back."

Kouros picked up a milking stool by the back door, brought it over by her, and sat. "How are you doing?"

She raised her eyes, stared into his for a second, and looked back at the potato.

"It must be tough," he said.

With her left hand she dropped the potato into the bowl on her lap and reached down to pick another out of the large basket, shaking the strand of peel encircling the blade off into the other basket as she did.

"Very."

Kouros nodded. "Would you like some water? Or coffee? I can make it." He smiled. "After all, I am a cop."

"Nice try, but I think you best leave the kitchen to professionals."

"So, you've heard about my coffee?"

She sighed. Put a half peeled potato and the knife into the bowl, and handed it to Yianni. "Here, hold this. I'll make us some coffee."

He watched his cousin labor off into the kitchen. She showed no signs of energy in her walk. Perhaps she was medicated? That would make sense. Her whole life had been about taking care of her mother and father. Now both were gone. Kouros tried to remember how old she was. Probably her late thirties, maybe older. Never married. Always lived with her parents. If she wasn't on medication, she certainly should be.

Kouros heard Calliope yelling from inside the

house. "Yianni, come inside. It will be easier to have coffee at the table."

He put the bowl on the chair, and went inside. His cousin had set the table neatly with the finest of her parents' china, a plate of cookies in the middle.

"There was no need to go to all this trouble."

She shrugged. "Why not? What else do I have to do? Besides why have the china if you don't use it?" She poured the dark Greek coffee into two cups. "You take it *metrio*, right?"

"Yes, medium sweet."

They sat across from each other, Calliope watching Kouros as he sipped his coffee. "So, cousin, what's on your mind?"

"What do you mean?"

"You may be a cop, but I've lived among the paranoid all my life. I know when there's something behind the eyes."

Kouros smiled. "Do you know a Father Carlos?"

"From Gerolimenas?"

"Yes."

"We went to school together." She looked down at her cup. "He once had a crush on me." She looked up. "My father said that was what drove him into the priesthood." She gave half a laugh.

"Not sure I follow that."

"His mother did not want her only child

marrying the daughter of a...well, you can guess what she said."

"What about the father?"

"He died at sea when Carlos was a baby." Calliope smiled. "Some say he killed himself to escape his bitch of a wife."

"How did you feel about Carlos?"

"It wasn't to be, so I moved on."

"What happened to him?"

"He drinks too much. Cost him his every chance in life. Now he is what he is. And his mother is still there, still making him suffer."

"Do you trust him?"

"What does that mean?"

"Do you think he'd ever do anything to harm your family?"

"By that do you mean my father? Do you think that he had something to do with his murder?" Her voice was rising.

"No, absolutely not. I'm just interested in your take on him."

"All right, Yianni, enough with this bullshit. What are you getting at?"

Kouros swallowed. "Did you know that your father was seeing women?"

"I would certainly hope so, considering the alternatives."

"I mean women who had boyfriends, maybe even husbands."

Her lips grew taut. "My father could take care of himself."

Kouros looked down at his cup. "Come on, Calliope, work with me on this."

"Okay, so my father was screwing Babis' girlfriend. It wasn't that hard to figure out. I lived with the man, I could tell from the way he took extra care getting dressed and preparing for his morning coffee at the taverna that he was interested in someone. And the only one down there was Stella."

"Someone showed Babis a photograph of your father and Stella coming out of a room in Panos' hotel."

"And you think that's why Babis murdered my father?"

"It sure gave him a motive."

"And you think Carlos took the photograph?"

"Or knows who did."

"I don't see why you think that."

"You've already given a reason to believe that he could. He's a drunk. He'd do anything for a drink. And probably not remember in the morning that he had. Look, someone took a photograph that ended up in the hands of the man who murdered your father."

She slammed her hands on the table. "NEVER.

Not Carlos, I cannot believe he would betray me or my family."

"Okay, then, who would?"

"How would I know?"

"You practically named names in your *mirologia*. Who did you mean?"

She crossed her arms and began to rock.

"Are you all right?"

No answer.

"Do you need something? Medicine perhaps?" There was real worry in Kouros' voice.

She stopped rocking and shook her head. "No, but thank you. The doctor wants me to take pills, but I can't. I don't want to lose my visions."

"What visions?"

"Of those responsible for my father's death. Yes, Babis was the assassin, but there are others. Of that I'm certain." She started rocking again, then stopped abruptly. "My father would say, 'Stop, enough. The killer is dead, end it there.'"

"And he would be right. But I am a cop. I don't have to end it. I don't want to end it. Tell me who you think did this to your father?"

She dropped her head and shook it. "Father never should have started up with the Ukrainian and this hotel business. I told him not to."

"You think the Ukrainian had him murdered?"

"Who else had a motive?"

This was not the time to trot out a list of other possible suspects for her and her brothers. "That's what I'm trying to find out. Any ideas?"

"Only the Ukrainian."

"But why? He had a deal with your father. Why kill the person giving you what you wanted?"

"I don't want to talk about this anymore. It depresses me. And I have cooking to do." She looked at Kouros' face. "Where are you staying?"

Kouros fought back a blush. "Not sure yet."

Calliope smiled. "Be careful. I have no ill will toward her. But the men attracted to her have not done well."

"What makes you think—?"

She raised her hand to cut Kouros off. "Cousin, please. If there's one thing you should know by now it's that there are no secrets in the deep Mani."

Kouros picked up his coffee, finished it, and put down the cup. "I'll remember that."

Kouros stopped by the edge of the road just over the crest of the hill beyond Vathia. He wondered how many more Romeo and Juliet-style secrets lay hidden in his family tree. The classic Greek version cast his doomed Great-aunt Calliope and her lover in the title roles. Next came the Uncle-Stella-Babis love-triangle production. And now he'd discovered the unrequited love version, starring cousin Calliope and her wacky, ex-boyfriend priest, Carlos. Not lucky in love, his family.

Kouros knew the pressures all too well. His mother had drummed them into his head since puberty. "You will marry a Greek girl. A good Greek girl." When he turned twenty-five she backed off her requirement that his choice be from the Mani.

It was almost enough to have him reconsider Stella's offer to spend the night with her. Almost.

He reached for his mobile and hit a speed dial button.

"Kaldis here."

"Things are getting interesting, Chief. Make that painfully so."

"Sounds like a Chinese proverb. What do you have?"

"It turns out that priest I told you about on my way over to see my cousin Calliope wanted to marry her when they were young."

"She told you that?"

"Not directly, but that's the way it was."

"What happened?"

"His family forbade it."

"Did your uncle?"

"Doesn't sound as if he did."

"If he had, that would give the priest a terrific motive for revenge against your uncle."

"My cousin said there's not a chance he'd harm her father. If his mother had been the victim, then I'd say we definitely had a suspect."

"Where do we go from here?"

"That's what I planned on asking you. My cousin thinks the Ukrainian is behind her father's murder, but she didn't come up with a reason. I didn't want to mention the Pirgos angle and get her agitating for a war against them, too."

"I'm still waiting to hear back from Tassos on what he's able to dig up from his arms dealer friend on the Pirgos boys who paid Stella a visit.

"So, what should I do now?"

"Just sit tight where you are until we see what Tassos turns up. Hope that doesn't wreck your plans on getting back to Athens."

Kouros glanced in the direction of the taverna. "No problem, Chief. It will give me time to brush up on my Shakespeare."

Chapter Nineteen

"Strip, it's Tassos. I hope I'm not disturbing you."

"As if you actually care. Give me your number—a land line—and I'll call you back in two minutes."

Tassos gave him the number and hung up. He knew Strip would be returning the call from a secure phone. No way Strip would ever trust a serious conversation to Greece's mobile phone system. Tassos couldn't fault him. Caution had kept Strip breathing all these years and never prosecuted for so much as jaywalking—so long as you didn't count the many courtrooms he'd seen for speeding tickets.

Tassos picked up the phone in Maggie's apartment on the first ring. "Thanks for calling back."

"I figured it was better than you showing up in the middle of Dimitri's granddaughter's wedding and asking me to dance."

"Whoops, I forgot about that, sorry."

"No problem. I've been to one of hers before."

Tassos laughed.

"And with the new *malaka* she's picked for a husband, I'm betting I'll be invited to another sooner rather than later. Why do they always go for the show and never the substance?"

"In my youth I tried selling that line to a lot of girls. It never worked with them either."

Strip laughed. "So, what sort of questions do you have for me to duck this time?"

"I always appreciated your honesty, Strip, but I don't think what I'm interested in is going to be a problem for you. I don't care about the Ukrainian. It's his competitors I want to know about."

"The ones from the Peloponnese?"

"Yes. What can you tell me about them?"

"That's a pretty broad question covering a lot of possible people. Anyone specific in mind?"

"All I have is some silly description of three hard-ass types."

"Silly's better than nothing. Shoot."

"A bear, a mole, and a skunk."

"What's this, some kind of 'pull poor old Strip's leg' bullshit?"

"Just tell me if you can think of anyone tied into arms smuggling on the Peloponnese who might be described as a bear, a mole, or a skunk."

"Damn you, Tassos, if this is a gag…hmmm. What do you mean by a 'skunk'?"

"A white shock of hair right down the middle of his head."

"Son of a bitch. You're talking about Niko. A bear and a mole I don't know."

"So tell me about Niko."

"He's one of five brothers. Niko's the only one I know. The others aren't in the arms business. It's a small-time operation, but he's a smart, careful, hard-ass son of a bitch who knows how to do deals that make him a pretty good living without attracting a lot of attention."

"What's a pretty good living?"

"Around a million a year, after expenses."

Tassos cleared his throat. "What about Niko's brothers, aren't they jealous?"

"Could be, but it's not their area of expertise, they're into agriculture."

"What sort of agriculture?"

"All kinds. Legit and otherwise. Though I hear they stopped growing the sort of stuff that led to their father serving time and dying in prison."

"What's Niko's last name?"

Tassos listened to the name. "Would Niko happen to be from Pirgos?"

"Yep, that's right. But his operation's based out of Kalamata."

Tassos shut his eyes and stroked his lids with the thumb and index finger of his left hand.

"Does the silence mean you're through with me or is there something else you'd like to know?"

"Yeah, how can I make a million a year?"

"Why are you asking me? You're a Greek cop. I should be asking you."

"*Malaka.*"

"Love you too, Tassos. Bye."

Tassos put down the phone. He picked up a glass of water, took a sip, and put it down. He picked up the phone and dialed.

"Hello, my love. Is your daytime boss available?"

"I hope you're not implying I have a nighttime boss," said Maggie.

"The thought would never dare cross my mind. But we can talk about it when you get home."

"Hold on."

A few seconds later Tassos heard Andreas say, "What did you find out?"

"It seems our skunk is reeking with one hell of a motive for revenge against both Yianni's uncle and Babis."

"Meaning?"

"His name is Niko, and his father was the guy set up by Babis to take the fall planned by the uncle."

"But that was years ago. Why go after the uncle and Babis now?"

"The only one alive likely to know that answer is Niko. And I doubt he's going to tell us."

"Maybe the girl knows something?" said Andreas.

"For her sake I hope no one else thinks that way. This guy Niko sounds like the type that doesn't like loose ends. But, yeah, I agree Yianni should talk to her. At least to warn her."

"I'll talk to him about it in the morning. He sounded exhausted. Good thing she seems the type who can take care of herself."

"Just like my Maggie."

"Why do I sense you want me to tell her you said that?"

"No need to, she's probably listening in on the line."

Click.

◇◇◇

The room was hot, the cot uncomfortable, the woman beneath him. They'd been at it for hours. She'd cooked dinner, they'd eaten quickly, made love, drunk wine, made love, drunk more wine, made love.

"I'm too hot," Stella said when Kouros paused to adjust his position on the cot.

He pushed himself up and off the cot and

opened the tiny window facing the road. "Is that better?"

Stella gestured no and stood up, holding out her hand to him. "Come."

She led him from the storeroom, though the kitchen and small dining room, down into the large room, and over to the windows looking out upon the water. Two nudes covered in silver moonlight, surrounded by the sounds of the sea. Kouros kissed the nape of her neck and she turned to him. He slid his hands down her back and pulled her close. But she stepped back and he moved with her.

Her bottom brushed against a tabletop and she lay back upon it lifting her legs onto his shoulders. He leaned into her. She reached out and gripped the edge of the table with her fingers as his arms clasped her legs to his chest and his body rocked in and out.

The grunts and moans of their lovemaking filled the room.

Until the *EXPLOSION*.

Closely followed by the crash of glass bottles shattering on stone floors and an orange glow flickering into the room.

Kouros scooped Stella off the table and ran with her to the doorway. He peeked around the corner. The glow came from beyond the small dining room and past the kitchen; from a fire burning in the storeroom they'd just left.

Kouros put her down just inside the doorway. "Stay here and don't move until I wave for you," he whispered.

Barefoot and naked, Kouros crept toward the kitchen listening for any human sound. He pulled a fire extinguisher off the kitchen wall and made his way to the open storeroom. What remained of the cot and anything else that could burn was in flames. He stepped back and waved for Stella to come.

He handed her the extinguisher and whispered. "When I point to you, pull the pin, aim the nozzle at the base of the flames, and squeeze the handle." He patted her on her butt. "Then stay out of the way."

Kouros undid the lock to the outside kitchen door and pointed at Stella.

The swoosh of the extinguisher swept away the sound of the flames almost as quickly as its contents did the fire.

Kouros heard a pair of feet running toward the kitchen door. He braced himself as the door swung in and a giant of a man wearing a ballistic vest and carrying an AK-47 came storming down the steps into the kitchen. A hard palm thrust to the man's right ear jerked his head back, distracting him long enough for Kouros to strip the weapon out of his hands and drive its butt up under his chin, sending him reeling back against the open door. He stumbled off the door, aiming a wild kick at Kouros' genitals, but Kouros pivoted away and took out the man's knee with a sweeping kick that sent him crumbling to the floor. Before he could move, Kouros had the muzzle of the gun planted firmly against the downed man's right eye.

"Move and you die."

The man froze.

"Who's with you?"

"Nobody."

"I see this is set for full automatic. If I just squeeze a little harder—"

"No, no. He gone." The man spoke rapidly, in badly broken Greek. "He ran when he saw flames go out. He told me to come back."

"And do what?" Kouros pressed the muzzle harder against the man's eye.

"See if she still alive."

"Stella, turn on a light and come here."

She walked over, flicked on a light switch, and stood above the man.

Even with a gun pressed against one eye, the man struggled to see Stella's naked body.

"Do you recognize him?"

"He's one of the three who came to see me. The bear."

"Where are the mole and the skunk?" said Kouros.

"I not understand."

Kouros kicked an ammo clip on the bear's vest. "Ahh. Ukrainian. What were you trying to do here? Perhaps, make it seem like a certain somebody else did in the lady who slept in that room you just torched? How about the bottle you used for your little Molotov cocktail? I bet it traces back to the Ukraine, too."

The bear's eyes kept darting between the gun and Stella's body.

"Stella, find something to put on so that I can get our guest to concentrate on what's about to happen to his miserable life."

She opened a cabinet, pulled out a tablecloth, and wrapped herself in it.

Kouros leaned in over the bear, pressing on the gun butt as he did. "I'm really hoping you'll try something crazy right about now. It will help make up for all the bullshit paperwork and explanations I'm going have to give my boss and cousins over this."

He pulled the gun muzzle off the bear's eye. "So, like I said, where are your buddies, the two who helped *you* set Babis up to kill my uncle and then got Babis to kill himself?"

"I not murder your uncle."

"Convince me."

Silence.

"Would you like me to get my cousin Mangas in here to ask the questions?"

The bear gestured no. "Only Niko part of your uncle's murder."

"The one with the white streak in his hair?"

"Yes, Urich and I not know anything until after your uncle dead."

Urich must be the one with the mole. "Urich doesn't seem the muscle type."

"He not muscle. He pain. He make big pain. Babis know Urich. That why Niko brought him with us when we go see Babis."

"The three of you found Babis fishing?"

"Yes. Babis not hard to find."

"And you gave him the choice of suicide or Urich?"

The bear nodded. "Babis to make it look like vendetta killing, so if heart attack and car accident not believed, your cousins think old enemies kill him. But your uncle never talk of vendetta and Niko worry your cousins go after Babis and Babis name Niko. Niko say Babis weak. He afraid Babis get him in war with your uncle's family. He call Babis fuck-up."

"How did Niko get Babis to agree to kill my uncle in the first place?"

He shrugged. "I not know. What I tell you I hear Niko tell Babis when he gave Babis choice of how to die."

"Was it Niko's idea to get you to kill Stella using Ukrainian ammunition and bottles?"

He nodded again. "Yes, make look like foreigners kill her. Greeks like to blame foreigners for anything bad, he said. Especially in Mani."

"Where's Niko now?"

"Not sure. Maybe Kalamata or Pirgos. But will run soon as Urich tell him what happened tonight."

"Run where?"

Another shrug.

Kouros looked down at his naked body, then at Stella wrapped in a tablecloth. He breathed in a whiff of the gasoline scented air and thought, *Where to run indeed.*

Andreas listened quietly to Kouros' middle of the night telephone explanation of what had gone down in the taverna.

"That's it. I turned him over to the local police and they took him to Sparta. They're looking for

Urich but by the time they catch up with him he'll for sure have an alibi for tonight, plus a dozen witnesses to back him up."

Silence.

"Chief?"

Andreas cleared his throat. "You're a very lucky man."

"I know. We'd both be dead had we been in that storeroom. Burned to death."

"No, I don't mean that. I mean because I'm lying in bed beside my wife at this moment and can't say what I'm thinking."

"Oh."

"Yes, 'oh.' About the only good news so far is there wasn't a TV crew running around filming while you were wrestling ancient Olympic-style with a gorilla in between bouts of playing hide the salami with our primary witness in a murder investigation."

"It was a bear, Chief. Besides, no one's going to find out about this."

"This isn't funny, Yianni. And how's this sound for an opening question by a defense lawyer, 'Detective Kouros, what precisely were you doing at the moment my client allegedly tried to incinerate the girlfriend of the man you'd linked to the murder of your uncle?' Answer. 'Uh, standing stark naked in the middle of the deceased boyfriend's taverna banging the shit out of said girlfriend.'"

"Okay, so I fucked up."

"Congratulations, the head on top of your shoulders is finally checking back in. Try using it the next time a hot body in a murder investigation gets your other one doing your thinking."

"I get it. Honest, I get it."

"It sounds as if your uncle pulled off quite a trick."

"What trick?"

"Revenge on his own killer."

"How's that?"

"He kept the vendetta threats to himself. He told you, but no one else. When he died, no one but you knew he'd received them, so Niko-boy panicked and took out your uncle's killer."

"Not sure that will satisfy my cousins when they hear what really happened to their father. And they will find out. No way to keep this quiet."

"I agree, so let's just try to keep it contained. We don't want your cousins starting a war with everyone in Pirgos. Just limiting their attention to Niko would be acceptable."

"And how do we keep it contained?" said Kouros.

"By you telling Mangas exactly what happened, who's responsible, and that we're going to get him."

"That should be a fun conversation."

"You had your fun last night. Now it's back to work, *Detective*."

"Anything else?"

"Yes. Get the girl out of there. It's not safe for her living down there alone. Certainly not after last night's story gets around."

Kouros coughed. "I know. She knows. She's leaving today."

"Where to?"

"Athens."

"Dare I ask where she's staying?"

"Not with me. She has friends there."

"How's she getting there?"

"Don't know. Bus, probably."

"Good. Stay away. You've helped her enough."

"Is that all, Chief?"

"Yes. Just let me know when you've spoken with your cousin. I'll get GADA looking for Niko and Urich."

"Fine. Bye."

"Bye, Yia—"

Click.

Andreas stared at the phone. "He hung up on me. Can you believe it? Yianni hung up on me."

Andreas heard a ruffling beneath the sheets beside him. "Yes," came a muffled voice. Two pillows plopped onto Andreas' side of the bed, followed by a *click* and burst of light from Lila's bedside table.

"If I were Yianni, I'd have hung up on you long before he did." Lila emerged from under the covers. She pushed herself into a sitting position up against the headboard.

"What are you talking about? He was having sex with a witness in a murder investigation."

"Yeah? So discipline him. You're his boss. But don't act like you're his father. He doesn't need to hear 'Good. Stay away. You've helped her enough.'

"Men are really dumb when it comes to women. They don't even know how to deal with other *men* when it comes to women. If one man tells another man that the woman he's attracted to isn't right for him, it drives the other man to find reasons why she is, if only to justify to himself why he was attracted to her in the first place. If you let Yianni work this out on his own he'll realize she's not right for him."

"And what if he doesn't?"

"Then may they live happily ever after."

Andreas shook his head. "I'll never understand women."

Lila nodded. "I know, I'm afraid you never read beyond the chapter on animal attraction." She smiled.

Andreas waggled his eyebrows. "Is that an invitation?"

Lila laughed. "Up until your Groucho Marx moment the thought had crossed my mind. Where did you pick up that eyebrow thing?"

"It made Tassaki laugh, so I thought I'd try it on you."

"Stick to flowers, chocolates, and—" Lila jumped.

Andreas had slid his hand under the covers and swept his fingers down between her thighs.

"And this?"

Lila slid down from up against the headboard onto the bed, put her arms around his neck, and whispered in his ear, "Forget about the chocolates."

"And the flowers?"

"Negotiable."

Andreas turned off the light.

"Deal."

When Kouros was a kid, he'd had all sorts of trouble with authority figures, though he never quite put his mother in that category. After all, she was different; she was his mother. His father learned early on that the best way to get his son to go along was to play to his conscience. "All I ask, son, is that you listen to what I have to say, and if you do, I'll back you one hundred percent in your decision, even if I disagree."

That put quite a burden on a headstrong teenager, for if he did the wrong thing he'd also bring shame upon his father. When his father died, that structural discipline to his life collapsed, and but for his fathers' military buddies convincing him to join the Navy, Kouros shuddered to think about how he might have turned out.

Or if he hadn't met the Chief.

Still, it riled him to be lectured by Andreas on his personal life.

Especially when the malaka *was right.*

Chapter Twenty

The early morning autumn air had taken on a noticeable chill and it didn't feel much different inside Uncle's house. Perhaps Calliope liked it that way, or maybe it was Kouros' imagination playing off the icy expression on his cousin Mangas' face.

"Sit," said Mangas, pointing to a chair across from him at the kitchen table. "Calliope, make us coffee and leave us be."

Kouros sat.

Calliope silently brewed and served the coffee. She put out no cookies, walked to the sink, leaned back against it, and crossed her arms. "I'm not leaving. I want to hear this."

"This is not for women," barked Mangas.

"I'm your sister and your father's daughter. I'm not moving."

Mangas gritted his teeth, drew in and let out a deep breath. He stared at Kouros. "You're lucky Calliope isn't chanting a *mirologia* over your body today."

Kouros nodded. "I know."

"What were you doing there?"

"Cut the crap. You know what I was doing."

"I mean besides that. It couldn't have been just to ball the girl."

Kouros bit at his lower lip. "We thought someone besides Babis might have been involved in your father's murder. I went there to find out what she knew."

"Who's we?"

"My boss, Andreas Kaldis."

"Did you get an answer?"

Kouros picked up his coffee and took a sip. "Yes." He looked at Calliope. "May I have some cookies, please?"

Calliope stared but did not move.

"Calliope, get your cousin some damn cookies."

She uncrossed her arms, opened a cupboard, took out a tin, placed it in front of Kouros, and returned to her place at the sink. She'd offered him no plate.

"Thank you." Kouros opened the tin, took out a cookie and bit into it. "Yes, we know who did it and why he did it. Now it's just a matter of catching him. Which we will do. I promise you he'll go to prison."

Veins bulged in Mangas' neck. "I want him."

"I know you do, but we don't do things that way anymore."

"He should die."

"Greece doesn't have the death penalty."

"The Mani does."

"Ease up on the drama, cousin. We're going to get him. No need to start a war. It's only one man, not a family thing."

"*I knew it,*" Calliope screamed. Both men jerked their heads around to look at her as she shook her fists at the heavens. "That miserable bastard. I told father to have nothing to do with him. That he was not of our kind. We should have killed him when we had the chance and father would still live."

"Who are you talking about?" said Mangas.

"The devil. That Ukrainian who wanted to build his hotel on our land." She spit at the floor.

Mangas turned his head to look at Kouros. "Is that true?"

Kouros gestured no. "It's not the Ukrainian. The one who killed your father also got Babis to kill himself, and hoped to kill the girlfriend in a way that would make you think the Ukrainian was behind all three murders."

"But why?"

"To stop the hotel project."

"I can't believe all this over a golf course."

"Come on, Mangas, you had to know about the Ukrainian and his arms dealing."

"How would I?" He banged his fist on the tabletop, spilling a bit of his untouched coffee. "I didn't know anything about the hotel deal until Father told us about it here the day before he died."

Kouros looked at Calliope. "But you knew."

"Of course she knew. She lived with him."

"They would meet here. Sit at that very table. I would serve him coffee." She spit again. "Father swore me to secrecy. He knew I'd find out about his plans and the Ukrainian's background. I pleaded with him not to trust the Ukrainian." With her right hand she pulled at the left sleeve of her black mourning dress. "It *had* to be the Ukrainian."

"No, it wasn't. I'll tell you who, but first, Mangas, you must promise you'll let us handle this."

Mangas smiled. "Well, since you said he'll end up in prison, that's almost as good as turning him over to us."

"I want your word you won't go after him."

"I promise not to interfere with the judicial process."

"That does not give me comfort."

"It's all you're going to get. Otherwise I start going after every miserable son of a bitch who could have done this."

Kouros swallowed. "An arms dealer out of Kalamata called Niko set up the whole thing."

"*No*," said Calliope.

"Are you talking about one of the sons of that Pirgos guy my father arranged to take a fall in a drug bust a half-dozen years back?"

"The same. Niko's father died in prison."

"What about the other sons?"

Kouros gestured no. "Only Niko and Babis had anything to do with killing your father. No one else.'"

Calliope stood shaking her head, arms wrapped tightly across her chest. "I can't believe this. It had to involve the Ukrainian. *It just had to*."

"The Ukrainian had no reason to want your father dead. He's a big-time arms, drugs, and human trafficker who wanted the deal to go through so he could build his airstrip. He planned on using charter flights in and out of the hotel property as cover for his operations in Africa. Niko found out about it and didn't want the competition."

"Why didn't he just take out the Ukrainian?" said Mangas.

"He likely didn't want to start a war with the Ukrainian mob any more than he wanted one with you. And by using Babis to kill your father before he signed the contract he also killed the deal."

"I don't believe this." Calliope walked out of the room.

"What's wrong with her?" said Kouros.

Mangas shrugged. "I have no idea what's going through her head. She's snapped or something. She knows she can live in this house for the rest of her life but all she keeps telling me is that she doesn't want to 'profit' from Father's death. I can only guess she somehow blames herself for not convincing Father to stay out of that deal."

"But it wasn't the Ukrainian who killed your father," said Kouros.

"Calliope only sees things in black and white. Somehow Niko found out about the deal and saw it as an opportunity for getting rid of both my father and his competition. No deal, no Niko, no murder of our father."

I hate somehows, thought Kouros.

"Any leads on where Niko might be?" said Mangas.

"You know better than to expect me to answer that."

Mangas smiled, "I'm only asking because if you'd like to know I can probably tell you. Unless, of course, you'd like me to find him for you."

"Where is he?"

"His wife's family is from Gytheio. In the old days his in-laws were almost as tough a crew as our family. I'm sure if Niko tells them he's hiding from us they'll protect him."

"Why?"

"The wife's family is related to a family from here. The same family whose son was murdered by our grandfather for getting Calliope's namesake pregnant."

"You must be joking."

"Nope, it's true. A lot of intermarriage among the Mani clans. And that family link gives those folks in Gytheio another reason for protecting Niko from us. But you're a cop, and who knows, the Petropoulakis clan just might be civilized enough these days to actually cooperate with the police."

Mangas walked around the table to Kouros. "Just be careful about using your last name. Even shortened they might guess you're one of us."

Kouros shook his head. "All these Byzantine interconnections."

Mangas put his arm around Kouros' shoulder. "Cousin, welcome to the real Mani."

Gytheio's history as a hideaway dated back to the Trojan War, but it had likely been longer since an Athenian cop successfully convinced a Gytheio local to turn in a family member to the police.

Andreas hoped it would improve their chances that Niko had only married into the family.

Tassos met Andreas and Kouros just outside the entrance to the Gytheio port. He'd hitched a ride there on the boat of a buddy from Syros rather than accept Andreas' offer of a lift on the helicopter Andreas had requisitioned to get him there from Athens. The three cops drove north toward Sparta for about two miles before turning right onto a narrow blacktop road at a sign marked HOTEL PETROPOULAKIS.

"The Gytheio police chief said it's about a mile up, at the top of the hill," said Andreas. "'Just follow the olives,' he said."

Kouros took his hand from the steering wheel and waved at the gray-green groves running across Tuscan-like hills of red earth. "They're everywhere."

Near the top of the hill, Tassos leaned over the front seat and pointed left at the crumbled skeletons of a few fieldstone buildings just beyond the first line of trees. "Looks like they went down in an earthquake."

Kouros smiled. "Finally, my chance to teach the teacher. Nope, they're what are left of what the Germans bombed in 1942. This whole area was hard hit. In fact, the first villages in Greece destroyed by the Nazis in reprisal for partisan attacks on German soldiers were here. On the road north to Sparta you'll see monuments to two villages the bastards wiped out. A lot of family trees lost entire limbs to the Nazis. They did almost as much harm as the Turks, and in a hell of a lot less time."

Tassos shook his head. "And right smack dab in the middle of the Gytheio port, I saw a huge sign for Chrysi Avgi."

"They have an office there," said Kouros. "Amazing how a political party openly praising the architects of Hitler's methods for inflicting such horrific suffering upon the Greek people has such widespread support among the children and grandchildren of the Nazis' victims."

"Go figure," said Tassos.

"I'd rather not," said Andreas. "I'd prefer guys like that and Niko simply disappear."

"Well, you're about to have your chance at making part of that happen," said Kouros. Dead ahead about thirty yards off the road sat a cluster of two-, three-, and four-story brown-beige-gray stone buildings.

"I don't see a sign," said Andreas.

"This has to be the place." Kouros pulled up and parked on the dirt under a huge mulberry tree close to the edge of a flagstone patio. Off to the right, an ancient three-story structure looked as if it had caught some of those World War II bombs.

Kouros pointed across the patio at an immaculately restored four-story tower about ten yards away. "That looks like it might have been a war tower for the Petropoulakis family. There's a sign on that almond tree over by the door. Maybe it's the office."

Andreas put his hand on the car door handle. "I think we have about as much a chance of pulling this off as winning the lottery."

"I prefer betting on a sure thing," said Tassos. "Like, if we don't get him, Yianni's cousin sure as hell will. So, don't worry, be happy."

"Yeah. But there could still be other players out there. And until we know how Niko learned about the hotel deal, we won't know for sure."

"And then there's the photograph of my uncle and Stella."

"The only living soul likely to give us an answer to those questions is Niko," said Andreas.

A dark-haired man in his mid-forties, approximately Kouros' size, and wearing a blue shirt and dark pants stepped through the doorway of the tower and headed toward them.

"That looks like the guy the police chief told you to see. You'd better move," said Kouros.

Andreas and Tassos jumped out the passenger side of the car and the man veered toward them, extending his right hand as he did. "Hello, I'm

Mihalis Petropoulakis. I understand you want to speak to me."

Andreas shook Mihalis' hand. "How did you know that?"

Mihalis shrugged as he shook Tassos' hand. "Come let's sit and talk." He turned and led them past the tower to a flagstone pool area lined with oleander, mulberry, and pines overlooking more Tuscan-like hills covered in olives.

"You have a spectacular place here," said Andreas.

"Thank you. The tower was built in 1750. It's been my dream and joy to restore it." He pointed at a taverna table and three chairs in the shade of a mulberry tree at the far end of the pool. "There's no one else here." He smiled. "And I don't expect any more surprise visitors this late in the season. Why don't we sit over there?"

They did, and a young girl brought them a bottle of water and three glasses. Mihalis put his arm around her. "This is my daughter." She smiled, he patted her on the back and she left. He leaned back in his chair. "So, what can I do for you?"

"I assume you know who we are."

Mihalis nodded. "Yes, and I assume I should be honored to be visited by two such distinguished members of the police."

Andreas smiled. "As are we that you agreed to see us."

"Always happy to help out the police."

Tassos waved his hand. "I don't have as big a sweet tooth as you two guys. How about we get through this huggy-kissy time and to the point."

Mihalis smiled. "I see your reputation is well-deserved, Chief Inspector Stamatos."

"As is yours, Mihalis. All I want to know is how long after we spoke to the local cops did it take for them to tell you we were down here looking to talk to the 'appropriate' member of the Petropoulakis family about a 'confidential matter'?"

Mihalis raised and dropped his shoulders. "Is it my fault you spoke to my second cousin?"

Andreas grinned. "No problem, Mihalis. Family is family. We understand."

He nodded.

"In fact, that's why we're here. To talk to you about a member of your family."

Mihalis pointed a finger at his chest. "My family? One of my children?"

"No, not your children. But a member of your family. Or rather someone who married into your family."

"Who's that?"

Andreas said Niko's name.

Mihalis nodded. "I see. Yes, he married a second cousin."

"You have a lot of second cousins," said Tassos.

"Even more third and fourth, as I find out every time someone gets married in this town."

"We need to speak with him," said Andreas.

"I don't know where he is. Why don't I give you his wife's telephone number and you can call her?"

"I doubt she'll know where he is."

"Then how should I?"

Andreas leaned across the table toward Mihalis. "This is not good for your family."

Mihalis' eyes flared for an instant. "What is that supposed to mean?"

"Your second cousin's husband is a dirtbag," said Tassos.

"That's between him and his wife."

Andreas shook his head. "I don't think so. Not when he tried to rekindle your family's famous vendetta with another well-known Mani clan."

"What are you talking about?"

"Do you know Mangas?"

"Yes, his father just died."

"Well, this is about your second cousin's husband setting up your family to look responsible for the murder of Mangas' father."

Mihalis crossed his legs. "I still don't see what this has to do with me."

"I'm just suggesting that if Niko should happen to show up around here looking for help from his wife's family, perhaps they should know that the bastard was trying to get some of your family killed just to protect his business interests."

"Why should I believe you? And even if I did, how could I ever get my family to agree?"

"I'm sure you can figure out a way," said Andreas.

"Yeah," said Tassos. "Like getting one of your 'second cousins' on the force up in Sparta to check out what a certain currently incarcerated employee of Niko had to say about Niko's plans for your family."

Mihalis bit at his lip. "Is there anything else you'd like from me?"

"Yes, sir," Andreas handed him his card. "A call when you know where we can find Niko."

"How did it go?" asked Kouros as Andreas got back in the car.

"Not bad," said Tassos from the rear. "I think we got him thinking about his cousin's choice in husbands."

"Does he know where Niko is?"

Andreas shook his head. "No way to tell. But if he wants to find him, he will." Andreas pointed toward the road. "Let's get out of here before he starts wondering what we're gabbing about."

Kouros started the engine, turned around and started back down the hill toward the main road leading back to the port.

"In the old days, if a family thought they had a traitor in its midst they'd take care of him themselves," said Tassos.

"We don't want that," said Kouros.

"I know," said Tassos.

"Let's just hope they're more civilized these days," said Kouros.

"It will be close," said Andreas. "Not sure it mattered keeping you and the Kouros name out of this, but no reason not to follow your cousin's advice."

"Yeah, Niko's wife might make a big fuss about turning her husband over to Yianni's cousins, but might not if it's to the police," said Tassos.

"Why's that?" asked Andreas.

"My buddy's boat got me into Gytheio early and I had some time to kill waiting for you guys to pick me up, so I put in a call to an acquaintance of Niko's. I'd put him away a few years back for drug running into Mykonos but he got out early because of prison overcrowding. I asked him what he knew about Niko."

"Why would he talk to you?" said Kouros.

"Because when I was asked for my opinion on whether or not he should be released early, I didn't object. He knew he owed me."

"Strange you'd be so nice to a drug dealer," said Andreas.

"It was either he or a lot worse types getting out. Besides, if I hadn't, we wouldn't know what a true dirtbag we're dealing with."

"So tell me, already," said Kouros.

"Niko has an irresistible appetite for very young girls and his wife is about fed up with him."

"How young?"

"Very. But he only goes after foreign girls. That way the locals don't worry about their own children."

"Nice understanding folks up in his neighborhood," said Andreas.

"He's a big customer of the sex traffickers."

"Do you think she's pissed enough to turn on him?" said Kouros.

"Let's hope she's just pissed enough not to object to us busting him."

"I think it's time for lunch," said Andreas.

"Took the words right out of my mouth," said Tassos.

Kouros smiled. "No doubt to make room for a lot of other things."

Chapter Twenty-one

They parked at the southern end of the harbor close to port police headquarters and strolled beside a seemingly endless row of two- and three-story buildings painted various shades of ochre. Tavernas, bars, hotels, and rooms-to-let lined the landside of the harbor-front road for as far as the eye could see.

"My rule is to try the busiest taverna," said Tassos.

"But not if there's a hustler outside pulling in tourists," said Kouros.

"I accept that modification."

"I prefer the one recommended by the harbormaster. It's up there on the left."

"You take away all the fun of the hunt," said Tassos.

"Don't worry, I'm paying."

"Do I have to remind you again that we're cops and cops—"

"Don't pay." Andreas nodded. "But today we're trying to be inconspicuous."

"Fine, pay."

"Here we are," said Andreas.

They entered the sort of place where all you'd remember about the décor would be the general concept of chairs, tables, windows, and a kitchen somewhere out back, but you'd never forget the food.

Fresh made *taramasalata, melitzanosalata*, and *skordalia*. *Rigonada* of the Cretan sort made with nuts, tomato, and feta, locally grown fried potatoes, Greek salad with caperberries, grilled calamari, sardines, and local sausage. All accompanied by locally grown and produced olive oil and Peloponnesian wine. Yoghurt with local honey and handmade spoon sweets made from reduced cherries and apricots would come last.

For twenty minutes everyone concentrated on the food and kept the conversation to small talk.

"Any word from Stella?" asked Andreas.

"As far as I know she's taken off for Athens."

"Can't blame her," said Tassos spearing a tiny deep-fried fish with his fork. "Things don't seem too hospitable for her down in that part of Greece. Which brings me around to asking what you guys have in mind if we actually get a lead on Niko's whereabouts?"

"Catch him," said Andreas.

"And then what?"

"Get him to talk," said Kouros.

"How do you plan on doing that?"

"Threatening him with a visit from my cousin ought to work."

Tassos shook his head. "I don't think so. Not with this guy. He's got his own family looking out for him. Besides, he had to know there was a risk of going to war with your uncle's family when he decided to go after him. But he still did it. He must have something up his sleeve. Or else he's expecting a very sweet deal to talk."

"He's not going to get one," said Kouros.

Tassos rocked his head from side to side. "Unless he's offered something better than taking his chances at trial, I don't think Niko cooperates. Let's not forget, the only firsthand testimony we have directly tying Niko to a possible murder charge is the word of that muscle guy who tried torching Yianni. Assuming we find Urich and he corroborates his accomplice's story, it's *still* going to be tough getting a murder conviction in connection with Babis' death without physical evidence of more than 'talk' on Niko's part getting Babis to take his own life.

"As for Niko implicating himself in the uncle's murder with what he said to Babis in front of those two guys, to me that's an even tougher case. At least with Babis' death we have Niko at the scene, standing around watching it happen. We have no physical evidence whatsoever directly tying Niko to your uncle's murder."

Tassos picked up another two *gavros* with his fingers. "It's going to be a tough sell to the court on the evidence we have. My guess is the current odds favor him walking."

"He won't live long if he does," said Kouros.

"Who's to say? As long as he's breathing he's ahead of the game. No telling what might happen. He could disappear and never be heard from again. It's romantic to think vengeance will hunt down the wicked no matter where, no matter how long it takes, but most often things don't turn out that way. Even in the Mani, memories fade, life events intervene."

"Not with my cousins."

"What I think Tassos is trying to say is that catching Niko may not give us the answers we're looking for."

Tassos nodded. "Talk only implicates him, and without a deal, why say a word?"

"I've lost my appetite," said Kouros.

"My God, don't do that," said Tassos. "I've given you the worst possible scenario. Speculation on what's going through a wanted man's mind. Thoughts of freedom and escape are the most common, but until we find this guy we don't know what makes him tick."

"Hard to imagine that a little two-bit shit like that could have brought down my uncle."

"Aye, there's the rub," said Tassos. "Getting the mouse that roared to talk."

Andreas leaned forward in his chair. "Not sure If I should thank you, Hamlet, or Peter Sellers, but you just gave me an idea on how we might get this guy to talk if we ever find him."

"What do you have in mind?" asked Kouros.

"It's percolating but about all I can say at this point is ''tis a consummation devoutly to be wish'd.'"

Kouros picked up a piece of *spanakopita* and took a bite. "I wish you two would stop."

"At least it got you eating again," said Tassos.

Andreas' phone on the table rang. The screen read BLOCKED CALLER. He picked it up. "Kaldis here."

He listened for twenty seconds before putting it back down on the table. "Well, we have an address for Niko."

"Where?" said Kouros.

"On Kranae, wherever that is."

Kouros turned and pointed off to the right. "You get there across that narrow, concrete causeway. It's an arrow-shape island two hundred yards offshore. The whole island's only about five hundred yards long, east to west, and one hundred yards wide at the broadest point."

"What's on it?" asked Andreas.

"Mostly dirt, rocks, and pine trees. There aren't many places to hide. It's got a lighthouse at the far end, a church on this end, and a battle tower and connected mansion from the early 1800s in the middle. The tower's been renovated and expanded to house the Historical and Cultural Museum of the Mani. And, aside from a couple of fishing shacks just beyond the church, a restaurant and taverna on the island end of the causeway, that's it."

"How do you know all this stuff?" said Andreas.

"My mother makes me take her to the museum practically every time we're down here."

"Whoever called you must be pulling your leg," said Tassos.

"We'll just have to wait until tomorrow to find out."

"Why's that?"

"Because someone other than Mihalis Petropoulakis just said to me, 'Niko will meet you at the tower on Kranae at ten tomorrow morning, right after it opens.'"

"He *wants* to meet with us?" said Kouros.

Andreas nodded. "Yes. But to be precise he also said, 'And please be sure to bring along that cousin with the shortened last name who works with you.'"

By nine the next morning Kouros and Andreas sat in a rental car off the edge of a gravel and dirt parking lot watching the seaside entrance to the museum.

Andreas lifted a two-way radio to his lips. "Anything yet?"

"Nope," said Tassos. "What about you?"

"Not a thing here, but we're hemmed in by pine trees. No telling who might be out by the lighthouse or back inside the church."

"Or on a boat tied up offshore," said Tassos.

"I think we'll take a drive around just to see if we're as alone as it looks. Give us a shout if anyone comes over the causeway."

"Will do."

They drove toward the lighthouse at the end of the island. Aside from rocks, trees, and a few crumbling sheds within a fenced in area securing the lighthouse, this part of the island offered no place to hide. The lighthouse doors and windows stood securely locked and showed no signs of forced entry.

Andreas turned the car around, drove past the museum, and parked thirty yards before a bright-white church with a terra-cotta-tiled dome roof. Next to the car, a half-dozen small, weather-beaten fishing boats lay scattered on the ground or propped up on pieces of scrap wood. Beyond the boats, down by the water, two tiny shacks looked in worse shape than the boats. They found no one in the shacks or boats.

The restaurant at the end of the causeway had a sign marked CLOSED, and none of the five men in the taverna next to it came close to matching Niko's description. Andreas and Kouros walked to the church and tried the front door. Locked.

"A lot of people come here to get married because this island is where Paris and Helen spent their first night together before sailing off to Troy."

Andreas smiled. "I sure hope things end up better for the newlyweds than it did for those two."

They turned and stared across the water toward the harbor-side road in Gytheio. That got them a quick wave from Tassos sitting in a parked car on the other side of the causeway.

By nine-thirty Andreas and Kouros were back in their spot by the entrance to the museum.

Twenty minutes passed, filled with small talk of the anxious sort cops do while waiting for all hell to break loose. Nothing serious about family or futures, just silly things to keep their minds off what might erupt at any second.

Tassos' voice barked through the two-way. "You've got company coming. A van full of tourists."

"He might be using that as cover." said Kouros.

"Anything's possible," said Andreas.

"You'd have thought our records guys could have found a photo of him," said Kouros.

"Never got arrested and keeps himself out of the papers. Let's just hope he hasn't dyed his hair."

They waited for the van to make it across the causeway and the additional three hundred yards to the museum parking lot.

"Motorbike coming now. It might be our guy," said Tassos.

"How can you tell?" asked Andreas.

"He's wearing a helmet, and since practically no one in Greece wears one, it makes me think our guy is trying to hide something."

Andreas smiled. "We'll keep an eye out for him."

They watched the motorcycle overtake the van just beyond the church, pull into the lot, and park at the head of the path that ran past them up to the museum entrance. The driver wore jeans, work boots, a light blue jacket and a full-face black helmet. He got off the bike and walked by them, up to the museum's front door without taking off his helmet.

"He must like his helmet a lot," said Kouros.

"Careful, Yianni, he's reaching in his jacket pocket for something."

Both cops pulled their guns and opened their car doors slightly in case they had to move quickly.

The driver never turned around. Just fiddled with the front door until it opened and went inside.

Andreas let out a breath. "He was reaching for keys." He spoke into the two-way. "False alarm. It was a museum employee opening up the place."

"First time I've been wrong today," said Tassos.

Andreas and Kouros watched a small group of foreign tourists unload from the van and head toward the front door.

"They look like pensioners from Germany," said Andreas to Tassos.

"They're about the only pensioners with money these days," said Tassos.

"Unless the bus driver's our guy, I'd say Niko's late for our appointment." Kouros pointed at his watch. "It's ten after."

"Tassos, we're going inside. Just in case Niko got here before we did. Let us know if more company shows up."

"Be careful."

Andreas and Kouros holstered their guns as they got out of the car. They scanned the windows of the museum buildings as they hurried along the stone path, down and up steps toward the entrance.

Inside, an elderly couple stood reading a poster on a wall next to a desk with a handwritten sign, TICKETS HERE. A pockmarked man wearing a black baseball cap marked MANI in white letters sat behind the desk in front of a door marked OFFICE.

"May I help you?" said the man in the hat.

Andreas walked over to him. "Yes, sir. My friend and I were supposed to meet someone here at ten."

"There are about a dozen visitors inside. Maybe your friend's in there."

Andreas shook his head. "No, we're looking for someone younger. In his forties. With a line of white hair down the middle of his head."

As they spoke a tourist couple moved in front of Andreas. "We'll take the senior special," said the woman, pointing for the man with her to get something out of his belly bag. "My husband has proof of our age." She spoke English with a heavy German accent.

The man in the hat smiled. "That won't be necessary. I believe you." He handed them two tickets, the couple paid, and went inside.

"Sorry about that, gentlemen."

"No problem," said Andreas.

"So, you're looking for a man with a silver streak in his hair?"

"White. Like a skunk," said Kouros.

The man nodded. "I see. You mean like this?" and he pulled off his hat. "You're late, gentlemen."

Andreas hoped he didn't look as startled as he felt. "That was you in the motorcycle helmet?"

"Yes, officer. It's the law to wear a helmet, and I obey the law."

"It's *Chief Inspector* Kaldis, and this is Detective Kouros."

"Pleased to meet you," said Niko extending his right hand.

Neither man took it.

"You know that whatever you say will be used against you?" said Kouros.

"Of course, but I have nothing to hide. Though I do think we should move into the office for this discussion rather than having it in front of the tourists. Some of them may understand Greek."

Kouros went behind the desk, opened the door, and looked inside. He nodded to Andreas.

Andreas gestured for Niko to get up.

Niko stood as tall as Andreas, but much slimmer in a sinewy, not lanky, way. Andreas followed Niko inside the office and closed the door behind them, never taking his eyes off Niko for a second.

Kouros pulled up a metal folding chair. "Sit."

Niko did. Andreas and Kouros did not.

"We're here to arrest you in connection with

the murder of two men and the attempted murder of two others."

"Including me," said Kouros.

"I assumed that's why you were looking for me. But for the life of me I can't figure out why. So, I asked one of my cousins to allow me to take his place here as a volunteer this morning. I wanted the chance for us to talk. To show you that everything I've done was an attempt at preventing harm from coming to anyone. "

"You have a strange way of doing that," said Kouros.

"Not sure what you mean."

"You and your buddies talked your family's old friend Babis into killing himself," said Kouros.

"Oh yes, poor, Babis. I tried my best to convince him not to take his own life, but he was so wracked with guilt at what he'd done to your poor uncle that I just couldn't talk him out of it. And, yes, perhaps the fact that he'd also betrayed my father made him feel doubly guilty. But I was there simply to end any further bloodshed in the Mani."

"Yeah, right. Too bad your buddy we arrested tells a different story. He has you pissed at Babis for screwing up my uncle's murder and leaving you exposed as his accomplice."

"I don't know what he told you, but his Greek isn't very good and he must have misheard. I went there to tell Babis he was crazy to have killed your uncle. That it would never get him back in the good graces of my family. Yes, I did for a moment lose my temper with him, but that was when he said he'd tried to make it look like part of an old family vendetta. I called him a 'fuck-up' because the idiot was threatening to get my wife's family involved in his crazy twisted thinking. And, yes, I might have said I'd see that he died far more painfully than he could ever imagine if he got my wife's family involved in his craziness. But I certainly wasn't suggesting he take his own life."

"Nice try," said Kouros, "but how would you know Babis murdered my uncle if you weren't involved? Only the chief and I had any evidence of that."

"I'm afraid I do have the advantage on you, Detective. You see, I knew long before it happened that someone wanted Babis to kill your uncle. So when he turned up dead I knew who must have done it."

For a second time in minutes Niko had Andreas struggling not to seem startled. He could see that Kouros felt the same. "And you did nothing to stop it?"

Niko shrugged. "What could I do? Someone came to me and asked if I thought I could get Babis to do a job. When I asked what kind of 'job' and was told it was to kill your uncle, I passed. The plan was well thought-out but required Babis to think all would be forgiven by my family if he took revenge on the man who'd set my father up to die in prison. I tried discouraging the idea by saying I doubted that would get Babis to turn on your uncle. After all, your uncle had been protecting him for all these years, so what reason would Babis possibly have for betraying him now? Besides, Babis didn't need my family's forgiveness as long as he had your uncle's protection."

Niko ran his fingers through his hair and stretched. "That's when I was shown a photograph of your uncle and Babis' girlfriend coming out of a hotel room together. Whoever planned this knew how to push Babis' buttons. But I certainly wasn't going to be the one to do the pushing."

"An even better story than before," said Kouros. "But why did they come to you and not go to Babis directly?"

"At first I thought because Babis would insist on direct assurances from my family that we wouldn't come after him once his protector was dead. But then I realized my family's guarantee didn't really matter, because if the kill went off as planned, he'd still not lose the protection of your uncle's family. What really mattered was that Babis never learn who was behind the hit. I thought that if I refused to act as middleman the plan could not possibly go forward. Obviously, I was wrong."

"Okay, I'll bite," said Andreas. "Who was your mysterious visitor with the plan and photograph?"

Niko stared into Andreas' eyes. "His cousin." He switched his stare to Kouros. "Your uncle's daughter, Calliope."

"You lying shit," said Kouros moving toward Niko.

Andreas raised his hand. "Easy, Yianni."

Niko raised both hands in a gesture of innocence. "I understand how you feel, Detective. But please, answer this question for me. How would I possibly know about that photograph if someone hadn't given it to me? And if you want to know who that someone was, ask the photographer."

"Do you have a name for this photographer?" said Andreas.

"No."

"I didn't think you would," said Kouros.

"But I have a description. Your cousin told me it was a legitimate photo taken by an old friend of hers. A priest. And if you can't trust a priest, who can you trust?" Niko crossed himself.

"Do you have anything else to say?" said Andreas.

"I've told you all that I know, freely and with a clear conscience. And I wanted you here," he said to Kouros, "so that you could share with your family all that I've told you. After all, I don't want there to be any misunderstandings on the part of your family that could have them thinking I had anything to do with their terrible tragedy. We all know how violent your family can be if they feel dishonored."

Andreas looked at Kouros. "Did you get the message?"

"Yes."

"Fine. Now cuff the bastard and let's get him out of here."

After briefing Tassos on their conversation with Niko, Andreas and Kouros hauled Niko up to Sparta and deposited him with the local police. They agreed to meet back in Gytheio in about four hours. Tassos said not to worry. He'd hang out with his friend who'd brought him there from Syros.

Niko didn't say much on the ride up. Nor did Andreas and Kouros. And at his booking Niko said little more than, "I want to see my lawyer." Everyone knew that as soon as he went before a judge he'd be released from jail while awaiting trial. Still, Andreas and Kouros stayed around to make sure all legal formalities were followed. No way they'd let a convenient official screw-up destroy this prosecution, no matter how weak it might now seem.

Andreas drove Kouros back to Gytheio. "He sure as hell gave us a lot to think about."

"Sociopaths can be very creative," said Kouros.

"Yes, but even a sociopath would have a hard time coming up with a story like that and expect it to fly. I thought the way to make him talk when we found him was to play up to his ego. Hardly needed to do that."

"He obviously knew everything the bear told us, and worked the details into his alibi story."

"Yeah, I'm sure he got the details from the bear's lawyer. No doubt Niko's paying him. But there is that other point…"

"I know. Calliope."

"Quite a story."

"I can't believe she had anything to do with her father's murder. No, not 'can't.' I *will never* believe that she did."

"Okay, I understand your reaction. But there is that part about the priest and the photograph. Hard to imagine he'd make that up since it's so easy to verify."

"Not so easy. The priest won't talk about anything having to do with my cousin. He even denied telling her about seeing her father and Stella together at that hotel."

"I know, but maybe this time things will be different."

"What do you mean, 'this time'?"

"While you were busy helping out with the paperwork on Niko, Tassos called me. His buddy who brought him to Gytheio is from one of those old Syros families that once did a lot of business with folks in Gerolimenas. Tassos wanted to know if I thought it okay to ask him if he knew the priest. I said, 'yes,' and it turns out he knows the mother even better. So, Tassos and his friend are on their way down to see the mother and the son."

"Why did you wait until now to tell me?"

"Because I'd rather you threw a fit alone with me in the car than in front of our suspect."

"Fuck you."

"Finished?"

"For now."

Chapter Twenty-two

The mother's apartment sat directly above the taverna, reached by a set of stairs inside a nondescript painted wooden door on the side of the building. At the top of the stairs stood a finely finished oak door with two hand-etched glass panes backed by a lace curtain on the inside.

Tassos and his friend Stavros showed up at the mother's door with a large box of sweets, flowers, and a bottle of seven-star Metaxa brandy. Her surprise at two unexpected visitors lasted only until she recognized Stavros. She insisted on cooking while they sat at her kitchen table, reminiscing about the old days and common friends. Tassos knew all her friends from Syros, and added some details about a few that surprised even Stavros.

Two hours into the visit, and a third of the way into the Metaxa, Tassos nodded at Stavros.

"*Keria*, I keep forgetting to ask. How is your son?"

"Ah, my joy. He is a man of the cloth. His prayers will surely send my soul straight to heaven."

Tassos leaned across the table and patted her arm. "I'm sure, *keria,* that no prayers will be needed to assure your place in heaven. Not after contributing your only son to the Lord's work."

She smiled and raised her glass. "But it doesn't hurt to have a friend on the inside. To my son, Father Carlos."

"To Father Carlos," the two men said raising their glasses.

"So sorry I won't have the chance to meet him," said Tassos.

"Why, of course you will." She picked up a mobile phone from the table, pressed a speed dial button, and waited. "No answer." She dialed a second number. "I'll try the taverna downstairs." She waited for an answer. "Costas. Have you seen my son?"

Pause.

"Then find him."

Pause.

"I don't care if you're busy, I want to see him *now*. Find him and tell him to come home immediately." She hung up without saying good-bye.

She smiled at the two men staring at her. "It pays be the taverna's landlord."

Five minutes later the front door swung opened and in hurried Carlos, scruffier than Kouros had described but just as bleary-eyed. On seeing the two men he turned quickly and headed back toward the door.

"Where are you going?" his mother said, and without waiting for an answer added, "come here, I want you to meet some old friends."

Carlos stopped, walked to the kitchen doorway, and stood acknowledging the men with a nod.

She pointed with a smile in her son's direction. "This is my boy, Father Carlos. Spiritual leader of Gerolimenas."

Carlos looked down at his dust-covered cowboy boots.

Tassos stood up, walked over to him, and extended his hand. "Hello, Father. My name is Tassos and my friend over there is Stavros. It is an honor to meet you."

Carlos hurriedly shook Tassos' hand. "Sorry, gentlemen, but I must run."

Tassos wrapped his arm around Carlos' shoulders. "I won't hear of it. Not after all the wonderful things your mother's been saying about you. I insist you sit with us for at least a few moments." He steered him over to a place at the table between his chair and Stavros.

Carlos' mother leaned across Stavros and patted her son's arm. "Why, of course my boy can spare some time for friends of his mother."

Had he been a deer he'd have bolted for the door. Tassos handed him a glass of brandy, and raising his own, "To your mother. A great lady."

Carlos mumbled some words and downed his drink without attempting to touch the others' glasses.

Tassos waited until he'd finished the drink. "I've always admired those who follow your calling, Father. So many souls lying bare to you the deepest of their despair. It takes a special sort of person to comfort their pain."

Carlos nodded, looking at the Metaxa bottle as he did.

"You must meet a lot of people here in the summers." Tassos picked up the brandy bottle. He waved it in the direction of the wall of photographs behind his mother. "And famous people, too. I recognize some from the pictures. Did you take them?"

"Yes, he takes a lot of photographs," said his mother. "It's his hobby."

"Is that so?" said Tassos moving to pour

brandy into Carlos' glass. When Carlos didn't answer, Tassos held off on pouring.

"Yes," said Carlos, "ever since I was a boy, I've loved taking photographs. It captures a moment that may or may not reflect a glimpse of the subject's soul, but it's as close as we can get to such revelations here on Earth."

Tassos filled Carlos' glass. "Very well said, Father."

"The camera makes life so much simpler, focused, understandable. At least for that instant it captures."

Tassos nodded. "I understand your thinking. I assume you capture candid moments."

"I try."

Tassos waved at the wall. "From what I see, I'd say you've been very successful. You must use a telephoto lens."

He nodded, and drank a bit of the brandy. "You capture reality best when the subject doesn't realize there's a camera watching."

Tassos stood up and walked over to the wall of photos. "I'm really impressed. You have a unique style in the way you place the subjects within the frame. Slightly slanted off the horizon."

"It's my trademark."

Tassos pointed at one photo. "This one reminds me of a photo I saw just the other day. In fact, I was told it was taken in this very port a few weeks ago. Perhaps you took it?"

"I doubt it. I don't sell my photographs."

Tassos nodded. "Well, it sure looks like one of yours. Maybe you gave it away?"

Carlos gestured no. "I don't do that either. I take them only for myself." He held the glass to his lips.

"And for your mother," she added with a smile.

Carlos forced a smile and began to drink.

"It was a photo of a young woman and an older man coming out of a room in that hotel across the harbor."

Carlos choked on the brandy.

"Are you all right?" said Tassos.

"Yes, yes." He put down the glass. "I really must run."

"I think the name of the woman in the photo was Stella."

Carlos stood up.

"The woman who gave me the photo," continued Tassos, "said the man in the picture was her father and that a friend of hers had taken it."

Carlos stared at Tassos.

"Please, Father, sit. I really need your help with this."

Carlos hesitated but sat.

"I can't remember the man's name, but I think his surname started with a K."

Tassos looked at Carlos' mother. "You know how hard it sometimes is at our age to remember names."

She nodded.

"It's going to drive me absolutely crazy if I can't remember the name of the man and his daughter. This getting old can be really discouraging at times." He smacked his right hand on his thigh. "I think the photo might be in my car. With your permission, *keria*, I'll run down to check, and if it is, perhaps you or your son will recognize the man in the photo."

"Of course. Go. Carlos and I will do whatever we can to help you."

Tassos thanked her and left. He waited downstairs outside the door and counted. At fifteen he heard footsteps racing down the stairs, at eighteen he caught Carlos coming out the front door on the fly.

"Whoa there, Father. What's the hurry?"

"I've got to be somewhere."

"I'm sure, but first we have to clear up that little matter of the photo we both know you took."

"I don't know what you're talking about."

"Why does everybody always say that when they know precisely what I'm talking about?" Tassos shook his head. "I know you want to protect your friend, Calliope, but if I have to go upstairs and get your mother all worked up over this, a certain mutual acquaintance has assured me it will turn your idyllic home life into hell."

Carlos looked up at the sky.

"If you're looking up there for an answer, that's fine with me. But, please, understand I'm really trying to help you out from down here, Father. I don't want to create more grief for you with your mother over Calliope and her father. All I want to know is why you took the photograph."

Carlos looked down at the ground. "I told Calliope I'd seen her father with the woman from the taverna going into the hotel, and she asked me to take a photo of them if I ever saw them together again."

"And did you?"

"Yes."

"And what did you do with the photograph?"

"I gave it to her."

"When?"

"A week and a half or so before her father died."

"To anyone else?"

"No."

"Are you certain?"

"Positive."

"How can you be sure?"

"Because I emailed the photo to Calliope and deleted it from my camera and computer."

"Why did you do that?"

"My mother's always snooping around my things. If you haven't noticed, she lives her life through me. I didn't want her finding a photo of Calliope's father. As our 'mutual acquaintance' no doubt told you, Mother doesn't approve of my having anything to do with Calliope or her family."

"How old are you?"

"I have to run."

Tassos paused. "Fine, but not too far. And do yourself a favor. Don't tell Calliope about our conversation. It won't help her, and definitely won't help you."

"Why?"

"Just trust me on that. For the time being just stick to praying for a poor soul in dire need of every bit of God's support you can muster."

"Who's that?"

Tassos patted him on the shoulder.

"The woman you love."

Tassos' friend Stavros turned into a gasoline station between Gerolimenas and Vathia, just beyond a small sign marked LAST GAS STATION IN EUROPE.

"Thanks, Stavros. I owe you."

"Are you sure you don't want me to hang around? I'm in no hurry."

"That's because you left the force."

"I prefer trolling for fish than bad guys."

"That's why I want you to get back to Gytheio, on your boat, and out of here. I'll see you on Syros." He pointed at a car pulling in. "Here come Andreas and Yianni, right on time." Tassos smacked Stavros on the arm. "Be safe, my friend."

Tassos got out of the rental car and into the backseat of the unmarked police car.

Kouros turned around in the front passenger seat and pointed back at the sign. "The owner has a sense of humor."

"I hope you'll still have one after you hear what I have to say."

"That bad?" said Andreas.

Tassos nodded. "Carlos took the photograph."

"We already guessed that," said Kouros.

Tassos cleared his throat. "Because your cousin Calliope asked him to. And she had the only copy. Looks like she's the only one who could have given it to Niko."

Kouros gritted his teeth. "*Fuck,*" and pounded his fists twice on the top of the dashboard.

Andreas made a calming motion with his hands and waited for Kouros to calm down. "I know this looks very bad."

"I still can't believe it," said Kouros. He spun his head around and looked at Tassos. "Are you sure?"

Tassos nodded. "I'm afraid I am."

"There could be other explanations," said Andreas.

"Like what?" asked Kouros.

"Like I don't know," said Andreas. "But there's one person who would know."

"Calliope?" said Kouros.

Andreas nodded. "But how to approach her? If she ordered the hit on her father, she's off the charts crazy. No telling how she'll react."

"Maybe we should first speak to Mangas?" said Tassos

"Wow, I don't even want to think of the sort of reaction that will trigger," said Kouros

"Nuclear?" said Andreas.

"At least. Even if she didn't order the hit, he'll never forgive her for whatever part she played in the murder. Nor do I see him showing much compassion toward Father Carlos."

"And let's not forget the messenger who blew his happy family apart," said Andreas

Kouros stared out the side window. "This most definitely will wear out my welcome in the Mani."

Tassos caught Andreas' eye as he said, "It's your family. What do you want us to do?"

Kouros scratched his head. "Talk to her. Now. Without her brother. If she did it, we'll take her in. Let the chips fall where they may."

Andreas gave a quick glance at Tassos. "Are you sure that's what you want to do?"

"Yes. I don't believe she did it, but if she did…" he shook his head.

Tassos looked at his watch. "It's after seven."

Kouros looked straight ahead. "She's probably preparing dinner."

"Alone?" asked Andreas.

"I certainly hope so."

Andreas pulled out of the last gas station in Europe and headed south, past another sign marked THIS WAY TO THE ENTRANCE TO HADES.

The sun had set by the time Kouros knocked on his uncle's front door. A minute later Calliope opened it, wearing a white butcher's apron over a black skirt and blouse.

"Ah, I see you've decided to become a regular

visitor to our humble part of the Mani, cousin."
She waved. "Please, come in. Your friends, too."

"I work with these men."

"My name is Andreas Kaldis. My condolences on your loss."

"*Ta sillipitiria mou*. I'm Tassos Stamatos."

"Thank you. Nice to meet you. If you'll excuse me for five minutes, I'm right in the middle of cooking." She pointed to the living room. "Please, make yourselves comfortable. Yianni knows where the drinks are if you'd like something."

"Thank you," the three said in unison.

She hurried off into the kitchen.

The men looked at each other, went into the living room, and took care to sit so that each faced a different direction from the others. No one said a word. They listened to Calliope working in the kitchen.

Five minutes passed. Ten minutes. Another five.

"Sorry to have taken so long." Calliope swung into the room carrying a large tray filled with plates of food. Kouros jumped up to take the tray from her and placed it on a coffee table in front of the couch.

"Since I was already cooking for myself I decided why not make enough for everyone?"

"That's very thoughtful, but we're really not hungry," said Kouros.

"Since when has that excuse ever worked on a Greek woman serving you food?"

Tassos smiled. "It's never worked for me." He picked up a fork, latched onto a stuffed grape leaf, and took a bite. "Hmmm, this could be the best *dolmadakia* I've ever tasted."

"Flatterer," she said smiling. "So, have another."

"I will."

"Cousin, we're here to talk to you about something very serious."

"I'm not surprised. This house isn't exactly the place I'd expect you to bring your friends for a good time in the Mani."

"Come, sit down. Please." Andreas pointed to a place on the couch across from him and next to Kouros. He waited until she'd sat. "It's about your father's murder."

"Have you caught that bastard Niko?"

Andreas nodded. "Yes. We found him with your brother's help."

"Good. May he rot in hell."

"He's told us quite a story." Tassos shifted in his chair. "He said that you're the one who arranged for Babis to kill your father."

"*That lying bastard.*"

"Calliope," said Kouros quietly. "He said you gave him a photograph of Uncle and Stella."

She dropped her head and clasped her hands together. "I guess I could deny that and there would be no way of proving that I did." She paused for a moment and looked up. "But I did give it to him."

Kouros pressed the fingers of his right hand tightly against his forehead. "How could you have done this to your father? To your family?"

Calliope looked at Kouros. "I didn't do it to hurt Father. I did it to help him. To save him. It was my duty."

Andreas moved forward in his seat and braced himself to react should she make any sudden move.

Tassos scanned the room to make sure they were alone.

"What are saying?" asked Kouros. "That you arranged for your father to be murdered to save him? Are you crazy?"

She looked down at her hands. "I am the Maniot woman of this family. Not my aunt or sister who live in Athens. I am responsible for deciding who risks death to save our family. If my plan had been followed, no one would have died. Certainly not father. Babis' target was the Ukrainian."

"The Ukrainian in the land deal with your father?" said Andreas.

She nodded. "He would destroy our family's

legacy. We've lived on this land for centuries. He wanted to destroy it to run his guns. His drugs. His women. Father's plan for assuring peace in our family came at too great a cost."

"And you had a plan to ruin the deal?" said Andreas.

She swallowed. "Yes. Convince the Ukrainian that he and his project were not welcome in the Mani. Warn him that great harm would come to him if he persisted. But I could not carry out my plan myself. I needed help, yet I knew if I went to anyone connected to my father they would tell him of it immediately."

"And so?" said Tassos.

"Father always said you could deal with your worst enemies as long as they saw profit in it. So I thought, who would never speak to my father but would want to stop the Ukrainian as much as I? The obvious answer was Niko, the Ukrainian's competitor in the arms business."

"How did you know these things?" said Tassos.

"I run this house. What *don't* I know?"

"How did you connect with Niko?" said Kouros.

"A friend's cousin is married to Niko. I arranged for the friend to set up a meeting with him in Kalamata. I went there and told him I had valuable information helpful to his business. He asked what I wanted in return and I said 'elimination of our mutual problem.' I told him my plan. He said he'd think about it and get back to me."

Kouros drew in and let out a breath.

"Two days later he called and we met again. He said he liked my plan, but there was a problem. If he were seen to have played a hand in it he'd be at war with both the Ukrainian and my father. That's when he proposed Babis. He said Babis' relationship with my father gave him the best chance of getting close enough to the Ukrainian to pass along the threat, and with the bad blood between Babis and Niko's family no one would think Babis was tied to Niko should Babis ever be discovered as behind the threats."

"The threats were intended for the Ukrainian?" asked Kouros.

"That was my plan." She bowed her head. "But Niko said there was no way he could think of to get Babis to betray my father. Otherwise he and his family would have tried it long ago."

She lifted her head and rubbed at her eyes with the palms of her hands. "I should have realized what that meant, but didn't. I was obsessed with getting rid of the Ukrainian. And when a few days later Carlos called to say he'd seen my father with Stella, I took it as a sign from above that Babis had been chosen to rid my family of the Ukrainian." She crossed herself three times.

"That's when I hit upon the idea of using a photograph of my father and Stella to enrage Babis. Inspire him to take revenge on my father by helping to destroy my father's plans with the Ukrainian. The obvious twist never occurred to me. All Niko had to do was convince Babis to kill my father instead of frightening the Ukrainian and he'd have it all— the deal dead and revenge on my father. He must have promised Babis forgiveness from his family if Babis made my father's death look like an accident or, at worst, that someone else was responsible. But I never imagined he would kill my father. *Never.*"

"What about killing the Ukrainian? Did you ever imagine that?" said Tassos.

She began to sob. "When Father died I was certain he'd been killed by the Ukrainian. That he'd somehow learned of the plot against him, thought my father was behind it, and killed him for it. I thought it was all my fault."

Her sobs turned to tears and she cried for several minutes.

No one made a move to comfort her.

She looked up. "It *was* my fault. I need to die."

Tassos waited until her eyes caught his. "No, my dear, what you need is serious psychiatric help."

◇◇◇

That night they drove Calliope to Sparta. They didn't want to arrest her, nor did they want her wandering free, if only to protect her from herself. They compromised on a charge that didn't implicate Calliope in her father's murder, but kept her under a twenty-four-hour suicide watch while awaiting psychiatric evaluation.

Kouros called Mangas to tell him his sister was on the verge of a nervous breakdown, and for her own good he'd taken her to Sparta. He made no mention of anything else. That could wait for another time. And he preferred not to be the teller of that tale.

As expected, Niko was out of jail the next day and back in Gytheio where he promised to remain until "vindicated." When the prosecutor learned from Andreas that Calliope had confessed to her role in the matter, and from Kouros of Niko's claimed statement of the facts, he told both cops there was a better case for convicting Calliope than Niko. Even more so after Kouros' wrestling buddy, the bear, denied ever telling Kouros of a link between Niko and the uncle's murder. He denied being part of anything more that an effort to convince Niko's old acquaintance, Babis, not to take his own life but rather turn himself in for the uncle's murder.

Andreas and Kouros knew where this was headed. With the actual killer dead, the victim a notorious bad guy, and prosecutorial resources strapped to the limit by across-the-board financial cuts, there was very little chance that Niko would ever see the inside of a prison cell. At least not this time.

Chapter Twenty-three

Andreas looked up to see who was coming through his office door. "You look pissed. What's wrong?"

"I just got word the prosecutor isn't taking my uncle's case to trial."

Andreas shook his head. "I hate this part of the job. We bust our asses catching scum everyone knows is guilty and some spineless prosecutor lets him walk because he doesn't have the balls to risk hurting his conviction rate. We knew this was a tough case, but I thought the prosecutor would at least try to put him away." Andreas pointed a finger at Kouros. "I want you to run a full financial background check on that prosecutor. If we find so much as a euro unaccounted for in his account I'm going to hang his crooked ass out to dry."

"No one's angrier than I am, but it isn't all the prosecutor's fault." Kouros dropped onto the couch.

"What are you saying?"

"My cousins are very worried about Calliope. Niko was out of jail within hours after his arrest, but she's been penned up in a psychiatric ward for nearly a month and a half. Mangas told me her doctors believe that if she testified it could send her over the edge forever."

Andreas shook his head. "And Niko's lawyers would make sure she testified."

"In vivid, excruciating detail. That's why Mangas told the prosecutor today that his sister wouldn't testify. And her psychiatrist backed him up on that."

Andreas blew out a rush of air from between his lips. "At least Babis is dead. That's some justice. Which reminds me, maybe someone should let Stella know that Niko and his two numb-nuts buddies are free? Just in case they might still consider her a loose end."

"I already told her. Her residency permit came through last week and she's moving north to Thessaloniki."

"What's the matter, she didn't like Athens?"

"No, she found a nice guy and he got a job up there, so she's going with him."

Andreas studied Kouros' face. "How do you feel about that?"

He shrugged. "Fine, we're just friends."

"I see. So, what are you doing for Christmas?"

"Not sure yet."

"Well, it's the day after tomorrow, and you're invited to our house if nothing better turns up."

"Thanks. I was sort of thinking of going down to the Mani to spend it with my cousins."

"Not a bad idea."

"But I'm not sure about that anymore."

"Why's that?"

"Mangas told me Father Carlos has visited Calliope every day she's been in the hospital and just obtained permission from her doctors to bring her home for three days over Christmas."

"That's terrific news."

"Yes, but I don't think I should be there for her homecoming. They don't need me as a walking reminder of all she's done and been through."

"Your family can't blame you for what she did."

"I hope not. But, still, I don't have be in her face the very first day she's out. In time, I want to talk to her. Perhaps give her something her father didn't think she'd appreciate." Kouros turned his head and stared out the window behind the couch. "I think he was wrong about that. It's a chest that once belonged to our Great-aunt Calliope."

"Do I take all that as a 'yes' for dinner on Christmas? Tassos and Maggie will be there."

"Sure. Thanks. Is the new kid you brought into the unit coming?"

"Petro? He's on Crete, making Orestes' life miserable. I told him to be his shadow until he found something to nail Orestes with big-time. Our new government says they want to fight corruption wherever it is, no matter who's involved. So I thought, wouldn't it be nice to start at the top for once?"

"May justice prevail in the end."

"While you're at it, don't forget true love," said Andreas.

"Yeah. Too bad this is real life, not fiction."

At four in the morning on Christmas Day, church bells rang out across Greece. Services followed, in some communities right then, but in most not before six. The ensuing three-hour service ended a forty-day fast forbidding fish, meat, dairy, and on Wednesdays and Fridays, olive oil. Beneath the altar, waiting to be blessed, lay bread, sweet red wine, oven-prepared lamb and roasted potatoes donated to the community by those who'd lost relatives over the past year. It served as an offering for the souls of the recently departed and comprised the traditional Christmas Day feast shared with the community at tables set up outside the church expressly for the occasion.

Saint Petros Church was packed. But that was to be expected. Especially with less than thirty minutes to go in the service. Neighbors nodded to neighbors, friends introduced visiting relatives and guests to other friends, and women all in black, some in full nun's veil, scurried around outside the church, readying the tables for the onslaught of diners.

One priest led the service and two others assisted. Lay participants and common worshippers performed their roles perfectly in rituals rehearsed since childhood, with a sort of clockwork-like precision rare to experience in Greece. As the service came to an end, worshippers hurried outside to find places at tables for their families. Some approached a table closest to the sea but were shooed away by a not-so-gentle-looking giant saying, "Sorry, taken."

Many came to this tiny island with its solitary white church and gentle harbor backdrop to exchange vows, promising to remain as one until death did them part. Some perhaps came wondering whether similar thoughts might have passed between Helen and Paris as they began their own epic journey from this place. While others, like many here today, thought only of the festivities to follow.

A group of six walked toward the taken table. A tall man in black trousers, white shirt, and a dark zippered jacket led them there. He smiled at everyone he passed, exchanging Christmas wishes. A few said "Congratulations," and he thanked each one.

He sat at the head of the table facing the church, his wife and two grown children to his right, his in-laws to his left.

Head-to-toe black-clad women hurried around distributing bread, wine, and platters of food to the tables. The sounds of toasts, rousing voices, and laughter filled the air. Priests moved from table to table, exchanging *Kala Kristougenna* greetings with the gathered, and men walked about, finding their friends and wishing Merry Christmas with a quick smack on the back or fast squeeze of the shoulders. Many came to greet the man at the head of the table. He smiled and toasted each one.

All the toasting had given Niko a buzz. No matter, he had much to celebrate. The prosecutor couldn't prove a thing. Too bad Babis had screwed up and failed to get the vendetta angle to play. The old man hadn't told anyone about Niko's carefully scripted threats, rendering pointless the message Niko had Babis put on the back of the old man's newspaper and the SMS Niko anonymously sent the day before the hit. The messages were supposed to emerge as part of an elaborate but feeble attempt by the Ukrainian to pass off a professional hit as a vendetta killing.

Niko remained convinced that, if the threats had gone public, Calliope so despised the Ukrainian she would have launched her hot-headed brother on a murderous vendetta against the Ukrainian—giving Niko free reign in the Peloponnese as he watched his two competitors kill each other off.

But the father's death was labeled an accident. Worse still, his cop nephew started poking around. Something Niko hadn't figured on. That limited Niko's options. Babis had to go because he was the only one who could have tied Niko into the hit. Maybe the girlfriend still could too, but he'd take care of her personally next week. Niko smiled. On her first New Year's Eve in Thessaloniki.

Of course there was also Calliope, but who'd ever believe her? The crazy bitch never for a second saw the switch coming. She remained convinced to the end the Ukrainian was the target.

Niko smiled. *Probably still does.*

The photograph she gave him had made it all possible. All he'd had to do was show it to Babis that afternoon outside the taverna. The rest was easy. He told Babis he'd be forgiven by Niko's family if he killed the man who'd betrayed them both. In exchange, Babis only had to stick the message in the old man's newspaper the next morning and use the poison as directed when Niko gave him the word.

Too bad the local cops found the poison. That

stuff was hard to come by. Expensive, too. One of their connected Maniot buddies would probably end up with it. Maybe he could buy it from the cops first.

Yeah, and too bad for Babis the threat messages didn't fly. But just like Calliope, the sucker never saw it coming until given the choice of a few minutes in the sea or days of pain with Urich.

Niko looked up at the church and mumbled to himself, "Thank you, Lord, for sending me two fools."

WHACK. Niko jerked forward from a hard smack on his back. "*Kala Kristougenna*, Niko. I hear you're moving to the Mani."

It was another forgettable cousin of his wife offering a *macho* Mani greeting.

"Maybe. I'm thinking of opening a hotel over here. One with a golf course."

"Good luck with it."

Black clad ladies started gathering dirty paper plates off the tables. One, dressed in a nun's veil, reached in between Niko's in-laws.

"Sorry, sister, we're not finished yet," said the mother-in-law.

The woman nodded and moved away from the table.

Niko followed her with his eyes. She never

turned around, just began gathering plates from another table.

WHACK. Another smack to the left of his back and a quick pinching squeeze to his neck. He turned quickly, only to see a crowd standing around the next table. It could have been any of them. He turned back to face his family.

"Who was that?" said Niko's wife.

"I don't know, I didn't see him."

"It wasn't a 'him.' It was a woman dressed in black. Maybe it was the mother of one of your baby girlfriends."

He raised his hand as if to strike her, but caught himself and forced a smile for everyone at the table. "No idea." He moved his raised hand to rub his neck. "But whoever she is has a mean pinch."

Three minutes later he felt a pain in the middle of his back. No wonder, after all the smacks he'd taken. He stretched his back trying to work it out, but it only grew sharper. He rubbed his stomach. Now he felt indigestion. That damn lamb didn't agree with him. Then came the pain in his jaw, the burning vise-grip on his chest, and the rush of adrenaline as he struggled for breath and realized he was about to die.

Eyes wide open, he stared straight ahead. Two tables away his eyes locked on a priest's staring right back at him. Next to the priest stood a woman all in black.

The priest nodded, smiled, and took Niko's photograph.